Artifact

OTHER BOOKS BY THIS AUTHOR

(historical thriller)

Code Name: Evangeline

Evangeline's Ghost Series:
(historical paranormal)

Evangeline's Ghost
Evangeline's Ghost: Houdini
Evangeline's Ghost: The Bridge (pending 2025)

Library of Illumination Series:
(young adult fantasy)

Chronicles: the Library of Illumination (first five books)
Second Chronicles of Illumination (books six and seven)
Third Chronicles of Illumination (book eight)
Fourth Chronicles of Illumination (book nine)
Fifth Chronicles of Illumination (book ten)
Sixth Chronicles of Illumination (book eleven pending 2025)

Over-Sixty: Shades of Gray brand:
(books on aging)

Over-Sixty: Shades of Gray – A Journey Through Life's Later Years (on the Road to Fossilization)
Over-Sixty: Shades of Gray – Mind Games & Soporifics
Over-Sixty: Shades of Gray – Our Coronavirus Diary
Over-Sixty: Shades of Gray – Book of Lists

Writing & Publishing

Indie Authors User's Guide

Artifact

by

C. A. PACK

Artiqua Press

www.artiquapress.com

This is a work of fiction. The characters, incidents, and dialogue are products of the author's imagination and are not to be construed as real. Any resemblance to actual events or persons, living or dead, is entirely coincidental. No part of this publication may be reproduced, distributed, or transmitted in any form or by any means, including photocopying, recording, or other electronic, digital or mechanical methods, without the prior written permission of the publisher, except in the case of brief quotations embodied in critical reviews and certain other noncommercial uses permitted by copyright law. For permission requests, email the publisher with: "Attention: Permissions Coordinator" in the subject line.

ARTIQUA PRESS
info@artiquapress.com
Westbury, NY 11590

TRADE PAPERBACK

November 12, 2024

ARTIFACT

Copyright © 2024 C. A. Pack
All rights reserved.

ISBN-13: 978-1-970028-14-0

Library of Congress Control Number: 2024916377

In an infinite universe, who can say an inconsequential object won't collide with a diabolical scheme that triggers a nuclear holocaust?

79 AD

FIERY ROCKS—LIKE an invading army of dragons—hurtled through Earth's atmosphere. The fragments of alien rubble struck Egypt's shoreline, sending up clouds of dust and steam near the place where Cleopatra's castle once stood. The glowing debris appeared to writhe as it burrowed into the sand.

Hero of Alexandria, mathematician and inventor, experimented with the intriguing new material he found on the beach, turning it into malleable ropes of metal. He hammered them flat so he could engrave them, but the strands always returned to their curvier shape. However, the inscriptions remained clear. And so, he wove together an odd record of his life's work, creating an intricate knot of formulas and theories out of the oddly shimmering material.

A sense of joy made him smile, and he thought this would be his legacy to humanity. *Little did he know.*

CHAPTER ONE

IF TRAYNOR LENNOX expected this to be the most wonderful weekend of his life, he was dead wrong. The bottom dropped out when he answered a cell phone call from his brother. "Carey—"

His identical twin's frantic voice cut him off. *"Tray. Thank God. I need your help. Someone's tailing me."*

Tray, a special agent on the FBI Art Crime Team, felt his pulse quicken. "Where are you?"

"East Hampton, behind whatever building you're in now."

Tray froze. "How did you find me out here?"

"I used a tracker app on my phone to locate your cell signal."

The agent's reflexes responded uncomfortably. *If Carey can track me that easily, so can everyone else.* Tray could think of multiple reasons why that could prove catastrophic. He skirted around a harried waiter toting a tray full of crockery. "I'm on my way," he said, with the phone still plastered against his ear. He heard an odd *tic-thump* sound and a groan followed by the phone crashing to the ground. A moment later, he rushed out the back door of the restaurant. Carey lay crumpled on the pavement, not ten feet away, his eyelids fluttering as a bloodstain slowly spread across his chest.

Movement caught Tray's attention. He glimpsed someone's back disappearing around a far corner. He had no time to give chase. Instead, he picked up the sweatshirt his brother had dropped and used it to stop Carey from bleeding out. Emotion made his voice husky. "Don't worry, Ca. I won't let you die."

Carey closed his eyes and winced as his brother applied pressure to stop the bleeding. Tray used his free hand to call the police.

"Nine-one-one, what's your emergency?"

"Shooting behind Chapter One on Main in East Hampton."

A glint on the ground—almost obscured by blood—caught Tray's eye. *A loose key.*

He looked at Carey again, only to see his twin brother shudder before his body completely slackened. He checked Carey's neck for a pulse but couldn't feel one. "I think he's… dead." Tray closed his eyes. The undeniable sting of loss warred with an overwhelming impulse to take stock of the situation and remain in control.

"Please stay—"

He disconnected the call. *There's no time. Especially if someone is after me because of the artifact and killed Carey by mistake.* He looked around, making sure no one else lurked nearby. He quickly checked Carey's pockets. The rest of his brother's keys were missing, along with his phone. However, Carey's wallet remained untouched. Tray stilled, his stomach clenching as he made a split-second decision. He swapped his wallet for his brother's, picked up the bloody key, and took off.

CHAPTER TWO

Three years earlier

Tray prided himself on being a highly skilled expert in art, archeology, and antiquities. That morning, he called upon every one of those skills as he examined an intricately jeweled egg while reflecting on its past and wondering how its history might affect the future.

The outer surface of the piece was glazed with two shades of white enamel and crisscrossed with diamond brilliants, making it appear multi-dimensional. It stood on gold cabriole legs and featured a sapphire gem on top that, when pressed, made the upper half of the egg pop open. Inside, a mechanized golden hen embedded with rose-cut diamonds dipped her upper body into a filigree nest and picked up a tiny sapphire egg in her beak.

"What do you think?" asked Maximilian Zane, owner of *Xanadu: Fine Art and Antique Acquisitions.*

They were standing next to the scarred refectory table that Max used as a workbench in the windowless back room of his business. Tray carefully set the egg back on its stand and turned toward the older man, whose Einstein-like hair seemed at odds with his impeccable suit. "Before we get to that, may I ask you a question?"

Max's shoulders sagged. "I was feeling pretty good until you said that."

Tray held back a grin. "Have you ever heard of Hero's Knot?"

"Is that a riddle?"

"No. It's an artifact I've been asked to locate. But I won't know how to find it unless I know what it is."

"Is it valuable?"

"I have no idea."

"If you've been asked to find it, it's valuable to someone."

Tray frowned. "I get the feeling it's more dangerous than valuable."

"Well, good luck finding it. Although to be honest, I've been in this business a long time, and I've never heard of it."

"Maybe my aunt will know something."

"Good. Can we get back to the egg?"

"Of course. The enameling is exquisite, as is the gold chasing." Tray leaned in with a magnifying glass to study the piece more closely. "The craftsmanship is spot on. There's light wear on the surface, in keeping with something made in 1886." He turned it over, and his face lit up. He pointed at a tiny symbol. "Michael Perchin's hallmark. In Cyrillic. If this is a counterfeit, it's better than the original. And that's impossible. I'd stake my reputation on this being one of the lost Faberge Imperial Easter Eggs."

Max's eyes widened. "Imagine what this could bring in at auction." His voice held traces of awe.

Tray slowly shook his head, not taking his eyes off the man. "You know I have to turn it in."

"To the Russians?"

"No. To the FBI Art Crime Team. They'll determine what to do with it."

"Just once, couldn't you throw me a bone?"

"You already know the answer to that. I'm employed by the FBI, which—I'd like to point out—did not prosecute you last year for possession of stolen merchandise because you cooperated with them by letting me work here. You get the benefit of my expertise for free, and I have a cover that allows me to identify stolen artwork."

"What if this egg isn't stolen? What if it's legitimately lost?"

"It's a Faberge Egg. It has a provenance, a history. The US government wants to reunite pieces like this with their rightful owners. However, if no one claims it, it's yours."

"'If no one claims it?' Everyone is going to claim it! Sometimes, having you as a *free expert* can be painfully expensive."

Attorney Walter Chichester personified the word *old*. He spoke slowly and moved at a snail's pace. He had so many age spots and wrinkles that Tray knew if he spent a month trying to catalog the lawyer's facial features, he wouldn't be able to do so. He realized he must look bored when he felt Carey's elbow jab the side of his ribs. *He should be poking Chichester. The guy looks like he could use a jolt.*

"I know it's not much, gentlemen, but most of your father's assets went toward paying off the debts he accumulated by marrying four women over the years," Walter explained. "He left them no bequests, per se, but the alimony he'd been forced to pay before he died literally bled him dry.

Tray fidgeted. He hardly knew his father. News of "Nate" Lennox's death was only a surprise because the man had died at a relatively young age. *Dear old dad* had bowed out of the twins' lives before they were old enough to walk. He may have spared no expense paying for their upbringing through college, but as far as Tray knew, his father had never tried to contact them.

He felt a pang of regret. His mother had died shortly after giving birth to him and Carey. He'd been told his father had been devastated by his wife's death, growing bitter and distant afterward and all but abandoning his twin sons. Their aunt Jane had raised them until they left for college. Carey had studied nuclear engineering, while Tray—like his aunt—had pursued degrees in archeology and art history. Apparently, their mother, Lily, had been the love of Nate's life, and he'd never found another woman who could completely fill the void left after her death.

"It's a good thing he never told anyone about his fishing cabin," Walter said, "or his exes would have tried to ensure that it was sold off as well." The attorney opened a manila envelope and poured out the contents. The deed to a cabin on sixteen acres of land near Roscoe, New York, fell onto the table along with a keyring containing two keys and a business-size white envelope that looked a little worse for wear. The attorney opened another file containing paperwork that needed the twins' signatures to transfer the property to them. When they were done, Chichester pushed the deed and the keys toward them. He also handed them the white envelope.

Carey opened it and removed a check for $43,000. His mouth dropped open. "What's this? I thought you said there was no money."

For a moment, Walter remained quiet, allowing the sound of birdsong to take center stage as it filtered into the wood-paneled office through an open window. He looked each twin in the eye for a second before speaking. "Your father was one of my oldest friends despite our age difference. He grew up next door to me, which incidentally was not that far from the cabin you now hold the deed to. Just before he died, he gave me his truck. It was only a year old and contained every option in the book. He said his eyesight was gone, and he couldn't drive it anymore, so he gave it to me for services rendered."

"I believe we've already spoken about this on the phone," Carey said.

Tray's chair creaked as he turned to look at his brother. "We did." He turned his attention toward Walter. "We said we didn't want it. It's yours to do with as you please."

"Good. Because I sold it, and I'm giving you the proceeds."

"No. We won't take it," Carey said, standing up to leave. He tried to hand the check to the attorney. "This is your money."

"That's a cashier's check. It's made out to both of you. I can't cash it. Only you can. Together. Use it to renovate the cabin. It could use a few updates before you sell it." He hesitated for a moment. "The same holds true even if you decide to keep it. Consider it my gift to you for the entertainment your antics provided me over the years. Your father always had the best stories about the scrapes you both got into."

Carey frowned. "How could he? He hardly knew us." Walter sighed, his jaw quivering a bit. "That's where you're wrong. Jane kept him in the loop. She knew how much he loved her sister and you boys as well. Unfortunately, Nate's heart broke a thousand times over—every time he looked at you two—because it reminded him of what he'd lost when your mother died. So, Jane quietly ran interference. But believe me, Nate spent two nights in an uncomfortable waiting room, Tray, when you were hospitalized with pneumonia. And he was in the stadium, Carey, when you scored the winning touchdown in your last college game. He loved the two of you. He just didn't know how to show it, especially after all those years of staying away from you. The estrangement—that he brought upon himself—was his undoing.

"Now, go." Walter slowly pushed himself up from his desk. "I'm an old man, and I need my rest." It was an understatement. He died peacefully in his sleep, two days later.

VERY FEW PEOPLE gathered for Walter's memorial service, which made it mercifully short. Jane, the twins, Walter's former secretary, and the minister stood around the grave site for the interment.

"I expected more people," Tray said.

"Most of Walter's friends and family predeceased him," the minister explained after the service. "You are the only ones left to prevent Walter's memory from passing into obscurity."

*

JANE AND THE twins remained quiet during the ride home until they passed a battered old sign saying *Country Auction Today.*

"Do you mind if we stop?" Jane asked.

"I don't," Tray answered. I love looking at old art and antiques. They tell a story about their previous owners and their journey through time. Art appreciation is the one thing I was always really good at."

"I don't mind stopping, but Tray's description of art is too esoteric for me. I tend to think of things in a more logical way. Art can be abstracted based on the temperament of its creator. You can't depend on it to give you factual information. I prefer something tangible that can be studied and dissected and reduced to its most basic components. I like to think I'm practical," Carey turned toward his brother, "while you're more of a seat-of-the-pants kind of guy."

Jane got out of the car. "You're both overthinking this. I just love looking at old treasures, and I think it might help lift my spirits. The thought of Walter having so few people left to mourn him is very depressing. It made me think of what *my* funeral might be like."

"We won't let that happen to you, Aunt Jane," Tray bit the inside of his mouth to keep from smirking, "even if we have to rent mourners to wail at your funeral."

Jane shook her head but didn't reply.

At the auction, they walked through what might have once been an impressive barn and started inspecting the various lots of merchandise.

"The two of you don't have to babysit me," Jane said. "I'm sure the items I'm interested in will only bore you.

Why don't we split up?"

Carey gave her a one-armed hug. "Whatever you want, Aunt Jane."

"Just don't let me forget to ask you about Hero's Knot," Tray added.

"I'm not familiar with it," Jane said.

"It's supposed to be an ancient Egyptian artifact, but I can't find any information on it. The topic came up at work, and I'd love to have some background."

"Enough said," she answered. "I'll see what I can dig up."

"Aunt Jane made an archeology pun," Carey joked.

"Ugh!" Jane cried, slapping the nearest twin in the arm. "Stop calling me *Aunt* Jane. It makes me feel ancient. Just Jane will do."

"Okay, Just Jane." Tray turned to Carey. "You think they have a snack bar here?"

"Go look. I see something intriguing." Carey circumvented a few tables filled with auction items until he reached a richly patinated head he had noticed peeking up at him. *Is this what I think it is?*

Propped up against a post, sat a beat-up wooden mannequin. *Lot 06* was written on a tiny card attached to the pole above it. Carey pulled the six-foot dummy off the ground, checking to see if it remained intact. He whistled when he saw the body clearly marked *Sierra Sam*. "This is a bona fide relic."

"*Whatcha* got, bro?"

Carey jerked, startled by Tray's sudden reappearance. "Nothing." He sat the dummy back on the ground and led his twin away. Lowering his voice, he said, "Just an early crash test dummy from the 1950s."

"Did they even have crash test dummies in the fifties?"

"The military used them to test aircraft ejector seats. No use popping the seat if it's going to kill the pilot."

"Your face was lit up like a kid in a candy store when you inspected that dummy. So, why are you suddenly acting so nonchalant?"

Carey pulled his brother away from other people. "I don't want my excitement to cause another buyer to take a closer look. I want that dummy for myself, even if I have to pretend it's a piece of trash."

Tray's eyes lit up. "You see a lot of yourself in him, do you?"

Carey smirked. "No. He reminds me of you."

"There is nothing dumb about me."

"How about when we were backpacking through France, and you kicked that man's dog—"

"I did not kick his dog! I didn't see it run in front of me. I tripped over it."

Carey picked up an old brass protractor. "A mistake anyone could have made."

"Yes!"

"But when the owner scooped up his little pet—"

Tray pulled the protractor out of Carey's hand and slammed it on the table. "What was a big guy like him doing with such a tiny dog?"

"—you said, *'pardonnez vous'* instead of *'pardonnez moi,'* and he punched you." Carey doubled over, laughing. "'Forgive you,' instead of, 'forgive me,' like it was his fault. It was hilarious."

"I don't remember you being much help. You took off."

"Yeah. Me and your girlfriend. God, she could run. She should have been in the Olympics. What was her name again?"

"Sophia Brodeur. And she did qualify—in both track and swimming. She was a triathlete. But her father was dying, and she forfeited her place on her country's Olympic team to be with her family. After his death, I don't think her heart was in it anymore."

Carey stooped down to look at a hand-carved wooden hobby horse. "She was hot."

Tray's features softened as he got a faraway look in his eyes. "Oh, yeah."

"Where did you meet her again?"

"Oxford. During my year abroad studying Classical Archeology."

Carey stood. "She's an archaeologist?"

"No. She was studying languages. She speaks a bunch of them."

"Russian?" Carey asked.

"I don't know if she speaks Russian."

"Urdu?"

"I'm pretty sure she doesn't speak Urdu."

"Okay. Don't tell me. She speaks pig-Latin, baby talk, gibberish—"

"Don't mock her. She's great at what she does." Tray picked up an old globe that sat amid at least a dozen similar spheres.

"Or says she is. You don't even know what she speaks."

"I know she speaks Arabic and French. And Mandarin. Can you speak Chinese?"

"Does she speak English?"

Tray placed the globe back on the table. "You're not even funny."

"I now know that she knows how to brush you off in several languages."

"There was no brushing off going on."

"Are you saying you were together in the biblical sense?"

"This conversation is over."

"Ooh … she really got to you."

"If you don't stop right now, I'm going to outbid you and then cut the head off your dummy."

"You always did have a mean streak. You'd better hope I don't die first because if it's the last thing I do, I'm going to come back and haunt you."

"Yeah. You do that."

They met up with Jane and found seats for the auction.

When *Lot 06* came up for sale, two other people had their eyes on Sierra Sam. The bidding continued in small increments until one man doubled the previous bid to one thousand dollars. Carey immediately offered fifteen hundred. The room went silent except for the wails of an unhappy baby. The man who drove up the bid shook his head, leaving Carey to claim his prize.

Back at the car, he strapped Sam into the back seat next to Jane, who shuddered, shaking her head. "What are you going to do with that thing?"

Carey's eyes lit up. "When I was in high school, I belonged to an after-school theater club, and we put on the play *Pal Joey*. The director wanted me to dress in some cheesy costume, but I went to a second-hand store and found myself a shiny blue suit and a black fedora, just like

Frank Sinatra wore in the movie. I still have that outfit—shoved in the back of my closet. I once trotted it out for a Halloween party, but other than that, it's just been hanging there."

"You are not—" Tray began.

"I'm dressing Sam in Joey's threads," Carey cut in, "and he's going to be my new best friend."

"If you wanted a doll as a child, all you had to do was ask," Jane teased, "and I would have given you one for your birthday."

"What are you going to call him?" Tray asked. "Sammy Joe?"

"No. Sounds too feminine. I think I'll go with Joey Sam." Carey laced his hands behind his back and smiled. "Joey Sam is going to look sharp, going for rides in my 1957 Cadillac."

"Your what?" Tray asked.

"My turquoise, 1957 Cadillac Eldorado Biarritz convertible. I bought it a couple of months ago at an auction. I just got it back from the body shop, fully restored."

"That must have cost you a pretty penny," Jane said.

"It was a planned expenditure. What hurts is the additional monthly fee I have to pay for another parking space in my building. But I lucked out. It's right next to my regular spot."

"Perhaps you should give me a key," Tray said, "in case you lose yours."

"Keep your dirty mitts off Elbi."

"Elbi?" Jane asked, her eyebrow quirked.

"EL-dorado BI-arritz. ELBI!"

*

SEVERAL WEEKS LATER, Tray and Carey met for drinks at the Tribeca Grill in lower Manhattan to discuss a trip they planned to take to the Cayman Islands. Carey admired the exposed brick and the industrial vibe of the space. Tray admired the long legs and the short skirt of a redheaded woman sitting not too far away.

Carey nudged his twin. "Don't let her boyfriend catch you staring, or you might find yourself on the wrong side of his fist. He's a pretty beefy guy."

Tray ignored the insinuation. "I can't believe you're already back in my neck of the woods. Usually, you're traveling all over the country for the Nuclear Regulatory Commission."

"I've been moving around a lot lately. It's exhausting. This week, I inspected Indian Point. Something was wonky with the radiation levels there."

"That sounds like a problem." Tray popped a pretzel in his mouth.

"It might have been. At first, I thought it was a system malfunction, but then I noticed a worker disabling a similar unit nearby. It was a stupid mistake; at least, that's what he admitted to. It could have resulted in a partial core meltdown."

Tray whistled. "How'd you handle it?"

"I had to report him. I hated doing it, but it was an error that could have cost lives. And if it wasn't a 'stupid mistake,' he needed to be caught."

"So, you came to the rescue."

Carey stared at the table, playing with the napkin under his drink. "They fired him. What if he has a wife and kids depending on that paycheck?"

"What if he was committing nuclear terrorism?"

Carey's tone became defensive. "I don't know that for sure."

Tray leaned back and studied his brother for a moment. "I think you're a hero."

"Some hero."

Tray finished his single malt scotch. "I think I'll call you Captain Beer Belly."

Carey closed his eyes before speaking through clenched teeth. "I do not have a beer belly."

"But you will if you don't start working out again. Your girlfriend is cooking you too many Italian dinners."

They paused while a waiter placed two fresh drinks and an appetizer on the table.

Carey snagged a piece of fried calamari before continuing. "You're just jealous. Although Caterina is also jealous that I'm going to the Cayman Islands with you and not taking her with me. As it is, we've been spending less time together because of my workload."

"No. No. No. This is bro' time," Tray said. "I can't wait to get away from the Realtors who keep calling to ask if we want to sell Dad's cabin."

"How do they even know about it?"

"Transferring the deed is public record."

Carey rubbed the back of his neck. "Do we want to sell the cabin?"

"I don't think so. It's the only thing of Dad's that we have."

"Yeah. I agree."

"One thing's for sure," Tray said. "I'm sick of people harassing me about the property. I think we should put it under another name. Maybe an LLC."

"Then they'll just call the LLC, and that's still us, right?"

"Not if we register it in Delaware, which will keep our identities private. Then, when we get to Grand Cayman, we can set up an offshore account and use the proceeds from the sale of Dad's truck to establish an escrow account to pay for the taxes and upkeep."

"That's a lot of cloak and dagger just to get a couple of Realtors off your back."

"I'm used to cloak and dagger. I work for the FBI. Besides, consider the cool factor of having an offshore bank account. And our own LLC. I like it!"

"Yeah? And what are we going to call this company?"

Tray doodled on a napkin. "Here." He pushed it over toward Carey. "LX2 LLC. Shorthand for Lennox times two—limited liability company."

Carey smiled. "At least it's not the *Captain Beer Belly Brothers.*"

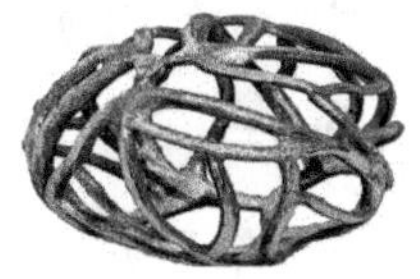

CHAPTER THREE

Tray received a tip that Hero's Knot had been tracked to Switzerland and headed straight to the special agent in charge of the Art Crime Team, Deneil Abernathy, to discuss following it up personally.

He knocked on the open door. Abernathy's office wasn't particularly posh, but it was private, and the wood shelves, desk, and credenza were a definite step up from the furniture most agents were allotted. "Do you have a moment?"

Abernathy nodded toward the upholstered visitor's chair across from his desk. His face remained expressionless while he quietly heard Tray out.

"What do you think?" Tray asked.

"Contact the bureau's legal attaché in Bern and have their people handle it."

"Their involvement could waste weeks."

"Try months."

"Then, sir—"

"It's out of your hands, Lennox. Hero's Knot has been floating around for thousands of years. A few more months won't hurt.

"What about the chatter saying it could be adapted to set off nuclear weapons?

"Right now, it's only wind. Call—"

"—I know, I know. The Legat in Bern."

He returned to his desk, shoulders slumped, and placed the call. However, every fiber of Tray's being told him he'd lose the artifact's trail by going through bureaucratic channels.

The next day, Tray submitted a vacation request. It was approved for the end of the month.

INSIDE THE GALLERIA BLANC auction house in Zurich, Switzerland, cataloger Mia Mair felt overwhelmed while working on the description for *lot 17*—an artifact from the "private collection" of an anonymous consignor. This offering, although unique, made her job tricky because of its inadequate provenance. She didn't want to give bidders the wrong impression about the item's history, nor did she want to scare them away from bidding robustly. Many rumors about the artifact's origin could not be authenticated, making the object less valuable to some potential buyers.

She opened an animal skin pouch and removed the object inside. Picking it up, she held the artifact close to her eyes, trying to look through the closely woven strands of inscribed metal. "What are your secrets?"

She turned it slowly, examining it from all angles, but it was oddly symmetrical, with no defined bottom or top.

The seller had been told the presale auction estimate for the piece fell between €350 and €400. Yet, looking at it, Mia sensed it was worth much more. The seller had mentioned that the writing on it appeared to be Ancient Greek, and he supplied paperwork from a scholar who said the inscription outlined the teachings of Hero of Alexandria.

Is it Egyptian? Is it Greek? Mia played up its old-world mystery while ignoring its lack of provenance and wrote a fairly fanciful description. When she finished, she returned the item to the shelf.

One more item. She started working on *lot 23,* which included a nineteenth-century matched set of diamond and sapphire jewelry. A graduated series of cushion-cut sapphires, each accented by rose-cut diamond sepals, made up a necklace, ear pendants, and a bracelet. The provenance was clear, and the description did not take long to write. The auction estimates for that particular set of jewelry ranged from €950,000 to €1.5 million.

Mia's stomach growled as she finished the detailed description of the bracelet. She stood and stretched. She still had several lots to describe, but she needed a break. She set the security alarm and locked the storage room door before leaving.

TRAY SQUIRMED, TRYING to find a comfortable position while doing reconnaissance in a too-small rental car. The artifact's sale was scheduled for the following week at the *Galerie Blanc.* He knew his superiors wouldn't approve of him being here, so he had told his boss he was taking vacation time to go backpacking with his brother. *I'm definitely backpacking, and I like to think my brother is here in spirit.*

He had already scouted the auction house and noted all the entrances and exits, as well as the number of security guards and closed-circuit cameras. He busied himself while continuing his surveillance, sketching a map that illustrated everything he'd personally observed.

He grabbed his coffee cup and drained it. If something didn't happen soon, he would face a very dry and sleepy afternoon surrounded by the mostly white and beige buildings that made up this section of *Borsenstrasse*, a nice place to visit for people in the market for expensive luxury goods, but not so great for those who wished to remain anonymous inside an unremarkable car. He turned the ignition key halfway and tuned the radio to a news station.

The anchor began talking about a young, ultra-rich financial wizard from India, Deepak Bhatti, who happened to be dating a beautiful French actress.

Tough life, Tray thought, remembering when he'd met the same actress on his last trip to Europe.

After a brief break, the anchor—sounding more urgent—announced that Iranian State TV had just broadcast a video by the Islamic Revolutionary Guard Corps. The IRGC declared the country's nuclear development program would launch a nuclear test missile in the near future at an undisclosed location.

If Tray had any doubts about what he should do about Hero's Knot, that report wiped them away. There wasn't enough time to get legal approval to confiscate the artifact, especially considering no one knew he was in Switzerland. He could only think of one option left open to him.

When the only worker he had noticed entering the

auction house locked the building before leaving at midday, he made his move. He casually walked around back to an open window he had spotted earlier. He stopped suddenly and stepped into a shadow when he saw a squirrelly-looking man making a beeline for the same window. Tray stayed back, watching the guy open the window before hoisting himself inside. Tray hurried over and looked in. The room was not illuminated and, at first, extremely quiet. Tray observed as much as he could until he heard the man's footsteps grow louder as he rushed back in Tray's direction.

"Halt! Dieb!" The building had a guard Tray hadn't noticed. Neither had the thief. The intruder shoved the top half of his body out the window, but the guard grabbed him by the legs and pulled him back inside.

Tray plucked a bundle out of the man's hand and ran off. He jumped into his car and drove away, blending into traffic. Twenty minutes later, he stopped the car on a narrow side street and unwrapped what the man had stolen. Tray's heart beat faster when he observed the ancient markings on the outside of the object. *This is it. It has to be!* He stuffed it in his backpack and peeled away from the curb, not stopping until he reached the airport. He wouldn't rest easily until his plane left the ground.

RETURNING FROM LUNCH, Mia was surprised to see police and security personnel streaming in and out of *Galerie Blanc.* She showed police her ID, before being allowed inside, and pushed through a dozen or so strangers until she saw a security guard she knew. He stood outside the office where the items for their next auction were stored. Her scalp tingled like a dozen ants crisscrossed its surface. "What happened?" she asked.

"Someone broke in and stole lot 17."

Mia's lips pulled to one side as she concentrated on pulling out her cell phone and searching for the auction catalog she had helped put together. "What about lot 23?" she asked. "It's one of the more valuable items up for sale that's small enough to be easily carried away."

"As far as I know, it's still here. The only item that's been confirmed missing is lot 17."

Mia tilted her head. "That's odd."

"There's no accounting for taste," the security guard replied. "Besides, everyone is more concerned that the thief managed to break in, rather than with what he stole. Apparently, a window was left unlocked."

Police Adjutant Liam Gerber had eavesdropped on their conversation. "I wonder," he asked, "if the stolen item's owner will feel the same way."

Mia turned to face him and shrugged. "Lot 17 wasn't worth that much. Not enough to qualify as a serious crime."

The police adjutant narrowed his eyes. "What do you know about 'serious crime?'"

"Only that it needs to be worth more than what *lot 17* was valued at."

"Which was?"

She located it on her phone and showed him. "Less than four hundred euros."

"At least they caught the thief," the security guard said.

"So, *lot 17* is safe," Mia replied.

"No. It's gone. The thief says someone grabbed it out of his hands while he was hanging out the window. He claims he was working alone and didn't know the man."

"But you got a description."

"Yes. Tallish. Normal weight. Wearing a ski hat,

sunglasses, and nondescript outwear, just like a quarter of the men in this country."

"What about cameras?"

The police adjutant shook his head. "We will look at whatever footage there is, but I doubt they'll be very helpful."

A FEW DAYS LATER, international power broker Zander Bakker waited for one of the most important auction purchases he might ever make—to become reality. He had one agent placed in the audience of the auction house, with another registered to make online bids for *Lot 17*. He thumbed through the *Galerie Blanc's* catalog while he watched the auction stream live online. He scowled when the auctioneer skipped Lot 17, and his jaw clenched when the event ended without a word about the missing artifact. Bakker fumed while texting his agents, trying to find out what had happened.

Their answers were less than satisfactory.

With one sweep of his arm, he knocked almost everything on his desk to the floor.

Adolfus raised his head. The fiercely loyal wolf dog sensed his master's distress. Rumor had it that Bakker saved the vicious dog from execution after it had killed a man. Bakker then trained Adolfus to answer only to him. His employees believed the animal was the only living thing that Bakker loved. Or tolerated.

Knock. Knock. His administrative assistant entered, saw her employer's enraged face, and clearly looked like she wished she had ignored the noise. The wolf dog growled at her.

"Clean this up." Bakker strode toward the door.

Adolfus whined.

The man turned and nodded at the animal, who immediately sprang to his side. After leaving the building, they entered the back seat of a discreetly armored vehicle before the driver had a chance to register Bakker's approach and open the door for him.

"Drive!" Bakker commanded.

The Lincoln Navigator pulled away from the curb, circling the block before finally parking not too far away.

Eventually, a back door to the auction house opened, and Godfrey Munk, a New York-based crime lord in Bakker's employ, took the seat across from him. "The auction house no longer has possession of *lot 17*."

"Who does?" Bakker hissed.

"They said they don't keep track of items that are no longer in their purview."

Bakker's voice remained controlled but cold as ice. "What the hell happened to it?"

"They said they don't know."

Adolfus sensed Munk's fear and growled.

Bakker smiled, stroking the animal affectionately before returning his attention to Munk. "Get out and wait for *Galerie Blanc* workers. They'll have to leave the building eventually. One of them must know what happened to it."

After Munk exited the vehicle, Bakker grabbed his cell phone and made a discreet call to the police *Oberst*. He learned about a reported break-in at the auction house and questioned why he wasn't informed.

"I was told it was minor," the colonel on the other end of the line answered. "The only thing stolen was a trinket of insignificant value."

Bakker threw his phone with such force that it broke when it hit the partition between himself and his driver.

Why would someone bother stealing a seemingly insignificant object?

He thought he knew the answer. Now, he wanted to know who he was in competition with for Hero's Knot.

Tray broke into a broad smile as he guided his car onto the exit for Roscoe, New York.

He arrived at the fishing cabin after two a.m. He didn't want to be noticed, so the timing suited him. There were no other cabins or houses within view, and he felt fairly certain he had arrived unseen. Instead of entering the cabin, he walked around back and unlocked the door to a root cellar on the property.

Slipping inside, he turned on a flashlight, brushing spiderwebs off his face and gagging on the smell of mold as he made his way to the back. He aimed the light at a dark crevasse under a corner ledge of the foundation. Opening his backpack, he removed an object securely wrapped in leather and shoved it into the small opening. He kicked old mulch and rodent droppings over it and doused the light before stepping out and locking the root cellar door. Taking a deep breath, he crept back to his car, driving a quarter mile before turning on his headlights.

Thank God, that's done.

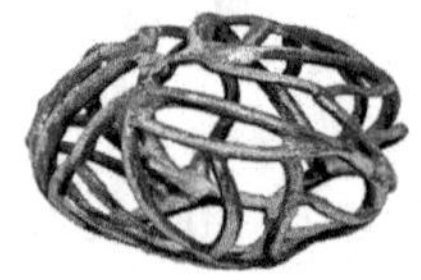

CHAPTER FOUR

Three years later

Carey stared at the power plant looming before him. Its two fat spouts belched white water vapor into a milky blue sky. *If all goes well, I may be able to shop for a ring this afternoon, take Caterina out to dinner at Marcel's tonight, and start planning our honeymoon tomorrow. If she says yes.* Two wrinkles formed between his brows. *What if she says no?* He shook his head. *Think positively.*

He inhaled deeply, girding himself for the day ahead. Everything about the surrounding area looked peaceful, even though he'd been warned there might be a problem. He'd spent the past two years investigating a troubling series of anomalies at nuclear facilities across the country as part of his job for the NRC. Today, he would conduct an unscheduled inspection of the Watts Bar Nuclear Plant in Spring City, Tennessee.

He flashed a badge and handed the security guard his federal ID. "Carey Lennox to see Ned Vonnegut."

The security guard stiffened, eyeing the ID suspiciously. "Do you have an appointment?"

"No."

"I need to make sure Mr. Vonnegut is here before I can let you in."

"I can wait."

The managing director told the guard to give Carey free rein.

Once inside, Carey announced his inspection. He observed the workers' reactions, trying to determine whether a problem at this plant might be part of a synchronized scheme. All he had to do was focus on ferreting out acts of sabotage and identify the culprits responsible.

As he waited for the head of engineering, he thought he saw a familiar face—a man he'd witnessed making an egregious error at a different nuclear plant a few years earlier. He racked his brain, trying to remember the man's name.

"Mark Allen, right?" he called out to the man as he approached him.

The worker looked up and froze momentarily. "Are you referring to me?" The man offered his hand. "The name's Pete Majewski. Who are you?"

Carey cocked his head, studying the man as he shook his hand. He felt sure this was the same man he'd previously had fired. "You have a doppelgänger." He kept his voice light. "I would have sworn that you're Mark Allen."

"Yeah? Well, everyone is supposed to have a double somewhere. Even you."

Carey thought of his twin brother and smiled. "I guess you're right. Sorry about the mistaken identity."

He walked away, thinking their exchange had seemed strained. He had seen the guy freeze when he first called his name, and for a moment, he had looked scared. *Something is going on here, and I need to find out what it is.*

The manager of engineering approached Carey and invited him to the other side of the vast space to start his inspection.

In the meantime, Pete Majewski picked up his tools—glad he hadn't started *work* yet—and headed toward a stairwell. Two steps above the landing, he launched himself forward on purpose and cursed loudly as he fell.

Someone out on the floor who heard him popped his head into the stairwell. "Are you okay? What happened?" He helped Majewski up.

"I tripped over my own two feet." Majewski stood there, clutching the arm he had landed on. "My whole side is throbbing."

"At least you can stand up, so it can't be too bad. You'd better get over to Health Services so they can check you out." He picked up Majewski's tools. "I'll carry this over for you."

"Thanks. I really appreciate it."

And Health Services is as good a place as any to hide out, at least until Carey Lennox is gone.

Once he was alone, Majewski pulled out his cell phone and called his boss—not his supervisor at the power plant, but the other *boss* he worked for—a man named Achille Pasquarelli.

Majewski had immediately recognized Carey as the man who'd gotten him fired from a previous nuclear job where he had worked under his real name, Mark Allen. Afterward, he had been blacklisted and unable to find another position until he remembered his college roommate, Pete Majewski. Pete had died in a car accident the year after they graduated. Mark could still picture the two of them at graduation, clutching identical engineering degrees. He initially assumed just enough of Majewski's identity to obtain another job. However, by that time, he was so overcome by debt it became easier to take on Majewski's entire persona and leave the burden of being Mark Allen far behind.

Unfortunately, Achille had learned about the impersonation from a constituent who complained about someone applying for credit in his late son's name. Achille found the source of the problem, but instead of turning him in, he told the *new* Majewski he would keep his secret if the engineer performed some special jobs for him.

Majewski was brought back from his reverie when Achille's voice on the other end of the phone demanded, "What is it?"

He cleared his throat. "Trouble just walked through the door."

ACHILLE PASQUARELLI HAD a reputation for getting things done. He prided himself on being a facilitator and a fixer, and more importantly, he worked as both administrative director and campaign manager for US Senator Phineas Paige.

On that sunny morning in Washington, DC, Paige sat behind his desk at the Dirksen Senate Office Building, busily editing new legislation he planned to introduce. People called him the "Anti-Nuke Senator." He had long ago declared nuclear reactors "dangerous" and worked diligently to have them all closed, even if it meant *proving* how dangerous they were. He was single-minded yet dedicated to his favorite issue and spent hours drafting legislation and writing arguments against the use of nuclear power.

He hated being interrupted while he worked. Achille usually provided a buffer between the senator and the "small," annoying details that plagued him. Whenever there was a bump in the road, Achille came to the rescue. So, when he told the senator, "One of our staffers is having a little problem with an NRC investigator," Paige replied, "See what you can do to fix the problem."

That made Achille smile. He knew Paige hated the day-to-day details of keeping his political machine running and had, perhaps unknowingly, ceded nearly autonomous authority to his administrative director. "Consider it handled."

DURING HIS LUNCH break at the Tennessee power plant, Carey called Dr. Caterina Volpicella. "Do you have time to talk?"

"Yes. Are you having a tough day?"

"I think I just saw a guy who should not be employed by any nuclear power facility—working at the plant I'm inspecting."

"And the problem is …?"

"He made a boneheaded mistake a couple of years ago that could have caused a meltdown. They fired him, and it should have been impossible for him to get another job in the industry. But I spotted him today. He told me I was wrong when I called out his name, and he said he was someone else. However, 'Mr. Majewski'—probably an alias—has the same scar on his right thumb and birthmark under his left eye as the previously fired Mark Allen."

"Wow." Cat leaned back in her office chair and gazed out the window at the various buildings within view of the Smithsonian. "No wonder spies aren't supposed to have scars or visible markings. They're too identifying."

Carey laughed. "Where'd you hear that?"

"I don't know. I think I read it a long time ago."

"In a spy novel?"

It was Caterina's turn to laugh. "Probably. Will you be home this weekend?"

"I sure hope so. Why?"

"I'm thinking of making a lusciously lavish lasagna using four types of cheese, three kinds of meat, two different wines, and thick, homemade noodles that stand upright rather than lie flat. It would be a shame to eat all that deliciousness by myself. So let me know as soon as possible because if you're going to be away, I'll need time to invite the handsome football pro who just moved in across the hall. I wouldn't want to rush him. He'll need time to select a good wine and possibly buy me flowers."

"You drive a hard bargain."

"But a delicious one."

As IT TURNED out, Carey had no time that evening to shop for a ring. Minor problems at the power plant, along with the accompanying explanations and paperwork, kept him busy all day.

His only reward was that he managed to have a quiet

dinner with Caterina, during which he never let on that he'd originally planned to propose to her that evening.

As the week progressed, he found he had no spare time to look for an engagement ring. The number of anonymous tips about issues at various power plants increased steadily, and he felt pressured to find the source of the problem.

A week later, he found himself at another troubled facility—this time, at the Oyster Creek Nuclear Generating Station in Forked River, New Jersey.

He needed to inspect the plant's underground tank rooms, which required full gear—an anti-contamination suit, respirator, and radiation monitor. Booties, gloves, and a hood completed the outfit. At best, the wearer looked like a hazmat worker, at worst, he resembled the Michelin Man. It didn't matter. The disposable suits were mandatory when inspecting tank rooms.

This was Carey's least favorite part of his job. He'd told his brother it made him feel like he was about to *descend into Hell.* Yet, for the second time this month, he needed to suck it up and check things out.

If he'd had a choice, he would have picked a different day for the inspection. His head wasn't in it, not after finding an envelope on the windshield of his car that morning with the warning,

YOU ARE A DEAD MAN

It was spelled out in letters cut from glossy magazine pages. *Who does that anymore? Why bother with all this drama when all the sender had to do was go to a library and print out the threat on a public printer?*

Still, he refused to allow the message to impede his mission. He picked up a camera and descended the ladder, taking pictures of the conditions inside the tank and mentally listing the questions he might have to ask when he finally climbed out.

He worked carefully, safety being his primary concern. He knew he shouldn't stay in the tank longer than two minutes, and he soon climbed out without a hitch.

I hope the next one goes as easily.

He changed into a fresh disposable suit for the second tank and climbed down. His radiation monitor started signaling almost immediately. Something was very wrong. It didn't take long to find the source of the problem, and it had no simple solution. The plant would have to power down so they could make the repair. Unfortunately, the resulting work would dangerously increase workers' exposure to radiation.

Carey emerged, removed the contaminated suit, and informed the supervisor about the need to cut power. "There's a valve down there that has to be dealt with."

"Are you sure the valve is not just doing its job?"

"It appears to be set too high. I need to know the name of the last person who worked in this section of the reactor. I'll also need a mechanic with me to handle the repair."

"You're going back down there? As an inspector, didn't you already do your job just by identifying the problem?"

"It's also my job to make sure it's resolved. I want to see a list of everyone who's worked in this area for the past few months."

"Sure, but it's mostly the same guys every day."

"Doesn't matter," Carey said. "I'd like to have it by the end of the day."

All hands were on deck for the plant's power reduction. It took hours to power down before Carey and a mechanic could descend into the tank room. Their goal was to work as quickly as possible. In the end, they discovered the valve was in good working order. That was good news. However, it meant someone had deliberately set it to produce major damage and cause a meltdown—a clear act of *sabotage*.

Later that evening, as the crew re-powered the plant, Carey studied the roster of workers. The name *Majewski* jumped out at him. He pointed it out to the senior manager. "How long has this guy been working here?"

"Majewski? He just started this week. We were lucky to get him. He used to work at a power plant in Tennessee. Why?"

"Where is he now?"

"He clocked out a couple of hours ago. He's gone for the weekend."

"When he returns, he needs to be held for questioning."

"You think he did this?"

"Just between you and me, this isn't the first time his name has been associated with trouble at a power plant." Carey handed his card to the manager. "As soon as you see him again, contact this number at the NRC."

It was close to midnight by the time Carey walked out the door. He climbed into his car and sent an encrypted email to his boss, outlining what had happened. Closing his eyes, he slumped against the headrest for a moment. *I can't remember the last time I felt this exhausted.* He should have found a nearby motel to crash at but decided to make the four-hour drive home while there was little traffic on the roads.

He pulled out of the parking lot, unaware he had a tail.

Speeding along I-95 in Maryland, Carey attempted to stifle a yawn. He couldn't help but think about the note he'd found on his car early that morning. *I bet it's tied to my hunt for a saboteur. I must be getting close.*

He glanced in his rear-view mirror. He was not alone on the road. There had been a car about a half-mile behind him for a while now. Sometimes, Carey would slow down as fog settled on areas of the roadway, allowing the car behind him to get closer, but then it would slow down as well. The other car had demonic-looking headlights and only one working fog lamp. He wondered if it was an omen.

Stop imagining things that aren't there.

He pulled off the interstate into a gas station with a twenty-four-hour convenience store. He topped off his gas tank and bought a can of Red Bull to keep himself awake.

Pulling back onto the road, he did his best Willie Nelson impersonation, singing, *On the Road Again.* It was the middle of the night, and the road appeared empty. He passed an on-ramp and saw a vehicle's headlights pulling onto the highway, followed by the blare of a horn. In his rear-view mirror, he saw a second pair of headlights pop on—the same evil-looking headlights he'd previously seen. That's when his paranoia set in. *I've got to lose this guy.*

He punched the gas as he approached the next exit and sped up the ramp. He blew a few lights before doubling back onto the highway, heading east toward New York instead of west toward his home in Arlington.

I need Tray. Together, we may be able to learn who this guy is and find out what he wants. If Carey turned out to be mistaken, he and his brother would have a good laugh over it.

He made it all the way to Trenton before he noticed the same pattern of headlights behind him. A few more cars were on the road now, even though the sun hadn't risen yet. He wished he knew where the local police stations were so he could get help. He pressed a button on his steering wheel and asked the hands-free assistant to dial Tray's number. No answer. *Where are you?*

Carey fumbled as he pulled out his phone. He could use the GPS tracker to locate his brother's cell. His jaw dropped when he saw Tray's marker out in the Hamptons.

Maybe Carey's tail would get tired, bogged down in traffic, or just give up.

If not, at least I won't be driving all this way for nothing.

Traffic got heavier as he drove east on the Long Island Expressway. He could see a glimmer of lighter sky on the horizon. If it weren't for the adrenaline coursing through his veins, he would have fallen asleep at the wheel hours ago.

He waited a while before calling Tray again. It went straight to voicemail, so he left a message.

"Hey, bro, I really need to talk with you. I may have some trouble on my hands, and I need your help to get me out of it. I've got a big weekend planned. I'm going on a huge shopping spree for a tiny box. But first, I need your assistance with this problem. Seriously. Call me as soon as you receive this message."

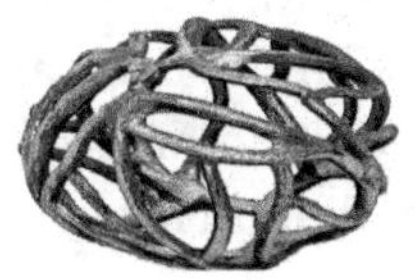

CHAPTER FIVE

TRAY TWIRLED AISLINN under his arm, sending her spinning across the dance floor of Gurney's Montauk Resort as they celebrated her cousin's wedding. The couple had clicked from the moment they'd met, and a whirlwind romance ensued. Call it love, lust, or chemistry—whatever category fit best—Tray wanted more.

"You're a good dancer, AY-sleen."

"Stop right there, Train-ERR. No one makes fun of my fine Irish name. It's pronounced Ash-lin, as if you didn't know. And I'd be careful about poking fun at other people's names when your own could be confused with someone who teaches animals how to jump through hoops. Besides, my name means *dream* in Gaelic. What does yours mean?"

"Son of the Strong Man," he said proudly, twirling her again.

"Either way, it sounds like you work for the circus."

Aislinn was the only person Tray knew when they first

arrived at the wedding. However, now that he'd met her extended family, he felt like part of the gang. And although he would never admit it out loud, he wished he had been lucky enough to have a family like hers to call his own. Not that he didn't love his brother and his aunt, but they hardly filled a table. Aislinn's family filled an emptiness he would never confess to, not even to himself.

He'd only known Aislinn for two weeks, but the couple had spoken over the phone every day they were apart, and he could already imagine carving out a future together.

Aislinn spun back into his arms, and he slipped both hands around her waist, pulling her close for a kiss. Even this admittedly chaste kiss on the dance floor made his testosterone surge. He touched his forehead to hers. "Perhaps we could go back to the inn."

She shook her head. "I can't. I still have bridal party duties. I need to toast Caitlyn and Nick, and I'm craving a slice of wedding cake. I don't usually eat cake, but this is a special Swedish almond concoction with a frangipane twist disguised under a layer of fondant. I've only had it twice before, but it can make the angels weep with happiness."

Tray sighed, dropping his chin to his chest for a moment before speaking. "All the toasts were an hour ago."

"Everyone else's toast was an hour ago, but I didn't want to get lost in the shuffle, so I'm toasting the cake."

Tray opened his mouth to speak, but nothing came out. He didn't want to alienate her by saying something stupid, so he shut his mouth and smiled. "And then?"

She winked. "And then I'm all yours."

They walked out onto the resort's ocean-front deck and watched as the waves rolled in. Off in the distance, a trawler slowly headed east. Above, a silvery moon—obscured by narrow wisps of cloud—ruled the twilight sky. "It's so peaceful here," Aislinn said, shivering as an offshore breeze brushed past them.

"You're cold." Tray unbuttoned his tux jacket and grabbed both sides, opening it like wings.

Aislinn slid her arms around his waist, and he closed the jacket around her. "I could stay here like this forever."

"I feel the same way," he replied, kissing the top of her head. He worked his way down to her neck.

A member of the staff coughed. "Excuse me, Miss Gilchrist? They're rolling the wedding cake into the reception."

"Duty calls," Aislinn whispered to Tray.

The cake resembled a lovely, traditional wedding confection on top, with muted pastel sugar pearls and edible flowers trailing down supporting tiers to a large bottom layer covered in a flamboyant riot of finger-painted fondant.

Ash tapped her champagne flute with a spoon. "Can I have everyone's attention?"

The room quieted down, and she launched into her speech. "When Caitlyn and I were little, she was always the outgoing princess, and I was the shy little handmaiden. She used to tell me I had no imagination. And at the time, she was right. However, she made it her life's work to ignite my creative spirit, and it all started with finger-painting in kindergarten." Ash removed a rumpled piece of artwork hidden under a linen napkin and held it up. It was covered with a finger-painted design similar to the base of the cake. "Caitlyn told me this is what life should look like. Then she told me *this,*" she turned the paper around so everyone could see the blank side, "is what *my* life looked like. She said—and I quote—'This will never do.'

"Thanks to my gorgeous, talented cousin, I have embraced her love of color and art, and I'm now a professional artist. Unfortunately," Aislinn paused for dramatic effect, "Caitlyn still paints like this." She flipped the picture around again and waited for the laughter to die down before continuing. "In her honor, I have recreated her original design on the base of her wedding cake as my special gift to her and her new husband." She held up her champagne glass. "Caitlyn and Nick, may your life together be as colorful, sweet, and as multilayered as this cake. You two are truly the best."

After the cake, Tray stood and held his hand out to Aislinn. "Shall we?"

"No, you shall not," her mother said before winking coyly at Aislinn. "You've danced with my daughter plenty. Now it's time for *me* to see what you're made of on the dance floor. Come on." She grabbed Tray's arm and led him away.

Aislinn's father took his daughter's hand and guided her toward the dance floor. "I like this young man of yours."

She smiled. "I do, too. He's so very … nice."

Afterward, Tray grabbed Aislinn's hand and said, "Now?" But before they got to the door, her cousin Caitlyn called all the single women to the center of the room for the bouquet toss.

"I have to," Aislinn argued. "I'm her maid of honor."

She stood off to the side, not wanting to compete with everyone, but Caitlyn never did have good aim. The bouquet sliced right, forcing Aislinn to either catch it or let it bounce off her chest. She refused to try.

An arm sprang out from the side at the last moment, catching the bouquet before it struck her.

Everyone stared at Tray, holding the bouquet.

"Not fair," a young woman cried.

Tray plucked out a passionflower and placed it behind Aislinn's ear before tossing the bouquet into a high arc over the heads of the unmarried women. They all lunged at once, like a giant centipede, with arms outstretched toward the collection of exotic blooms. Tray pulled Aislinn out of the room. "Let's go."

AISLINN AND TRAY had their arms around each other's waists as they entered The Old Salt House lobby, a three-hundred-year-old inn in East Hampton.

"How was the wedding?" owner Emily Brooks asked, walking out from behind the desk where she checked in her guests. One of the wide plank floorboards creaked, and she shook her head. "I'll fix that one of these days. But for now, spill!"

"Caitlyn looked beautiful," Aislinn gushed, "and it was the perfect day for a ceremony on the beach. They had the afternoon sun behind them, and a chamber music quartet was set up on a small deck playing classical melodies. It was exquisite. We moved inside for the reception because, according to my aunt, the mosquitoes weren't invited. Having first-hand knowledge of the tenacity of our local bloodsuckers, I was fine with that."

Anna laughed. "As far as I know, your cousin's wedding is the biggest one in the Hamptons all year. I'm sure she'll get plenty of mentions in the press."

"Trust me—if she doesn't—my aunt will probably send video highlights to the media that they can stream."

"I remember your aunt being like that when I dated your cousin Jude. She sent our prom picture to the New

York Times and the East Hampton Star. The Times couldn't care less, but the Star printed it."

Anna noticed Tray taking a step toward the hallway and immediately recognized the universal male signal for *can we get going?* "Do you need anything before you settle in for the night? Bottles of water? Fresh baked oatmeal cookies?" She looked at Tray. "We make them with chocolate chips instead of raisins."

He hesitated. "Okay. You've twisted my arm."

Aislinn hit him in the shoulder with her clutch. "How can you think of eating anything? We just worked our way through a huge feast."

"It's the chocolate." He held up his forefinger for a moment before continuing. "The wedding cake was good. No. It was great. But there was no chocolate. I need a little chocolate to sustain my energy."

"It won't take me a minute." Emily disappeared behind the kitchen door and emerged a moment later with a white paper bag. She handed it to Tray. "Four cookies, in case you want to share."

He laughed, thanking her.

"Come on." Aislinn linked her arm through his. "Our little hideaway awaits."

They disappeared down the hall and used a polished brass key to open the very last door, *Room 2*. It had a king-size bed covered with a fluffy duvet and eiderdown pillows. The floor had the same wide planks as the reception area and was covered by a huge area rug the color of sea glass.

Tray opened the French doors to their private patio before turning to look at Aislinn. "Are you okay with a little fresh air, or do you agree with your aunt about mosquitoes."

"Let's leave them closed for tonight. Too many people here know exactly who I am, and I don't need them listening to me in the throes of passion."

"Good answer."

After making love, they nestled against each other, not quite ready to say goodnight. "If you hadn't been at that *last hurrah* bash before Caitlyn and Nick got married," Aislinn said, "I would never have met you. I'm so glad you were invited."

"I wasn't invited. I was at Gosman's Dock and overheard one of the bridesmaids talking about the party to a stockbroker I know. I figured it was free booze."

Aislinn hit him with her pillow. "I can't believe you were an interloper. I thought you were a friend of Nick's, or else I would never have left with you."

He rolled onto his side, lifting his head so he could look down at her. "Be careful about what you say to me. Your mother loves me."

Aislinn laughed. "I think my parents like you better than they like me."

"I wonder if your mother would like me as much if she knew we didn't come up for air all last weekend in my condo."

"She'd be more interested in why someone who appraises antiques doesn't have a single antique inside his entire home."

"It's only five rooms, and it's in a very modern building. Besides, not all chicks are into antiques."

She pouted. "Is that what I am? A chick?"

He nuzzled her neck. "You're an extraordinary chick," he whispered in her ear. "You, my dear Aislinn, are a chick of the first caliber." He made a big show of turning off his phone. "And tonight, I'm dedicating myself entirely to you because you deserve no less.

"Besides, I'm surrounded by antiques all day long at the auction house where I work. When I go home at night, I prefer to rest my eyes on bright, shiny, young stuff. Pretty stuff. Like you."

"Now, you're just being ridiculous. Shut up before I—"

He kissed her before she could say anything more.

Dust motes danced in the morning light as Aislinn combed her hair. She caught Tray's reflection in the bathroom mirror. "We should take a walk on the beach before meeting up with my family."

"What time is the brunch?"

"Not until noon. We have more than an hour for a nice stroll along the sand."

Tray picked up the dress pants he had carelessly thrown on the floor the previous night and placed them on a hanger. "Okay, as long as we can avoid being targeted by seagulls with gastrointestinal distress."

"Ew."

He laughed. "Just wanted to make sure you were paying attention."

"Thanks for the imagery."

On the marble top of the flamed mahogany antique dresser lay a miniature watercolor that Aislinn had given him the previous day. Tray picked it up. "You're an excellent artist, you know."

"I try," she said, grabbing a mesh market bag. "Let's go."

As soon as Tray locked their room, she pulled him over to her little sports car. "I'm driving."

"You don't like my driving?"

"Do you have an East Hampton parking permit?"

"Uh … no."

"I do. I'm driving," she said with a smile. "Get in."

Tray spotted a pair of men's glasses on the ground. He picked them up.

"Come on," she yelled from the front seat.

He slipped them into his cargo pants pocket. *I'll hand them in when we get back.*

He practically folded himself in half to get into Aislinn's Miata, bumping his head on the top of the doorframe. "It would be so much more comfortable to take my SUV and pay the parking ticket."

"No."

"Fine," he relented, rubbing his head.

CAREY HAD BEEN driving all night. He wasn't sure what had happened to the vehicle with demonic headlights that had been tailing him since midnight; sunlight made seeing the unique pattern in his rearview mirror more challenging. For all Carey knew, his unwanted tail may have turned off his lights or left the highway for his destination.

He studied the phone he'd used to track his twin brother's location. By the time he'd arrived on the tip of Long Island, Tray had physically moved. Carey found his brother's empty car, but the tracker showed Tray was now somewhere in the village of East Hampton. *Please stay in one spot. I need you.*

AISLINN POKED HER toe into the wet sand on Main Beach, stooping to pick up the seashell she'd unearthed. "This one is huge. I can paint a little beach scene on it and sell it at one of the local gift shops." She slipped it into the market bag.

"Are you happy doing that?" Tray asked. "Selling small works of art at local shops?"

"It's not like I'm *not* negotiating to get some of my larger canvases into galleries and exhibitions. But everything takes time, as well as connections. The profit from little touristy things like this seashell keeps my landlord at bay."

"I wish I could do something to help."

"Thank you, but I can do it on my own."

"How long have you lived in East Hampton?" Tray asked.

"I was born here, but I live in Sag Harbor now. Although technically, I'm still in the town of East Hampton, if not the village. I've only been staying with Caitlyn's family for the wedding. But after we leave the inn, I'll be heading back to my studio in Sag Harbor."

Tray's face lit up. "You have your own art studio."

"No!" she said a little too emphatically. Her shoulders slumped. "My studio *apartment*. It's tiny. Claustrophobic. Which is why I suggested we stay at The Old Salt House instead of inviting you to my home."

"If it's anything like the rest of the area, I'll bet it's still charming. There's something intrinsically enchanting about the Hamptons and the ambiance of the local villages."

"It *is* inspiring. I do a lot of waterscapes and bucolic windmill scenes. And I've sold several paintings through restaurants that put them on display because it's free art for them. However, the term *starving artist* did not come from two disparate words that randomly ended up next to each other. Eking a living out of being creative can be challenging. That said, there's a big exhibit planned at the end of the month at Guild Hall. If I could get into that, it would be like getting my foot in the door."

"Would it help if an established antique and art appraiser from Manhattan called to ask if they'll be exhibiting anything by local prodigy Aislinn Gilchrist?"

"I don't know about 'local prodigy,' but it might light a fire under someone."

"I'll do it as soon as I return to work, so they'll see the business name on caller ID."

Her smile turned brighter than the sun. "I like the way you think."

CAREY SCRUTINIZED THE map app, too busy to notice that the car following him had pulled over on the other side of the street. Without the headlights on, no one could tell they appeared demonic, nor that one of the fog lamps didn't light up. The car was easy to identify in the dead of night but not so much in the pure light of day.

He got back in his car and concentrated on tracking Tray's signal on his phone. With his attention diverted, he failed to see the person tailing him make a U-turn and continue following him from a distance.

Tray's signal jumped to a new location. *Not again,* thought Carey. *You've got to stay still, Tray. But that's not in your nature, is it. You were always afraid of missing out on the next big thing. Please find a place to roost for just a little while. I'm counting on you.*

Carey turned right onto North Main Street. Tray's signal had once again come to a rest a few blocks ahead. He saw a car pull away from the curb, and Carey maneuvered into the parking spot. He could walk the rest of the way, as long as his twin brother stayed put.

*

Tray and Aislinn had arrived fashionably late at Chapter One on Main, the restaurant her aunt had chosen for a post-wedding brunch. The bride and groom were *in absentia*, having departed for their honeymoon the previous night. The remaining family members huddled around tables with mimosas in hand to share one final meal before leaving the celebration in the Hamptons for their respective homes.

Aislinn leaned against Tray as they looked over the menu and whispered, "The lemon ricotta pancakes with edible flowers are to die for."

"I don't know if I feel like dying today. Someone last night said something about 'chocolate croissant bread pudding.'"

"That's more of a dessert than a breakfast."

"You're right. I'll have steak and eggs with breakfast potatoes first. Then I'll have the chocolate croissant bread pudding for dessert."

"You're incorrigible."

"I just know how to live life."

While they waited to be served, Tray turned on his phone and saw several missed calls. He scrolled through them and clicked on the last one from Carey. While he listened to the voicemail, the ringtone reserved for his twin brother rang out.

"I've got to take this." Tray slipped out of his chair and walked to the back of the restaurant, taking the call in private. "Carey—"

His identical twin's frantic voice on the other end of the phone cut him off. *"Tray. Thank God. I need your help. I think somebody is following me."*

Tray felt his pulse quicken. "Where are you?"

"East Hampton, behind whatever building you're in now."

Tray froze. "How did you find me in East Hampton?"

"I used the tracker app on my phone to find your cell."

Tray's reflexes responded uncomfortably. *If Carey can track me that easily, so can others.* Tray could think of a thousand and one reasons why that might be catastrophic. "I'm on my way." As he hurried toward the back door, he heard an odd *tic-thump* sound, then a groan followed by the phone crashing to the ground. A moment later, he rushed out of the building. Carey lay crumpled on the pavement, not ten feet away, his eyelids fluttering as a bloodstain slowly spread across his chest.

Movement caught Tray's attention. He glimpsed someone's back, disappearing around a far corner. He had no time to give chase. Instead, he picked up the sweatshirt his brother had dropped and used it to stop Carey from bleeding out. Emotion made his voice husky. "Don't worry, Ca. I won't let you die."

Carey closed his eyes and winced as his brother applied pressure to stop the bleeding. Tray used his free hand to call the police.

"Nine-one-one, what's your emergency?"

"Shooting behind Chapter One on Main in East Hampton."

A glint on the ground, almost obscured by blood, caught Tray's eye—a *loose key.*

He glanced at Carey again, only to see his twin brother shudder before his body slackened. He checked Carey's neck for a pulse but couldn't feel one. "I think he's … dead."

"Please stay—"

He disconnected the call. *There's no time. Especially if*

someone is after me because of the artifact and killed Carey by mistake. He looked around, making sure no one else lurked nearby. He quickly checked Carey's pockets. The rest of his brother's keys were missing, along with his phone. However, Carey's wallet remained untouched. Tray stilled, his stomach clenching as he made a split-second decision. He swapped his wallet for his brother's, picked up the bloody key, and took off.

CHAPTER SIX

AT THE POST-WEDDING brunch inside Chapter One on Main, Aislinn's cousin Jude entertained her with stories about his recent trip to Machu Picchu. It didn't bother her that Tray's chair remained empty until the sound of sirens interrupted the conversation. A moment later, police pulled up in front of the restaurant.

Jude put down his fork. "I wonder where the police are going." He walked to the window to look outside. He needn't have bothered. Chapter One on Main turned out to be their destination.

Customers appeared both annoyed and excited by the sudden police presence.

"This will give the rumor mill and gossip mongers something to feed on for days," Aislinn's aunt said.

Sergeant Jefferson Williams approached the man standing next to Jude and identified himself. "We received a tip about a possible shooting behind your establishment.

Do you know anything about that?"

The owner's eyes widened in surprise. "No."

"Mind if we pass through to the back?"

"I'll show you the way," the owner replied, leading them to the rear exit.

Jude returned to the table and sat down next to Aislinn. "Somebody got shot out back. Police are here to investigate."

Aislinn jumped out of her seat. "Tray!" She ran for the back door.

A waiter stopped her. "Can I help you? The restrooms are over on the right. Only the kitchen is back here."

"My boyfriend came back here to take a phone call—a while ago."

The waiter stiffened. "Oh." His brow knitted. "Okay. You know the cops are out there."

"Yes." She pushed past him and opened the door. She saw Police Officer Holden Fisher, an old classmate, standing watch nearby. "Hey, Holden, what's going on?" She didn't see any victim. Or Tray. It wasn't until she turned to go back inside that she noticed Sergeant Williams examining someone lying on the ground.

Fisher stepped in front of her, blocking her view. "It's best you go inside."

"I'm looking for someone." She leaned to the side to look past him, but the sergeant shifted his weight, blocking her view again.

Williams used his pen to pick up a narrow silk cord and bagged it as evidence. He searched the victim's pocket and found his wallet. He notified the county they had an apparent murder victim and gave them the address in East Hampton.

Aislinn couldn't help but overhear the sergeant say, "His name is Traynor Lennox. He appears to have been shot."

Suddenly, Aislinn felt the sounds of life all around her fade until all she heard was her own scream. "Nooo!" She grabbed Fisher's arm, at first to push past him but then to hold herself up as her world went dark.

PO Fisher caught her as she sagged to the ground, lifting her into his arms.

Williams turned around. "What's going on?"

"She overheard you. I think she knows the victim. I'll take her inside." Fisher carried Aislinn into the restaurant, attracting everyone's attention.

"Oh my God, Aislinn," Monica Gilchrist cried, pushing her way toward her daughter.

"Does she belong to you?" Fisher asked.

"She's my daughter. She's here with her boyfriend." She looked around. "Where is Tray?"

"Traynor Lennox?" Fisher asked, looking for a couch or oversized chair for Aislinn. Seeing nothing better, he placed her on a regular restaurant chair at her family's table. Jude put an arm around her to keep her from sliding to the floor.

"Yes," her mother replied. "Don't tell me he hurt her."

Aislinn stirred, regaining consciousness.

Fisher lowered his voice. "Not as far as I'm aware. What can you tell me about Lennox?"

Monica's mouth hung open for a second before she answered. "Not much. We only met him the day before yesterday at my niece's rehearsal dinner. He seems like a nice man who makes my daughter happy."

Aislinn craned her neck and tried to get up. "What happened?"

"I think you kissed the pavement," Jude answered. When she looked at him quizzically, he added, "You passed out."

Fisher pulled over a chair and sat next to Aislinn. "EMTs are on their way. In the meantime, what can you tell us about Traynor Lennox?"

She looked at him quizzically. "I don't need an EMT." Suddenly, tears rolled down her face as she remembered hearing that Tray was dead. She took a few choking breaths. Her voice quavered as she did her best to explain who Tray was, and when Fisher asked for his address, she told him where to find Tray's condo in Manhattan and gave him Tray's cell phone number.

Sergeant Williams walked in from outside. "Backup is securing the perimeter until the medical examiner and forensics team arrive, but that won't be for a while. Did you find the victim's cell phone?"

"No," Fisher replied, "but Ash . . . Miss Gilchrist just gave me his number."

"Do you have your boyfriend's cell phone?" Sergeant Williams asked Aislinn.

"No. He was taking a call on it when he walked out back."

"Who was he speaking to?"

Her tears intensified. "I don't know," she answered between sobs.

Her family comforted her while police questioned everyone in the restaurant. No one saw anything other than Tray walking out back with his cell phone in hand.

By the time homicide detective Miles Molyneaux

arrived, village police had finished interviewing restaurant patrons and local businesses, taking note of their contact information. Molyneaux had a lengthy discussion with Sergeant Williams and Officer Fisher, during which the medical examiner and forensics team pulled around back.

Aislinn's relatives were told they were free to leave. Aislinn said she needed to be alone. She grabbed her mother's arm. "Could you drop me off at the inn?"

"I don't think you should go back there. Come to Aunt Jen's with us," her mother said.

"No. I need to be alone. If you don't want to take me, I can drive. I have my car outside."

Her father shook his head. "I don't think you should be driving. We'll drop you off and wait for you."

"No. Don't wait. I'll get an Uber back to the house when I'm ready."

Her father took a moment before answering. "Do you have your phone with you?"

"When don't I have my phone with me?" she replied, almost making him smile.

Her parents drove her to The Old Salt House. "Call if you need us," her mother said, squeezing her hand.

"I will," Aislinn replied, watching the car until it drove out of sight.

Steiger Bob couldn't get away from the scene of the Lennox shooting fast enough. *That silencer came in handy. Glad I brought it.* He stashed the gun in a fanny pack so he would look like a tourist. As he rounded the corner from behind the restaurant, he slowed to a walk to avoid looking guilty of anything. This was the last place he wanted to be taken in for questioning.

He casually got into his car and drove away, heading further east as if to do more sightseeing. After a few blocks, he doubled back toward the Long Island Expressway, thirty-five miles away. It wasn't until he was about to enter the LIE that he sent a quick text to Achille Pasquarelli.

Subject terminated.

Tray didn't have his car, and he couldn't use his phone to call an Uber. He would have to dump the phone so it couldn't be used to trace him.

He ran back to the inn, staying off the main roads. He couldn't wander the streets as himself; he needed to hole up somewhere, where nobody knew him. He stopped by his car only to remove cash he had stashed in a locked compartment. *Can't use the car.* He snuck into Room 2 at the inn via the back patio. People might guess he was still alive if he removed his belongings, so he checked his tablet, deleting anything he didn't want someone else to see. He would have to buy a new one. More than that, he would have to create an entirely new identity for himself until he caught Carey's killer. He ducked back out onto the patio.

Aislinn unlocked the door to the room she had shared with Tray. She froze when she thought she saw a shadow outside, but upon closer inspection, no one was there. Tray's duffel bag sat on a chair. She closed her eyes and rubbed her hands across the leather bag, tears rolling down her face. She picked it up and placed it on the bed, unzipping it. Only one clean shirt and a pair of black boxers remained inside. The corner of the liner on the bottom of the bag was bent. It bothered her. She pressed her fingers against it to straighten it out, but instead, the entire bottom shifted.

She lifted it out to fix it and discovered a large envelope marked *Classified Information; Restricted Data,* jammed inside the base of the bag. "Why would Tray have this?" Too curious to heed the words, *Classified Information,* she opened the envelope. It contained a confidential file about something called *Hero's Knot.*

A noise sounded outside, and she froze. Unwilling to stay in the room any longer, she stuffed the file in her tote bag and quickly exited the inn, requesting an Uber to take her back to the restaurant.

OF THE SMALL cadre of employees in Senator Phineas Paige's orbit, Steiger Bob was the low man on the totem pole. The senator, of course, was the central figure of the group. Achille, his administrative director, handled the day-to-day details and employed his own special brand of finesse to get things done. Pete Majewski, AKA Mark Allen, devised specific ways to reduce the public's trust in nuclear power plants and, in most cases, acted as a saboteur. When any of them needed extra help, Steiger Bob stepped in to handle various odd jobs. Unfortunately, Steiger often tackled assignments like a bull in a china shop; breakage was a given.

STEIGER BOB'S LIFE hadn't been easy. He had dropped out of high school, successfully running away from "home" after his *last* foster mother's boyfriend had badly beaten him one too many times. For the past decade, he'd supported himself by being a *dogsbody*—picking up small, menial jobs wherever possible. There wasn't much he wouldn't do to keep himself in beer and cigarettes. He'd met Achille when he bested the administrative director at a game of darts in a

DC bar. Steiger had collected fifty dollars for his win, and Achille had paid for his drinks for the rest of the evening. Before the night ended, Achille had offered Steiger some work, and the two had been associating ever since.

As much as he liked Achille, Steiger hated Senator Paige. The first time they'd met, the senator had wrinkled his nose like he smelled something sour, saying, "Steiger Bob? What kind of name is that? Is Steiger your last name? Surely, it's not your first. Or is it some sort of private joke? It sounds as if you don't know the difference between your first and last names. Why would you do that? It makes people feel uncomfortable."

Steiger immediately took offense. "For your information, Steiger is my real first name. My mother was fond of her father's name, and it's all spelled out clearly on my birth certificate."

He'd left it at that, and Paige hadn't asked any more questions. If the senator had, he might have learned that Steiger's last name was actually Roberts. It was a name Steiger refused to use because, after having run away from foster care, he didn't want to be caught and returned to the system. By the time he'd become an adult, his shortened last name was as much a part of him as his arms and legs, and he had the counterfeit documents to prove it. As far as he was concerned, Steiger Bob *was* his name—his only name—and the senator could take it or leave it. Like most people, Steiger hated feeling belittled, and he hated the senator for putting him in that position.

Still, it wasn't Paige he should have been worried about.

PAIGE MAY HAVE paid the bills, but Achille wielded the real power. No one realized he kept a detailed journal of every side job Steiger and Mark Allen performed at his request. Achille also kept notes on every bit of business he brokered for the senator.

In addition, the journal listed *favors* Achille had done for other powerful people—moving money, amassing weapons, providing heroin for a party. Achille considered himself a man of many talents; his journal was insurance. It could get a lot of people in trouble in Washington.

CHAPTER SEVEN

AISLINN RETURNED TO Chapter One on Main, relieved to see the police were still questioning diners. Detective Molyneaux noticed her by the front door and walked over. "Is there something you've forgotten?"

"I think there's something you need to know," she whispered. "Can we sit down?"

Molyneaux's eyes lit up. He led her to an empty table in a corner by the bar and pulled out a chair for her. "And what is that, Miss Gilchrist?"

She placed her bag on the floor next to her chair. "Um . . ." She twisted a mini vase holding a single bloom. "It's about Tray. The victim? I … uh … once noticed he had a top-secret file in his apartment. It was marked *classified* and *restricted*. Do you think he might have been a government agent or something?"

Molyneaux rubbed the stubble on the side of his face. "You saw this file in his apartment, you say?"

Aislinn felt herself blushing as she thought about the file in the bag at her feet. "Yes."

"In Manhattan?"

She couldn't look at the detective. "Yes."

"And what exactly was in the file?"

She cleared her throat. "I don't know. It said it was restricted."

"And the two of you drove out here from that apartment?"

"Tray did. I met him at The Old Salt House, where we stayed the last two nights for the wedding."

Molyneaux's jaw dropped. When he spoke, his voice had hardened. "You didn't mention anything before about staying at The Old Salt House."

Aislinn finally looked him in the eye, surprised by his sudden vehemence. "You didn't ask."

"I asked you for your address."

"And I gave you my address in Sag Harbor. I don't live at The Old Salt House."

The detective huffed. "Right. What room were you staying in?"

"Room 2. Our stuff is still there."

"Do you have the key?"

Aislinn took out her key but didn't hand it over. "Tray had one too. Couldn't you use his, so I'll have a way to get back in to pick up my stuff?"

"Once we've finished our initial investigation, we'll return everything that hasn't been entered into evidence. You can pick it up at police headquarters in Yaphank." Molyneaux held out his hand for the key as he studied the woman sitting across from him. "Or I could deliver it to your address in Sag Harbor."

*

Sitting at the bar—less than six feet away—a young woman named Jin Rumi nursed a Bellini as she listened in on everything Aislinn told the police detective. Jin turned to retrieve a mirror compact and lipstick from her shoulder bag, twisting in her seat to get a better view of Aislinn. She retouched her lipstick as she used the mirror to continue to spy on Aislinn and Molyneaux. Once their conversation ended, Jin calmly made her way outside and called her boyfriend, Calam Fergus, to tell him about the room at the inn. "You need to act quickly and search the place for the artifact before the police get there."

Are you going to meet me there? he asked.

"No. I'm going to stay here just in case anyone else has important information to share. Meet me here at the bar as soon as you're done. I need to order food, so they don't kick me out. The quicker you get here, the more there will be for you."

Yeah. See you in a few.

Just blocks away, Tray paid cash for a motel room. It was a place to keep out of sight while he figured out his next course of action. The room was clean, and bland, and certainly didn't look like a Hampton's resort, but what it lacked in luxury it made up for in concealment.

Being dead isn't all it's cracked up to be. The freedom he sought to investigate Carey's murder was sharply curtailed by losing the use of his car and credit cards, not to mention his FBI connections. And being isolated on the far end of eastern Long Island didn't help.

Tray suddenly remembered promising his brother that he wouldn't let him die. His face crumpled. He couldn't fight the sting of tears. Carey was more than his brother—he was a part of him, the other half of his brain, an extension of his conscience, someone who loved him unconditionally. When they were together, they interacted like a pair of highly trained swordsmen. Their thrust and parry brought to mind a well-choreographed scene. Tray disintegrated into sobs.

After several minutes of being enveloped by a black haze, his thinking grew more rational. *I hate men who cry. Carey is the one who always said men shouldn't be afraid to show their emotions. But I think it makes them look weak.* He looked up as if toward heaven. *I hope you're satisfied, Captain Beer Belly. You've reduced me to a blubbering fool.*

Tray took some deep breaths to bring back a sense of calm. *I need a plan of action.*

Sitting on the edge of the bed, he pulled out Carey's wallet. Inside, he found a pile of cash. *Why did he have $25,000 on him?* Tray suddenly thought of Caterina. He knew Carey had been serious about her and racked his brain to pick out bits and pieces of past conversations. Tray dropped his chin to his chest as he groaned. *The money is for a ring. That's what he meant when he said he was going on a huge shopping spree for a tiny box.*

He nearly choked when he groaned a second time— for a totally unrelated reason. He suddenly remembered the classified file he'd left in his duffel bag. He looked at the clock by the bed. *Can I make it back to The Old Salt House to retrieve that file before the police get there?*

EMILY BROOKS HAD a problem. The woman who usually helped her with weekend housekeeping at The Old Salt House had taken the day off to visit her new grandchild.

It shouldn't have mattered, considering everyone staying at the inn had either checked out or was already off-premises enjoying their day. Unfortunately, when the people in her only two-bedroom suite had settled their bill, they told her the toilet was clogged. Another family had already reserved that suite and could arrive at any time.

The inn owner felt the weight of responsibility pressing on her shoulders. *Into the breach,* she thought as she grabbed a plunger and the box of cleaning supplies and headed upstairs, leaving the lobby unattended.

WHILE EMILY WAS otherwise occupied, Calam Fergus easily broke into Room 2 without being seen. He quickly searched Tray and Aislinn's room, stopping in the bathroom to admire a sterling silver shaving mug and razor. He picked up the razor, running his finger near the blade's edge. *This is nice.*

His whole body jerked when his phone rang.

"Is it there?" Jin asked.

"Dammit, Jin, you scared the hell out of me. My phone wasn't on vibrate, and anyone could have heard it ringing. There's nothing here that fits the description you gave me."

"Look again."

He disconnected the call, then stilled when he heard the door open. He peeked outside the bathroom, irritated to see someone going through a duffel bag. The tickle of an impending sneeze ruffled the inside of Calam's nose. Before he gave himself away by sneezing, he rushed out and grabbed the man from behind. Tray threw him off. They knocked over a night table in the ensuing fight, sending a lamp crashing to the floor. Calam landed a punch on Tray's face, but it was only enough to draw blood without doing any real damage.

Upstairs, Emily froze when she heard the fight. After a moment, she came to her senses and called the police. She locked herself in the room she'd been cleaning and quietly strained to hear what was going on below.

Down in Room 2, Tray lunged for Calam, who pulled a pistol out of his waistband. The two men struggled, and moments later, the gun went off. Calam slumped in Tray's arms.

Before anyone could come to see what all the noise was about, Tray took off through the back patio.

It didn't take long for the police to arrive at the inn. Emily heard the sirens and prayed the sound would scare away whoever had been fighting. She hurried downstairs to let the police inside, giving them permission to search all the rooms.

They found Calam clinging to life on the floor of room 2.

Molyneaux joined the investigation after local police revealed the victim had been found in Tray Lennox's room. The detective arrived in time to see the forensic team bagging and tagging evidence. He clamped his lips together. He would have preferred to see everything first-hand. Instead, he could only look on while EMTs tried to stabilize the victim before taking him to the hospital.

Aislinn drove to Thorne Hall, her aunt and uncle's estate. Her mother had grown up at 'the Hall,' and Aislinn had spent nearly every summer there playing with her cousins.

She inhaled the familiar scent of her mother's perfume as Monica enveloped her in a bear hug. "We were so worried about you. We should have never allowed you to return to that empty room after what happened to Tray."

"What she said," her cousin Jude agreed, nodding toward her mother. He looked at her empty hands. "I thought you were picking up your stuff."

"The police said they'll return everything that isn't evidence after they're done investigating."

"They kept everything?"

Aislinn nodded.

Monica shook her head. "I doubt that was necessary."

"I don't know. I just need to be by myself for a while. Maybe take a nap. I'm exhausted."

"Of course you are, sweetie," her mother said. "I'll walk you upstairs."

"I don't need to be tucked in, Mom. I can find the room on my own. I'll see you all later."

Once Aislinn had left, Jude grabbed his car keys from the wooden bowl on the counter. "I'm going to the inn to see if I can retrieve her belongings," he told Monica. "Why should she have to wait?"

BY THE TIME Jude arrived at The Old Salt House, the police had already finished boxing everything as evidence.

"I just need to pick up Aislinn Gilchrist's belongings." He stopped when he noticed the blood on the floor. "What happened here?"

No one answered.

Detective Molyneaux took Jude's arm and led him outside. "Your cousin's room is off-limits. There's an active investigation going on. Please stay away and ask the rest of your relatives to do the same."

"Aislinn needs her stuff. You know, toothbrush … underwear."

"I'm sure she has enough to hold her over at home."

"But she's not home. She's in East Hampton with my family."

"She lives in Sag Harbor. It's only a fifteen-minute drive."

"She's too distraught to drive," Jude yelled over his shoulder as he jumped into his car and peeled out of the inn's driveway. An oncoming car swerved, and the driver leaned on his horn, signaling his anger. Jude wondered if the police would bother to chase him for almost causing an accident.

He drove to Aislinn's apartment, but the door was locked. She was the only person in the universe who didn't hide a key under the mat, or beneath a potted plant, or inside a fake rock. He knocked on a few doors, but none of the neighbors had been entrusted with a spare key to his cousin's apartment. Frustrated, he returned home, surprised to find three police cars in front of Thorne Hall.

He almost tripped over one of the front steps as he rushed inside and gasped when he saw a police officer slapping handcuffs around his cousin's wrists.

"Aislinn Gilchrist, you're under arrest for the attempted murder of Calam Fergus. You have the right to …"

He moved to stop them, but his father pulled him back. "Don't do anything stupid. I've already called our lawyer. Aislinn will have the best attorneys protecting her rights. I don't need to end up paying even more to get you out of jail for obstructing justice."

"But—"

"Stand down."

*

AT POLICE HEADQUARTERS, Aislinn didn't bother doing anything to help herself. She felt a mixture of shock, exhaustion, and guilt, although her guilt pertained to having read a classified file and not from murdering anyone.

Police prevented her father from entering the interrogation room. She could hear him complaining until the door closed, muffling outside sounds. She wrinkled her nose. The small room was more homely than homey, with a mixture of cinder block walls and panels that looked like oversized acoustic tiles. The vinyl tile floor felt a little tacky under her shoes, and the room smelled of disinfectant and sweat. She looked down at the table in front of her and wondered how many bodily fluids it had come in contact with over the years. She dropped onto a chair that appeared to be bolted to the floor. From above, cameras surveilled her every move, and—she imagined—anyone could be watching her through what she thought might be a ubiquitous two-way mirror bolted to the opposite wall.

Detective Molyneaux took the seat directly across from her.

"We believe you're withholding evidence, Miss Gilchrist," he said.

"No," she whispered.

"You left the restaurant and headed back to The Old Salt House. Not an hour later, you returned to the restaurant and said you thought your boyfriend was a government agent. I feel like you're trying to throw us off track. Tell me, how did you meet Calam Fergus?"

She blinked before saying, "Who?"

"Calam Fergus, the man you shot when you returned to The Old Salt House."

"I. Didn't. Shoot. Anyone. Not to mention, I don't know anybody by that name."

"We believe you do."

"Who is he?"

"You tell me."

"I can't."

Knock. Knock. Knock.

Sergeant Williams pushed the door open, approaching Molyneaux. "The lady's attorney just arrived."

Molyneaux pinched the bridge of his nose. "Show him in."

The rest of the session was cut short. Officials were forced to release Aislinn for lack of evidence.

Her father and her attorney accompanied her back to Thorne Hall to discuss how she should handle police encounters in the future.

Aislinn had never been so happy to see the inside of the bunk room. The guest rooms and cottages at the estate had been filled with visiting family for the wedding, so she'd taken refuge in the bunk room. It had just been vacated by two younger cousins, who had returned home with their parents after the reception. Aislinn had the place to herself and was grateful for it. She closed the door and blocked it with a chair in case one of her relatives paid a surprise visit to console her.

She opened the classified file and found bios of several people, none of whom she knew. There were also several pages dedicated to something called the *Hero's Knot*. It sounded familiar, but she couldn't quite place it.

She heard someone out in the hallway and looked for a hiding spot. She used to stay in this room when her cousin had sleepovers, and she knew there was a one-inch space under the drawers of the bottom bunks when they were pulled all the way out. She and her cousin had left notes there for each other when they were younger. She slipped the file into that space and replaced the drawer as quietly as possible.

She felt reluctant to remove the chair but did so anyway and closed her eyes for a few minutes while she waited to make sure no one would pop in for a visit. It didn't take long for exhaustion to overwhelm her.

Just before falling asleep, she asked herself, *who is Calam Fergus?*

At her home in Scarsdale, Jane Deveraux's heart rate thumped out of control. She had been packing to leave on a long-planned cruise to the Mediterranean when she'd been interrupted by a visit from Suffolk County police saying her nephew Tray had been murdered.

After they'd gone, she sat on the couch in her living room—the one she had purchased after both boys left for college—and sobbed into the sweater she had been about to place in her suitcase. The couch was a symbol of passage, marking the end of an era of overactive boys and roughhousing teenagers abusing her furniture and the beginning of her return to life as a sedate adult. What she wouldn't give to have that old, tattered couch back again, with Tray and Carey bouncing off the walls behind her.

It took her a while to get herself under control. *I need to call Carey,* she thought. She dialed his number, but it immediately went to voicemail. "Carey, it's Aunt Jane. I know you must be feeling overwhelmed, but please call me." She tried not to sob. "I need to hear from you, or I'll go out of my mind. You know I love you, and I'll always be here for you. Let me know if you want me to help with the funeral arrangements." She paused. "Call me."

She spent the evening unpacking her trunk after contacting her travel agent to cancel her booking. For once, having travel insurance had paid off.

She repeatedly tried to call Carey, but her calls didn't go through. *He's probably rushing around, taking care of the funeral details by himself.* She stared down at the phone, willing him to call her back. *Where are you?* "I can help you," she whispered. "Call me."

Back in East Hampton, Tray prayed that he would anonymously blend in with shoppers at a local store. It had been a hot day, and the store was nearly devoid of customers, probably because most people had gone to the beach. He needed a new computer tablet to stay connected to the real world, but it had to be inexpensive because he had limited cash.

Half an hour later, with a tablet and a couple of burner phones in hand, Tray returned to the motel. He turned on the TV to see if news of the murder had been made public and listened while he set up the tablet. Using the motel's Wi-Fi, he searched Carey's social media until the news anchor's words caught his attention.

> *"... the arrest of Aislinn Gilchrist for the attempted murder of a man identified as Calam Fergus."*

Tray felt his heart skip a beat. Unfortunately, he had missed the beginning of the story, and the anchor had already moved on to the next one. He switched through the channels, but instead of news, he found mostly regular programming. Finally, he located a local twenty-four-hour news channel, but it kept regurgitating the same report, which didn't tell him anything new. *I need to help Aislinn. But how?* He spent the next hour staking out the police station but couldn't risk being seen. *How am I going to spring her?*

Little did he know her family's attorney had already taken care of that.

AT HIS OFFICE in Zurich, Zander Bakker slowly seethed. For the past three years, he had paid a team of professionals to track down whoever had stolen Hero's Knot right out from under him, and finally, now that they'd learned the thief's identity—it was too late. The thief was dead, and Bakker didn't have a clue about the location of the artifact. He wanted Hero's Knot in the most extreme way. Instead, he found himself back at square one.

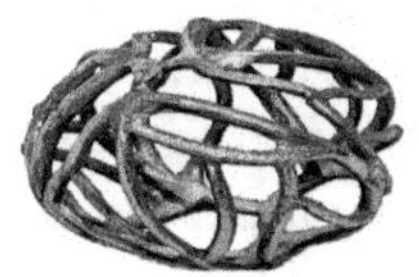

CHAPTER EIGHT

J{\scriptsize ANE} {\scriptsize SAT} {\scriptsize IN} front of her TV the following morning, so engrossed in the news coverage of a local tire factory explosion that she hardly touched her coffee. She thought she might know people who worked there or, at least, some of their relatives.

> *"… The explosion occurred shortly after 10:00 a.m. when workers filled the factory. The plant had recently received a large delivery of methyl isocyanate—a colorless, highly flammable liquid often used to manufacture tires. Officials say a significant amount of the toxic chemical was released into the air as a result of the explosion, killing more than a hundred people almost immediately—"*

She lowered the volume of the TV when her cell phone rang. "Jane Deveraux," she said automatically. She had set up her phone to answer video calls but tensed when she saw a stranger on the screen.

The caller identified himself as a Suffolk County Coroner's office representative. "As the only next of kin we can get in touch with, I'm calling to ask you to identify and claim the body of Traynor Lennox."

Jane's eyes overflowed with tears. She pulled tissues out of a box on the coffee table and wiped her face. "Have you tried contacting his twin brother Carey?"

"We haven't been able to locate him. According to his employer, he's working out of town. They didn't give us a date when he'd be back nor the means to reach him."

"Well, that explains why I haven't been able to get in touch with him. Do you need me to come right away? I don't live on Long Island, and getting there would take some effort. Besides, I really shouldn't do anything without his brother's input."

"You don't need to come here at all. First, if you could give us the name and address of a funeral parlor that can pick up the deceased, we can start the process."

Jane used the remote to turn off the TV. "I guess I could do that. I'll need to call them first, won't I?"

"Yes. And second …" The coroner took a few steps, the video going astray until it settled on her nephew's vacant, white face.

"Oh my God," Jane cried. "You could have warned me."

"You said the trip would inconvenience you. I just need to be sure that this is Traynor Lennox, ma'am."

She glanced quickly, barely able to look at her nephew's face, her vision clouded by new tears. "I believe so."

"Good. Have the funeral home contact us at this number." He gave her the information she would need for the body's release before saying goodbye.

"Wait—"

"Yes."

A wave of exhaustion swept over her—even though it was early in the day. "How long do I have to do this?"

"Twenty-four hours. The autopsy is scheduled for this afternoon."

"That's all? What if I didn't answer the phone?"

"But you did, and you have twenty-four hours. We'll ship the body as soon as the funeral home contacts us."

She rested her head against the back of the couch. What she wouldn't give to be able to crawl back into bed and pretend Tray's death never happened.

LATER THAT DAY, Jane visited a local funeral parlor. She explained the need for a wake and funeral but emphasized her desire for a delay until she could notify the victim's brother.

The funeral director asked Jane to fill out paperwork and then entered the information on his computer. He busily scrolled through several screens before looking up. "I'm sorry to say this, but due to an explosion at an area tire factory, we have little in the way of openings. It was an incredible tragedy." He paused as he continued searching his computer. "We don't even have space to store the body." Tapping his fingers on the desk, he picked up the paperwork she had completed and excused himself to make a phone call.

Jane looked at the empty seat next to her. She had never felt lonelier. It didn't matter that the funeral director was there, helping her arrange Tray's burial; Jane had expected to hear from Carey by now. She didn't want to make choices he wouldn't like. She shook off the feeling. *Considering he's out of town, all I can do is make the best arrangements possible.*

"Good news," the funeral director said when he returned a few minutes later. "I just checked with Gate of Heaven Cemetery, and if you're willing to forgo a wake, they can hold a memorial service in their chapel tomorrow, immediately followed by interment."

Jane shook her head ever so slightly while she wrapped her brain around his words. "Good news?" she finally responded. "How can that be good news when I can't get in touch with my nephew's twin? Can't you freeze the body for a week or two until I contact his brother?"

The man referred to his computer screen once again. "Normally, I would suggest that course of action to someone with your needs. However, with the factory explosion and toxic chemical release, it's impossible. Quick interment at the Gate of Heaven is the best we can do."

"Perhaps another funeral home …" Jane said, standing up.

He waved his hand dismissively. "You'd be lucky to find one within a hundred miles of here that could provide more than a graveside service. These are difficult times."

Her shoulders slumped, and she dropped back into the chair. "Fine. Just … do it."

"I'll be right back with your copy of the paperwork."

At least Tray will be buried near his father. That was what Carey would probably want. Besides, without his input, she had no other choice.

*"WE HAVE BREAKING news on the East Hampton
murder of Manhattan art appraiser Traynor
Lennox."*

Hearing his name, Tray focused his attention on the
TV in his East Hampton motel room.

*"As we've previously reported, he was in
town for what Hamptonites are calling the
society wedding of the year. Lennox attended
the lavish event with the bride's cousin, Aislinn
Gilchrist, whom police had taken into custody
in connection with the shooting. According
to a source close to the investigation, police
have since released Gilchrist due to a lack of
evidence.*

*"Lennox was killed Sunday behind the
popular restaurant, Chapter One on Main.
Police say the motive is still not clear, and the
murderer remains at large."*

Video of the wedding, Aislinn walking out of the
police station, and still images of Tray from his social media
accounts—ended. The anchor reappeared.

*"A funeral service will be held tomorrow
at the Gate of Heaven Cemetery in Hawthorn,
New York."*

Tray closed his eyes to block out the TV, stunned after
hearing about his sudden funeral. The only person who
could have claimed the body, considering how little family
he had, was Aunt Jane. But why would she hold the funeral

89

so quickly and without hearing from him first? *Unless the FBI claimed the body.* His heart skipped a beat.

I need to attend that funeral.

He grabbed what little he owned and stuffed it into a shopping bag. It only took him five minutes to walk to the train station, where he caught the LIRR into Manhattan. While waiting for a New Jersey Transit connection to Newark Liberty International Airport, he purchased a backpack and a laundry list of small personal grooming items, including a sewing kit, self-tanning lotion, and isopropyl alcohol. He shoved everything inside the bag before looking for his train platform.

TRAY NONCHALANTLY STUDIED the crowd at Newark Airport as he munched on a bag of trail mix. *I can either steal someone's wallet and use their credit card to rent a car, or I could risk using one of Carey's credit cards since no one knows he's dead yet.* He made a face. He hated using Carey's card because it might lead back to him. However, the easiest person to pickpocket would be a harried father, traveling with young kids, or an elderly man. Both options seemed grossly unfair to the victim.

Walking out of the terminal, he watched a man leave his car at the curb—with the door hanging open and the motor running—while he ran after a woman who had left something behind.

Tray nonchalantly walked over to the vehicle. As soon as the driver disappeared inside the terminal, Tray slipped behind the wheel and drove away.

He searched for a large shopping center where he could switch cars. Pulling into an out-of-the-way space, he quickly removed the license plates from the car he had just taken. He stored them in his backpack and went inside to do some shopping. He picked up a small pillow and a baby sling. On his way to the checkout, he grabbed a pair of matte-black metal earrings and a cheap canvas duffel bag. He asked the cashier to pack his new purchases in the duffel rather than waste a shopping bag.

He studied the vehicles he passed, pretending to talk on his phone while walking to the opposite end of the parking lot. He finally settled on a nondescript SUV as his next car. Ducking low, he swapped its license plates with the ones from the airport vehicle. *This should do the trick.* He entered the car, hot-wired it, and continued his journey back toward New York. He stopped one last time to do another vehicle and plate switch before crossing the state line. He used as many secondary roads as possible, hoping there'd be less of a chance of being caught by a CCTV camera.

Eventually, he found himself at a thrift store. He looked through the racks, acquiring a pair of old sneakers, the ugliest shirt he'd ever seen, a belt, and an ill-fitting second-hand suit that was a size too large.

Time to find my own personal spa.

He continued to drive around, looking for a cheap motel near the cemetery. He found one by a liquor store, where he conveniently picked up a bottle of whiskey.

"WHAT DO YOU charge for a room?" Tray asked the motel manager. He counted out enough cash to cover two nights. "This should do it."

"Your room is on the second level, right up the back stairs," the man said, pointing across the courtyard.

Tray wrinkled his nose when he entered the room.

The overwhelming stench of cheap cigars couldn't hide the stale odor. A back window faced the parkway. He pushed it open, preferring to deal with the road noise over the stuffiness. He was almost ready to get to work.

He pulled out the whiskey. *I think a drink is in order.* He took a quick trip to the ice machine near the lobby and bought snacks from a vending machine for dinner.

The alcohol relaxed him, but he stopped after one drink. He had a lot to do to prepare for the funeral. Standing in front of the bathroom mirror, he hacked off his hair with scissors from the sewing kit. When he had hardly any hair left, he shaved his head and face. That done, he slathered self-tanner all over his face, head, and upper body. *Can't forget my hands and arms,* he thought, rubbing them with lotion.

It would take hours for it to take effect. He killed time by using a sewing needle to poke a hole in his left earlobe. He grimaced, grabbing an ice cube to soothe the pain. He realized that he should have done that first to numb his ear. *Asshole.* When he felt it was numb enough, he jammed in one earring. *It's a look,* he thought, as he dabbed at a drop of blood. *The rest can wait till morning.*

Jane hung up her phone, leaning her head back against the sofa cushions. She closed her eyes. She felt guilty calling people at the last minute to tell them about Tray's funeral. Even worse, she felt guilty arranging it because she was only the victim's aunt. She wasn't even sure her other nephew knew his twin brother had died.

Jane allowed herself to wallow in misery for a while before making her next call. She dialed the antique business where Tray had worked, informing the owner of Tray's death. She gave him the time and place of the funeral.

"I didn't want to believe it when I heard it on the news," Max said.

"Do you know of anyone else my nephew might have been close to that I should contact?"

"Not that I can recall at the moment. If I think of anyone, I'll let them know."

"Thank you. I appreciate it."

Afterward, she sat in silence. *Poor Tray. He was such a vibrant guy. Now, he's going to have the most pitiful funeral imaginable.* "No thanks to you, Carey," she said out loud. He had always been such a loving, caring brother. And nephew. And now he seemed to have dropped off the face of the earth.

IN WASHINGTON, ACHILLE Pasquarelli locked the door of Senator Phineas Paige's office. He accompanied the statesman to his car, talking in a calm and controlled voice, even though he hated telling Paige what Steiger had done.

Achille explained how Steiger may have erred on the side of caution when he *eliminated* a nuclear investigator.

The senator paled, breaking out into a cold sweat. "Define 'eliminated.'"

"Permanently."

Paige gasped. "What have you done?"

"What are you worried about?" Achille asked. "No one will make the connection between us and Steiger Bob. Besides, the victim, Carey Lennox, was getting way too close for comfort. Don't give Steiger a second thought. I'm sending him on vacation."

*

The senator asked his administrative assistant to look for articles, tweets, mentions, or whatever else she could find concerning a murder in East Hampton, New York. It neither happened in his state, nor close to Washington, DC. However, he explained it away by saying the son of one of his buddies had known the victim and asked him to find out what he could about it.

That night, he went through the clippings she had collected. Each item referred to the victim as *Traynor Lennox*, an antiques appraiser from New York, not Carey Lennox, an investigator for the NRC in Washington.

He hated using his own computer for *research*, but he took a chance and searched for both Traynor Lennox and then Carey Lennox. *They're twins, and that idiot killed the wrong one!*

Paige's blood pressure rose as he erased the cache and memory on his computer. He shredded the clippings and popped a Lanoxin in his mouth, trying to get his heart to stop tap dancing. Then he called Achille to express his "extreme displeasure" about the incident.

Achille hated late-night calls from Paige. They usually involved more work for him, and this time was no different. He kept his voice controlled and calm while discussing the problem with the senator, hanging up before his blood boiled. He immediately called Steiger.

"Yeah?"

"Whom did you kill?"

"The guy you told me to take out, Carey Lennox."

"Wrong. You killed Traynor Lennox, an antiques appraiser."

"How is that possible? I followed this guy from the Oyster Creek Generating Station in Forked River, New Jersey. Why would an antiques appraiser be visiting a nuclear plant?"

"They're twins!" Achille slammed his hand down on his desk to call attention to the point, even though Steiger couldn't see it. "Did you have your eyes on the guy every single second?"

"Well, not when I was parking. And then there were people around, and I had to look casual and blend in. But I picked up his trail again easily enough."

"Apparently not. You eradicated his brother."

"I can make this right."

"No!" Achille shouted. He consciously lowered his voice. "One death might be considered random. Killing Carey Lennox now could point a finger at us." He picked up a stapler and waved it in the air, emphasizing his next words. "I want you to lie low."

"What do you mean? You want me to sit here, twiddling my thumbs? I've got expenses."

Achille pulled a book out of his desk drawer and paged through it until he found the information he wanted. He shoved it back in the drawer. "You'll be receiving an envelope from a courier service. It will contain a new passport under a different name, a plane ticket to Belize, and two hundred and fifty thousand dollars. Take the year off."

"And what happens when I run out of money?"

"That's enough money to keep you going for ten years in Belize if you're not stupid with it. I just need you to stay out of the picture for a while so no one associates you with the Lennox brothers."

"What about the power plant jobs? Majewski has a list of tasks for me."

"Let Majewski handle his own 'tasks.' He gets paid enough to do them himself. Your flight is tomorrow. Be on it, or you just might find yourself being questioned for murder."

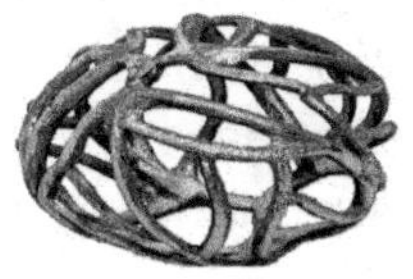

CHAPTER NINE

Tʀᴀʏ ᴜsᴇᴅ ʜɪs motel room in Hawthorne as a staging area. He found changing his appearance turned out to be more involved than he had anticipated. Miscellaneous items cluttered every available surface.

He inspected himself in the mirror. His second application of self-tanner considerably deepened the not-too-funky bronze color he already had. It also disguised the whiteness of his newly shaved head. He struggled with the baby sling, trying to figure out the best way to attach it across his stomach. *Hope this works.* He ripped open the pillow he bought the previous day and stuffed the sling with its contents, moving the stuffing around until he was happy with the way it looked. He covered it with the hideous mustard-yellow shirt that did nothing to compliment his complexion. *Perfect.* He slipped into the suit, cinching the pants with the belt. They bunched up, but he didn't care. They would enhance his newly created paunch.

He splashed whiskey on his face like aftershave. *God, I hope this doesn't remove my fake tan.* He patted his face dry with a tissue just to be on the safe side. For good measure, he took a slug straight from the bottle, using it like mouthwash. He also sprinkled a few drops on his shirt.

Time to road test this get-up. He walked down the block and bought a bacon, egg, and cheese sandwich at a fast-food donut shop. He paid attention to how people reacted to his disguise. They kept their distance, considering he reeked of whiskey, which was the desired effect.

After he ate, he didn't bother brushing his teeth. The whole point of the disguise was to keep people so repelled that they wouldn't get close enough to recognize him.

JANE ARRIVED EARLY at the cemetery chapel to make sure everything was in order. No one else was there. She walked around for a little while, finally taking a seat and staring at the front of the room. *I wonder if I'll be the only one here.*

"Mrs. Deveraux?"

She spun around. "Yes?"

"I'm sorry if I startled you. I wanted to introduce myself ahead of time. I'm Reverend Clarence White. I'll be officiating at the memorial service. Will you be giving the eulogy? No one is listed on the paperwork."

"I have … had … twin nephews. One of them, Tray, is the deceased. I haven't been able to get in touch with his brother. I have no idea if he even knows Tray is dead. This funeral was all so rushed. I would have never planned such a hasty and ill-thought-out memorial service, but the funeral home said—because of the tire factory explosion—I'd have to take it or leave it." She broke down in tears, unable to hold herself together anymore.

The reverend took Jane's hand. "My dear woman, I am so sorry. No one should be placed in such a position."

"Thank you," she said, retrieving her hand. "It's just that I may be the only one here. What would be the point of giving a eulogy if no one else comes?"

"I do believe you may have spoken too soon."

Jane heard footsteps behind her and turned to see who was there.

Two couples, one older and one younger, walked into the chapel.

Jane stood up and approached them. "Hello. I'm Jane Deveraux, Tray's aunt. I don't believe we've met."

Aislinn tried to hold back a sob. "I'm Aislinn Gilchrist." She sniffed. "Tray's girlfriend." The woman accompanying her handed the young woman a packet of tissues. "These are my parents, Monica and Andrew Gilchrist, and my cousin Jude."

"Thank you for coming. Please have a seat up front. Everything happened so quickly, I'll be surprised if anyone else knows to come here today."

"Would you care to say a few words about Tray during the ceremony?" Reverend White asked Aislinn.

The young woman's eyes widened. "What would I say?"

"As his girlfriend," Jane answered, "you probably knew him better than most."

Aislinn's breath stuttered as she turned first to her parents and then to Jane before answering Reverend White. "We've only been together a couple of weeks."

Jane's face saddened. "Oh."

Aislinn paused as she gave it some thought. "It would be short."

"That's fine," Reverend White replied. "Tell me your name again, and I'll call you at the appropriate time."

More footsteps sounded behind them. They belonged to Maximilian Zane and a couple of young women who worked with antiques.

The reverend took Jane aside. "Now that you can see there will be other mourners present, shall I call you up to the podium to say a few words about your nephew?"

She studied the people in the room. *How could I possibly shortchange Tray of the respect he deserves at his funeral?* She nodded. "Okay. Where will I need to go?"

He turned and pointed to the podium. "Right there. I will be speaking from the same podium. Just walk up to me when I call your name, and I will relinquish my place to you. Is it okay if I call you first, considering you've known the deceased the longest?"

The corners of Jane's lips lifted, but her smile was barely visible. "Yes. That would be fine."

Jane was so engrossed in her conversation with Reverend White, she didn't notice the slovenly man who entered the chapel and sat down in the back row.

TRAY SELECTED A SEAT on the aisle where he could easily watch the proceedings. He was looking for anyone who didn't look like they belonged. Ironically, he fit the bill perfectly.

He didn't expect to see many people—a half dozen at best—with his family being so small and the funeral being so hurried. He was surprised by the number of mourners who showed up. At least half a dozen people arrived together as a group. He recognized one of them as a friend of Carey's. *Do they know Carey is dead and think this funeral is for him?* Then Tray saw people he worked with as well, including a couple of former girlfriends. *Does everyone think we're both dead?* Neighbors from his condo building walked in next. *No. They must believe it's me.* He assumed some of the other people were police officers in street clothes.

In fact, Detective Miles Molyneaux, Sergeant Jefferson Williams, and Officer Holden Fisher were all in attendance. They spaced themselves out, noting all the mourners. One of them appeared to be studying Tray but eventually looked away.

The reverend took his place at the podium, and subtle organ music began playing in the background. He paused when he saw the door open.

Godfrey Munk entered, followed less than ten seconds later by Jin Rumi. They each took a seat in the shadows on opposite sides of the chapel.

Tray didn't recognize them, but their appearance unsettled him. They looked shady—like they were up to no good. He noticed each of them surveying their surroundings and turning away from the people he assumed were police.

DETECTIVE MOLYNEAUX STARED at Jin Rumi. She looked familiar. He thought back to the day of the murder, working to place her face. *In the restaurant. But she wasn't one of the primary suspects. She acted like an innocent bystander. So why is she here? And why is she sitting so far away? Are you a ghoul or a person of interest?*

*

AISLINN CRIED SILENTLY throughout the funeral. Jane put her arm around the girl's shoulders but noticed it didn't help.

"I didn't think it would be like this," Aislinn whispered. "He's gone. And the casket is closed. I can't even say goodbye."

Jane thought back to the sight of the vacant, pale face she had seen on her phone when the coroner had asked her to confirm Tray's identity. "It's probably for the best." She patted the girl's arm.

"I just wanted to see his face one last time," Aislinn replied, breaking down into sobs.

Jane took out another packet of tissues and handed them to Aislinn.

The young woman gave Jane her used tissues in return. Jane initially grimaced, then schooled her features into a more acceptable expression as she shoved them in her handbag and removed a small bottle of hand sanitizer. *This one needs to get her grief out of her system. Thank God her family is here to support her.*

NEARLY EVERYONE TOOK part in the caravan that traveled to the grave site afterward.

Reverend White continued with his ministrations, ending with a quote from Benjamin Franklin.

> *"It is the will of God and Nature that these mortal bodies be laid aside, when the soul is to enter into real life; 'tis rather an embryo state, a preparation for living; a man is not completely born until he be dead: Why then should we grieve that a new child is born among the immortals?"*

The mourners each said a last goodbye while tossing a flower onto the casket. Then, released from the formality of the service, they drifted away.

One of the last groups to approach the casket included a couple of Carey's fellow nuclear inspectors. As one of them leaned over it, his shirt pocket began blinking red.

"Your radiation detector is going off," his friend said.

"Was Carey's brother killed by radiation poisoning?"

"I heard he got shot."

The other man removed the detector from his pocket and shut it off. "Maybe it needs new batteries. I'll look into it later."

"Or we could just stay until after dark to see if the casket glows," his friend joked.

"Too soon," the man with the radiation detector whispered, leading the second man away. "Where is Carey, anyway?"

"Good question," his friend replied.

JANE HAD BEEN standing far enough away from them and hadn't heard their conversation. She had been struggling all morning to remain strong for everyone but couldn't hold back any longer. Her tears fell freely as she mourned Tray's short life and his brother's inability to make it to the funeral. She also cried for her own aloneness, unable to take solace in the words spoken or the sentiments shared with her. She had not prepared for a post-funeral meal, thinking no one would show up. *If Carey had been here, he would have understood.* That thought made her cry harder. She felt herself spiraling down a rabbit hole created by Tray's unexpected death. She walked back to her car alone and awaited her turn to escape from the cemetery.

Tray hung around. He'd sniffed back enough tears over the past hour. The sight of Aislinn had made him second-guess what he was doing. He had also felt the need to go to his aunt and console her, but he couldn't unless he wanted people to know he wasn't dead. He knew the police were studying him, even now. *I bet they're trying to figure out if I'm a suspect. I doubt they know I'm the victim or, at least, the victim's brother.* He watched as police retreated to their vehicles. They were parked away from the others and situated in such a way that they could see each car and its license plate as it left. *That could be a problem.* He looked back at the grave site just in time to see Jin heave a clump of dirt at the casket before spitting on it. It took all he had in him to hold himself back. *Who the hell are you?*

Jin stomped back to her car. She hated Traynor Lennox. If she and Calam hadn't been told Lennox probably had the artifact, and Munk hadn't asked them to steal it from him, Calam would not be clinging to life somewhere. *If he's still alive.* For all she knew, he could be dead, but Godfrey Munk had expressly forbidden her from going to him. He said it would throw her—and Munk's entire operation— into the crosshairs of the police.

Munk grabbed her arm in a vice-like grip, pulling her to a stop. "You're calling attention to yourself," he whispered harshly.

She stared at the hand clutching her arm. "And you're not?" she replied through clenched teeth.

Police had a different line of sight than Tray and didn't see Jin spit on the casket. But they did see Munk grab her. They knew exactly who he was because they had uploaded his photo earlier, and facial recognition software had matched him to an extensive rap sheet. It appeared most of his more recent charges had been thrown out. Although, there was a notation that said the dismissals were probably due more to political connections and payoffs than his actual innocence.

Munk let go of Jin's arm and got in his car, pulling out of line and trying to cut off the rest of the people who were ready to leave.

Police had the advantageous position of being able to follow him easily.

Tray was grateful they found someone else to tail and wouldn't see his stolen car. It also allowed him to follow Jin back to her apartment in Queens.

ACHILLE'S PHONE RANG, allowing him to delay dealing with the pile of paperwork that cluttered his desk at the Dirksen Senate Office Building. He cursed when he recognized Steiger's number. "What is it?"

"I've got keys from that Lennox guy." Achille could hear Steiger jingling them on the other end of the phone. "What do you want me to do with them?"

"Where'd you get them?"

"I took them off his body."

"Get rid of them. Find a dumpster and throw them in, now!"

Steiger looked around the crowded departure terminal. He'd already waited in a long line to pass the security checkpoint and didn't want to have to do it again. "I don't know if I can find a dumpster here in the airport unless I leave the terminal. Should I reschedule my flight?"

"No. Go to the men's room, wipe any prints off the keys, wrap them in a paper towel, and throw them in the trash bin when nobody's looking. Then leave. And get rid of that phone. Don't use it again. Destroy it now. You can buy a new one in Belize."

"Okay. I'll call you with my new number."

"No. Don't call. Not until a year is up." Achille paused, thinking about the implications. "You don't want anyone to know where to find you, okay? If they can't find you, they can't charge you with murder."

"Okay. Trash the keys. Trash the phone. Talk in a year. Later."

Achille released a huge breath after the call disconnected and used his shirt sleeve to wipe the sweat that had accumulated on his brow. Steiger had turned into a massive loose end.

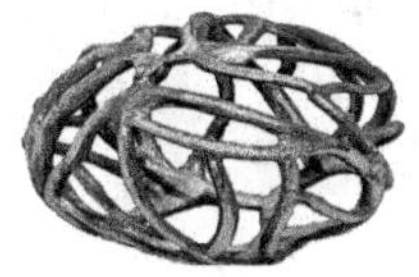

CHAPTER TEN

POLICE FOLLOWED MUNK'S car back to his house in Beechhurst, Queens. He lived in a large Mediterranean villa with views of the East River. It had been built to impress but fell shy of its mark if only because of a lack of acreage. Located in one of the five boroughs that made up New York City, the property sat on a decent-sized lot, but it could not compete with the houses in Kings Point, right on the other side of Little Neck Bay.

Sergeant Williams and PO Fisher traveled together in one car. Detective Molyneaux drove alone. After parking within sight of Munk's house, the detective walked over to the other officers' vehicle, knocking on the window before sinking to his haunches. He didn't want to be seen from the house.

Fisher rolled down the window, saying, "I'm willing to bet he purchased that little hacienda with dirty money."

"I'm not betting against you on that," Molyneaux

replied. "The question is, what does this guy have to do with the death of our art appraiser? Unless they were both smuggling less-than-legitimate artwork into or out of the country."

"We may be jumping the gun here," Sergeant Williams said. "Perhaps we should plug both their names into the system and see if we get any hits that include both Munk and Lennox."

"Stop being the voice of reason, or I may think you're gunning for my job," Molyneaux said to Williams.

"No, thank you. I have no desire to give up life in the Hamptons for Yaphank."

UNAWARE OF WHAT was going on outside his home, Munk sat down at a nineteenth-century mahogany partner's desk. The impressive piece of furniture had been a source of joy for him ever since it mysteriously disappeared from a truck on its way to a prestigious New York auction house and miraculously showed up in his home. He rubbed the rich wood as if it were a good-luck talisman before dialing Jin's number.

"Yeah."

"Snap out of your snit. I need you to go to the dead guy's condo and search for the artifact."

"Don't you think the police have found it by now? They probably searched his place right after his death."

"They wouldn't have been looking for an ancient artifact. I need you to get inside and bring back anything that looks like it might be our prize."

"Some prize," she said, picking at a piece of duct tape used to repair a tear on the arm of her faux leather chair.

"I may not know much about the object, but it *is* a

prize—and not of the penny arcade variety. Come straight here afterward with whatever you collect."

Like Munk, Jin also lived in Queens, but her apartment was a far cry from his *nuevo-palatial* house. She and her brother, Dai, had grown up in a one-bedroom apartment with their parents. Dai had moved to Japan several years ago. Her mother and father had both died during the pandemic. Jin continued to pay the rent because her "family home" was all she knew.

Muttering obscenities about being forced to go out again, she stuffed a garbage bag inside her knapsack for any goodies she had to *relocate* from the dead guy's home to Munk's. She was still muttering when she boarded the Number 7 train to Manhattan.

Finding Tray's Hudson Yards condominium was easy for Jin. Getting past the security guard might be more difficult. But she had a plan.

She mussed up her hair and took a few fast, deep breaths before running into the lobby screaming, "Call 911. A man just got hit by a car." She ran out again but didn't go far, doubling back to hide in a space right behind the entry. Just as she expected, the security guard ran out a minute later, taking off down the block to look at the accident. She caught the door before it closed and headed up the stairs.

Tray had been watching Jin's building since following her home from the funeral. He followed her when she left and wasn't surprised to see her enter his building. He instinctively knew that she was about to break into his apartment. He anonymously called police from one of his burner phones, saying he was visiting a friend when he saw someone picking the lock of an apartment down the hall. He gave the address and apartment number and hung up.

When an NYPD patrolman responded, he found a fellow officer already in the modern marble and brass lobby, questioning the building's security guard about reporting a false incident.

"I'm telling you," the guard said, "a girl came running in here, screaming her head off that some guy got hit by a car. I was trying to save a life, not call in a false report."

The patrolman cut in, "I wonder if that's connected to the call I'm checking out about a young woman breaking into apartment 1410."

The guard led them both upstairs, where the patrolman pounded on the door. "NYPD," he called out. "Open up."

No response. The guard used a master key to unlock the apartment. As the door swung open, they saw Jin holding a heavy plastic bag, scrambling for a hiding place.

"That's her," the guard said. "The woman who asked me to report the accident."

Jin swung the trash bag high, hitting the closest cop with a heavy crystal geode she had collected for Munk. It sent the patrolman sprawling into the living room. She rapidly swung around, kicking the security guard in the gut. He doubled over and slumped to the marble tile floor. She pulled out a gun she had found in Tray's closet. The other cop tasered her before she could use it. As she writhed on the floor from the shock, he grabbed his handcuffs. As he secured her wrists, he stated her Miranda rights.

Tears rolled down Jin's face as she sat in an interrogation room at NYPD headquarters, wishing she were anywhere else but there. Officials left her alone to molder in the hot, airless room for more than an hour. She regretted taking Tray's gun and trying to use it, if only as something to throw at someone's head. At least she wasn't sitting in a cell.

The door opened silently, and the patrolman entered, accompanied by a detective. The door banged shut behind them.

"We can do this the easy way, or we can do this the hard way," the detective said, standing over her. "The easy way is you tell us what you were doing in Traynor Lennox's apartment."

"I will not answer questions without a lawyer present." It was bad enough she had given them her name, but she didn't have a record and hoped that fact would help her case. Why had she taken that gun?

"So, you want to do things the hard way." The detective turned toward the patrolman. "Lock her up. No visitors other than her attorney. Schedule arraignment for tomorrow."

"What about my phone call?"

"Let the lady make a phone call. One phone call," he emphasized for Jin's benefit.

She phoned Munk, who arrived several hours later with an attorney.

MUNK GRITTED HIS teeth when police said only the attorney would be allowed to see Jin. He pulled the lawyer aside before he was taken to confer with his new client. "Tell her to say she's that guy's old girlfriend," he whispered. "Tell her to say he has compromising pictures of her. The stuff she removed from the apartment were gifts from him to her."

The gun was a sticking point. Jin claimed it wasn't loaded. Police checked, finding the weapon empty. But she had pulled it on police after trying to knock the hell out of them.

The following morning, after conferring with the defendant, verifying ownership of the gun (Traynor Lennox), and hours of negotiating a possible deal, an assistant district attorney offered Jin community service and one year of probation in return for a guilty plea to misdemeanor breaking and entering. Neither side was happy. However, Jin and prosecutors each thought it was the best deal they could get.

Afterward, police told Munk he could have five minutes to speak with Jin but said they still had to hold her until after arraignment.

"Well, you really screwed this one up," Munk hissed at the desolate young woman.

"Next time you have a 'small side job,' call someone else," she replied, more upset than he would ever know. In the past, she'd always worked under the radar.

"I thought you'd want to pair up with Calam—to watch his back—considering you two are fucking each other."

Tears welled up in her eyes, but she refused to let them fall. "And now he may be dead." Her tone was bitter. "And now I have a record in the police system. The only good news is they're not charging me with a felony, so they can't take a DNA sample. You expect me to watch out for you, and I do. But where were you when I needed you to watch out for me?"

"I'm right here!" Munk shouted.

The guard jerked to attention. "Five minutes are up."

"We'll talk after the arraignment," he said, pushing past the guard and heading toward the door.

Because of the Tray Lennox homicide connection, NYPD made sure the Suffolk County Homicide Squad received a copy of Jin Rumi's mug shot and police report.

Meanwhile, Jin curled into a tight ball in the corner of a cell and couldn't help but reassess her relationship with Godfrey Munk.

She had been hired as a receptionist for I & O Import & Export and had only been working there for a week when a couple of thugs pushed past her, barging into Munk's office. They slammed the door shut behind them with such force it banged back open. "Where is it?"

"You gentlemen aren't on my schedule for today—"

One of them walked behind Munk's chair and used a choke hold to pull him out of it. "Mr. Guarino says you 'appropriated' his shipment of Middle Eastern antiquities."

Jin popped her head in the door. "Mr. Munk—"

An armed thug tried to grab her, but Jin spun away from him. She might not be a great secretary, but her older brother had drilled her in Krav Maga and MMA while they were growing up. She kicked the gun out of the man's hand when he came after her and successfully threw him headfirst into a wall, knocking him out.

That evened the odds for Munk, who subdued the other man.

Later, Munk asked, "Where'd you learn to fight like that?"

"My brother."

"Impressive. Unexpected, you know? You suck as a secretary, but you obviously have other skills. I like the element of surprise, so I'm giving you a promotion to bodyguard. Just don't tell ANYBODY."

Tray headed back to the motel in Hawthorne. He packed all his stuff in the duffel bag, placing a bottle of alcohol and a washcloth—stolen from the motel—on top.

He threw his duffel on the passenger seat and drove to the train station before wiping down the car's steering wheel, door handles, and any other surface he'd touched. Abandoning the vehicle, he used public transportation to head back to Arlington.

Onboard the train, he stared at the window but only saw a reflection of the well-lit interior.

He sighed with frustration, knowing he couldn't use back channels to learn what had happened with Jin breaking into his apartment.

Being dead sucks.

The weather in East Hampton was picture-perfect, and Aislinn could have kicked herself for not going to the beach. Instead, she found herself walking into her aunt's white and gold living room, where Detective Molyneaux awaited her.

"Detective," she said, "what is it this time?" She dropped into an antique French Bergère chair as if the weight of the world were on her shoulders.

"Frankly, Miss Gilchrist, I think you know something you're not telling us. Perhaps you don't understand its importance to the case. Or maybe you're protecting someone. Until we're satisfied that you've been completely upfront with us, we'll be checking and double-checking the information we have. As it is, there's not much we can do without further evidence. Although we did receive an anonymous tip that a burglary arrest in Manhattan may be related to your friend's murder."

"What burglary?"

"At a Hudson Yards condo. Apartment 1410."

"Tray," she whispered.

"What do you know about it?"

"Nothing. It wasn't me."

Molyneaux sat across from her in a matching chair. "I didn't say it was. But we are wondering who called in the tip."

"Not me."

"According to NYPD, a young woman named Jin Rumi was found on the scene. Unfortunately, a background check reveals almost nothing about her after her graduation from Queens Community College. Only that she got a job as an administrative assistant for a Queens business called I & O Import Export LTD. A company representative says they have no record of her working there.

"But here's the twist," Molyneaux continued. "She claimed apartment 1410 belongs to her ex-boyfriend, who had compromising pictures of her, and she was there looking for them. She also had a selection of pricey baubles in a sack, but she claimed those were gifts he had given her that she was picking up.

"Perhaps your friend had compromising photos of you as well? Did you kill him because of that?"

Aislinn paled. "No. I was in the restaurant with my family when he was killed. I had nothing to do with his death."

Molyneaux crossed his arms over his chest and stared at her for a moment. "You could have hired an accomplice. Perhaps this Jin Rumi is a friend of yours."

Aislinn's father stormed into the room, the leather soles of his Italian shoes slapping noisily against the herringbone hardwood floors. "Stop speaking, Ash. Now." He turned toward Molyneaux. "Detective, you have no right talking to my daughter without her attorney present. Leave."

Molyneaux stood, clearly unhappy about Aislinn's father's sudden appearance. "Just doing my job, trying to find out who killed your daughter's boyfriend." He turned to Aislinn before walking out the door. "Goodbye. For now."

AISLINN PICKED UP her tote bag. She refused to stay cooped up in the house a minute longer. *It's time to do a little investigating of my own.* She removed Tray's classified file from its hiding place and slipped it inside her bag. "See you later," she called out to her family. "I'm going out."

Aislinn loved the East Hampton Library. She'd gone there every two weeks like clockwork as a kid, allowing each book she read to take her on a new adventure. But she wasn't looking for an adventure today. She wanted information and planned to use a library computer to anonymously search for what she needed.

Social media described Tray as a sophisticated New Yorker, well regarded as an antiquities appraiser. His personal accounts allowed a glimpse into his travels and almost served as a catalog of intriguing artworks and artifacts. She didn't see much in the way of information about his old girlfriends. However, her jaw dropped when she found a photo of her and Tray emerging from his condo building after their long weekend together. It included the caption, "Traynor Lennox brushes off the dust of old relics for something younger and fresher."

She searched for references to the woman whose name sounded like a cross between a drink and a card game. Gin Rummy. *Nope.* Jen Rummy. *No.* Gyn Rumby. *Uh-uh.*

This was going to be more challenging than she'd thought.

She looked up news of the murder. She read each article, most of them sounding the same, but none mentioned anyone with the unusual name the detective had stated earlier. *This is a waste of my time.*

She was about to log off the computer when she saw one last follow-up item in the *East Hampton Star.* She clicked on the link and began reading. Her eyes widened when she hit pay dirt. *Restaurant customer Jin Rumi said police presence following the murder was very disruptive for diners, who were just trying to enjoy their meals.*

She opened a new search page and typed in J-I-N R-U-M-I. Only one thing came up: a program saying she had graduated from Queens College. No social media accounts. No pictures.

It's almost as if she died right after graduation. But she didn't. So, what are you trying to hide, Jin Rumi?

Exasperated, Aislinn removed the papers marked *Classified Information* from inside the envelope. She'd paged through them previously, looking for Tray's name, but hadn't seen anything about him. This time around, she started reading the pages word-for-word and learned the unsettling story behind *Hero's Knot*.

She felt confused. Why would Tray have this? Unless he had been asked to appraise Hero's Knot? Could he have been killed because he had possession of the artifact? She looked for citations online about Hero's Knot, but references to it were vague. There was practically nothing that she could find. She learned quite a bit about Hero of Alexandria but nothing about Hero's Knot, *per se*.

Finally, she packed up the classified papers. Her neck and shoulders ached from the tension she carried. Maybe she should have gone for a massage instead.

Miles Molyneaux called headquarters in Yaphank and asked to speak with the Chief of Detectives.

"Detective?"

"I probably already know the answer to this question, but is there any way to rush the results of the DNA tests on the blood found in The Old Salt House in East Hampton?" He received the answer he expected.

"No. We probably won't get anything back for a couple more weeks."

"The times of death for both victims are within the same one-hour window. It would help if I knew who died first."

"Do you have a working theory?"

Molyneaux scratched his head. "I think Lennox killed Fergus at the inn. And I think Fergus had an accomplice who killed Lennox in retaliation."

"Do you know why Fergus was at the inn?"

"No."

"What do you know about him?"

"Only that he's a low-level hood working out of Queens, allegedly for a guy named Godfrey Munk. We have no proof of that connection. Nor do we have any proof of an accomplice. But Munk was at Lennox's funeral."

"Dig deeper."

"I'm trying."

The chief shuffled papers around on his desk. "Did you see the report from NYPD about one of the people who was in East Hampton on the day of the murder?"

"No. What does NYPD have to do with it?"

The chief smiled like a Cheshire cat. "Apparently, some woman named Jin Rumi got herself arrested for breaking into your murder victim's Manhattan apartment."

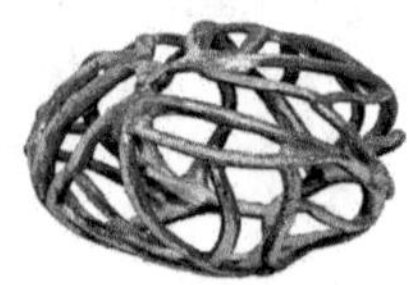

CHAPTER ELEVEN

Jane brewed enough fresh-ground beans for a very robust pot of coffee. She was scheduled to speak at a seminar on the Library of Ashurbanipal, named after a mid-600s BC king of Assyria with a passion for collecting texts. She'd spent the entire morning getting her notes in order. Unfortunately, her eyes began drooping before she completed her task. She needed to finish her research so she could commit some of it to memory before the event.

She cursed under her breath when an unexpected knock on the door forced her to leave her coffee on the table.

Her eyes widened when she saw Tray's girlfriend. "Aislinn." Then, they narrowed. "How do you know where I live?"

"I found your address on the internet. Can I talk to you?"

"Of course." Jane opened the door the rest of the way.

"I just made some coffee. Would you like a cup?"

"I'd love it," Aislinn replied, realizing she'd had nothing to eat or drink all day.

"I have to warn you, it's very strong."

"The stronger, the better." After a few sips, Aislinn steeled herself for what she wanted to say. "Like I said at the funeral, I haven't known Tray very long, but I've known him long enough to have fallen in love with him." She looked down at the coffee in her cup. "And it's hard for me to understand why he was suddenly ripped away from me." She looked up at Jane with tears in her eyes. "I feel like I owe it to him to find out what happened."

Jane turned and grabbed a box of tissues off the shelf behind her, pushing them toward the young woman.

Aislinn wiped her tears and blew her nose before continuing. "Have you ever heard of Hero's Knot?"

Jane paled, hesitating before answering. Tray had once asked her the same question. What she had learned in the interim bothered her—the current speculation even more than the established facts. *Would Tray have trusted his new girlfriend with this information?* She tried to appear blasé. "What makes you think I know anything about it?"

"Tray told me his aunt was an archeology professor who lectured on ancient civilizations. I just figured that had to be you. And this *Hero's Knot* sounds like something an archeology professor might know about."

"I'd never heard of it before Tray first asked me, but it's my nature to do research. I've learned quite a bit since his initial question. However, I don't know how much of what I've learned is true. There is a lot of information afloat that seems to be nothing more than innuendo and rumor. What do you know of it?"

"Nothing! Except I think Tray was interested in it, and I want to find out if it's related to his death."

Jane sipped her coffee as she gathered her thoughts. "I've since corroborated some of what I've learned with a contact I have at the Egyptian National Library. She says the most credible information she's heard is that it's an artifact created at the time of Hero of Alexandria's death.

"A man—believed to have been a colleague of Hero's—supposedly left a written account of the mathematician's demise, in narrative form. The Museum says it cannot disprove its specifics. They are theorizing that Hero found space debris made up of nanoparticles of extraterrestrial biological origin.

The corner of Aislinn's mouth turned up. "Nanoparticles? E.T.'s body parts? It doesn't sound scholarly. It's more like something you'd see on that William Shatner show, *The UnXplained*."

"Yes, well, if Hero were alive today, he'd probably watch it.

"Anyway, he supposedly experimented with it and turned it into metal strips that he inscribed all his formulas on. But," Jane removed a folder from the drawer of a sideboard, "his colleagues turned against him because the metal looked like it was writhing. They thought it was possessed by evil.

"He named it *herotite* after himself. Isn't that just like a man?

"Read this. Tell me what you think. I should point out that it reads like a short story, augmented with modern-day references by ENL—the Egyptian National Library."

She handed the folder to Aislinn. "Here. Start with his," Jane made air quotes, "friend Decimus. We all need friends like this."

Decimus called on Hero, inviting him to taste a new wine that had just come into his possession. Glad that Decimus had not spurned him like others had, Hero gladly accepted the offer and sampled the drink, remarking on its rich, honeyed flavor. Little did he know that Decimus had added honey to the wine to disguise the taste of nightshade berries. As Hero drank, Decimus walked around the workshop, surreptitiously dumping his own wine before adding more to their cups.

It didn't take long for Hero to become inebriated. As the poison coursed through his veins, he slumped to the floor and stared at his friend, who did not appear to be affected. Hero no longer had control over his body. His mind became muddled. Slowly, the nightshade paralyzed all his organs— including his heart—killing him. The look on his face conveyed one emotion. 'Betrayal.'

Hero's other colleagues may have feared the herotite, but that didn't stop them from descending on his workshop that night to destroy the substance. "We must remove all evidence of Hero's existence." One of the turncoats grabbed an axe and started battering the strands of herotite. While it didn't affect the older portions, an errant axe mark on a newer strand changed a formula Hero had inscribed earlier that day.

Decimus stopped him, taking the inscribed strand of herotite and weaving it into a massive cage-like knot. He melted the ends and joined them together. Decimus handed Hero's Knot to the dissenters. "Throw it into the sea," he told them. "Be rid of it, and never speak of it again.

POMPEII, ITALY – SUMMER – 79 AD

Out in the Mediterranean Sea, bottom crawlers nibbled on a sack that held the promise of food inside. Cloth fibers finally gave way, releasing Hero's Knot. Unlike some metals, herotite floated, and Hero's Knot rose to the surface. Battered by the currents and sometimes transported great distances by large fish—the artifact's journey was circuitous. Still, it didn't take long for it to land on a distant shore near Pompeii, Italy.

Perhaps it was fate, perhaps it was a natural geological event, perhaps it was Hero's alchemy, whatever the reason, minutes after a fisherman saw the artifact washed up on a beach, the surrounding area rumbled. Nearby, Mount Vesuvius regurgitated, darkening the sky with ash and pumice, which rained on Pompeii and the surrounding region. By the end of the following day, the prosperous city had been destroyed, and Hero's Knot became lost in obscurity.

ENL Note: After Pompeii's devastation, rumors regarding the artifact were not heard for centuries—not until the Antioch earthquake in 526. Again, there were reports of a glowing metal mass with odd markings washing up on the Syrian coastline just before a quarter of a million people died in the devastation. It's also believed Hero's Knot is responsible for the Aleppo earthquake in 1138 and another Vesuvius temblor in 1631.

Aislinn returned the papers to Jane and pulled out the classified file she had found in Tray's duffel bag. She handed it to Jane. "It sounds like science fiction. I wouldn't believe it, except for this."

Jane stared at the outside of the envelope, almost afraid to open it, but her curiosity got the better of her. She read through the file, her face growing more serious with every word. She returned her gaze to Aislinn. "This says Hero's Knot poses a credible threat to national security."

Aislinn nodded. "That's why I'm here. Do you think this is why Tray was murdered?"

CHAPTER TWELVE

MOLYNEAUX OMINOUSLY WHISTLED while looking at a copy of the NYPD's mug shot of Jin. He knew her face. He had spoken with her at Chapter One on Main the day of the murder. He read the police report. *Authorities caught her inside Traynor Lennox's apartment in Manhattan. She had a trash bag filled with art. She pulled a gun on responding officers. She was proficient in martial arts. Officials offered her a plea bargain.* "Damn."

He looked around for PO Fisher, handing him a copy of Jin's mug shot. "I need you to show this around The Old Salt House and Chapter One on Main and find out everything you can about this woman. She was here the day of the murder, and the NYPD caught her breaking into Traynor Lennox's apartment."

Fisher took the photo. "I remember her from the restaurant. She was a tiny little thing who looked harmless until I noticed the Krav Maga tattoo on her inner arm. You think she's our perp?"

Molyneaux grimaced. "Why would someone proficient in martial arts carry a gun?"

"Ahh. Good question."

"Get out there and see what you can find. Ask if Ms. Rumi was seen in the company of anybody else."

"Will do."

THE MANAGER OF the Old Salt House didn't recognize Jin from her photo, but the bartender at Chapter One on Main said he'd served her drinks on the day of the murder. "She was sitting at the bar alone, drinking mimosas. I remember her because I thought she was cute. But when I tried to chat with her, she acted cold. Standoffish. Although I have to say, she perked up during the police investigation. *That* interested her."

"Does she come here often?" PO Fisher asked.

"As far as I can recall, the day of the murder is the only time I've ever seen her here. But I'm only here evenings and weekends. For all I know, she might come in every day for lunch."

Fisher called Molyneaux from the squad car, relaying the bartender's information.

"It makes sense," Molyneaux answered, "considering she's from Queens. But just to be on the safe side, return to both places tomorrow during the day and see what they say."

MOLYNEAUX CALLED NYPD to inform them that witnesses saw Jin Rumi in East Hampton on the Sunday Traynor Lennox and Calam Fergus were both shot. "Thought you might like to note that in her file."

"Did you say 'Calam Fergus'? Wait." Molyneaux picked at his cuticles for several long minutes before the NYPD officer returned to the phone. "You need a link?"

The detective blinked. "What do you mean?"

"Both Calam Fergus and Jin Rumi—rumored to be lovers—work for a crime boss known as Godfrey Munk."

"Really!" Molyneaux, taken by surprise, moved suddenly—knocking over a cup of stale coffee on his desk. He grabbed some used napkins and tried to sop up the mess before it seeped into his files. "Does Mr. Munk have a specialty?"

"Mr. Munk is an importer. As near as we can tell, about a third of what he sells is stolen. Another third is comprised of fakes—jewelry, art, and artifacts. And the rest is made up of very real illegal firearms. Unfortunately, like some other notable cons, Munk is like Teflon."

The detective groaned. "Just when I thought there might be some light at the end of the tunnel."

Tray didn't want to return to his apartment in Manhattan or go near the cabin. Instead, he headed to Carey's Arlington, Virginia, condo where he planned to claim he had "viral meningitis" to anyone who might knock on the door.

As he inserted the spare key Carey had given him long ago, Tray noticed scratches surrounding the door lock. That should have prepared him for what he saw inside. Carey had always been neat and methodical with a designated place for everything. However, Tray opened the door to chaos. Drawers were pulled out, the contents spilled on the floor. Papers littered every surface. The furniture cushions were slashed, and pictures had been removed from the walls.

Then there was the stench. Tray followed his nose into the kitchen, where frozen food boxes were ripped apart and the food thrown on the floor. Dairy products had soured. No food container was left untouched.

Did Carey have something somebody wanted? Tray contemplated his options. He couldn't call the police. Or the Bureau. However, for the first time since Carey was shot, Tray wondered which one of them *had* been the intended target.

He had plenty of time to consider it while he searched for a broom and a box of garbage bags. He had a lot of housekeeping ahead of him.

Even though the intruders had shredded Carey's couch, Tray was able to duct tape enough of the cushions back together, so he'd have someplace to sit. The same held true for the guest room mattress. However, when the building manager discovered the mountain of trash bags stacked against the dumpster, he would be none too pleased with the person responsible.

Tray used his twin's food delivery accounts to keep himself fed and his Internet connections to learn all he could about who might be after either of them.

He had exhausted a lot of his time rushing around, trying to protect his own identity while looking for clues into his brother's death. The only thing he knew for sure was it wasn't a street robbery that killed Carey. Either his brother had access to information at the NRC that someone would kill to protect, or it was a case of mistaken identity, and the murderer had been after Tray. After all, before his improvised death, he had been deeply embedded in a case involving the illicit trafficking of antiquities.

He couldn't stay in Arlington very long; he needed to be *in the field* to find Carey's killer. However, lying low to throw people off the scent was the best way to handle the matter at the moment.

Besides, the more Tray investigated Calam Fergus, the more he became certain Calam and his friends were after him and not his twin.

NOT SO FAR away, in a private room at Walter Reed Hospital, a patient lay in the stillness of a medically induced coma.

He had been pronounced DOA before being wheeled into a Long Island morgue four days earlier—a shooting victim who had lost a great deal of blood, severely reducing his heart rate.

If it weren't for an almost inaudible moan made by the "corpse" as the medical examiner approached, the man would have surely expired as a result of his autopsy.

Instead, the ME performed lifesaving emergency surgery while morgue workers tried to locate the victim's next of kin. They had no luck contacting his family but did connect with the FBI, which was very interested in the victim's welfare.

"We appreciate your call about *Patient X.* That is how you will refer to him from here on in. You are not to discuss this victim, his identity, or his injuries with anyone. We are notifying a Washington, DC, medical facility, which will be ready to receive him, no questions asked. Contact us when he's stabilized. We'll send an unmarked van to make the transfer."

Patient X had both entrance and exit wounds, the bullet had made a clean pass. It had missed his heart but nicked his lung, causing it to collapse. He had also lost a lot of blood and had lost consciousness after slipping into shock.

130

Now, he was emerging from the fog of his medically induced coma. Being shot at point-blank range had been traumatizing for both his body and his mind. In this twilight haze, he could remember the muffled sound of the gunshot and time slowing down. *It was so cold.* Yet, at his very core, he had felt calm afterward, lulled into a sense of peace by his own heartbeat, which had become louder than the sounds around him.

Pneumothorax. It was a word he had heard, but he wasn't sure what it meant. He just remembered it had been difficult to breathe after the initial pain and burning of the bullet.

He felt like he was floating on air. Mostly. A tinge of pain lingered at the edge of his universe, and outside noises tried to break into his peace and tranquility. He wanted to stay in this twilight forever, but there was something he had to do. What was it?

If it's important, I'll remember it. Eventually.

But not today. Patient X willed himself to sink deeper into the cloud on which he floated, his mind once again going blank.

Aislinn sat in the bunk room of her aunt and uncle's East Hampton estate with a pad and pen on her lap, outlining the few facts she knew about Tray's murder. She looked up when she heard a knock on the door.

"Detective Molyneaux is waiting downstairs to see you," her aunt said.

Aislinn reluctantly followed her aunt downstairs. The detective stood by the living room window, looking over the grounds.

Aislinn slumped onto the couch.

Her aunt invited Detective Molyneaux to have a seat. "I'll just pop into the kitchen and ask Anita to make you some coffee."

"Should I call my lawyer?" Aislinn asked.

"That won't be necessary. You're no longer a suspect. But I believe you know something important that could help crack the case. Once again, what can you tell me about Traynor Lennox's occupation?"

"That sounds so formal and cold. Could you just call him Tray? Everyone else does … did."

"It's his legal name, Miss Gilchrist."

"Traynor sounds so … dehumanized." Closing her eyes, she pinched the bridge of her nose, willing her tears to recede. She looked at the detective and continued, "So does 'Miss Gilchrist.' Please call me Aislinn."

He smiled. "Can you tell me about his occupation, Aislinn?"

"I don't know much about it, just that he appraises art and antiques. I've never been to where he works. I think it might be an auction house. Or an import-export business. I've never seen him actually appraise anything. I've never even been to a museum with him. We've never discussed antiques. Huh." She studied her fingernails for a moment. When she looked up, her eyes glistened with tears. "I guess I don't really know him that well after all."

Molyneaux felt a tug of emotion but knew he had to stay tough. He leaned forward. "If that's *all you know*, why did you say you thought he worked for the government?"

Aislinn stiffened. She took a deep breath while she thought about how to answer the question.

Molyneaux wanted to keep her talking. "Miss Gilchrist?" He waited. "Aislinn?"

"It was something I saw in his apartment," she lied. "A large envelope marked *Classified Information, Confidential Files, Restricted Data.*" At least that part was truthful. "Who has files like that?" she asked. "Spies?"

Molyneaux pulled back as if someone had slapped him. "You seem to have a pretty good handle on what was written on that envelope. Do you also know what was inside?"

Aislinn reddened but said nothing.

Molyneaux leaned forward slightly, his eyes narrowing. "Aislinn, do you even *want* to know who killed your boyfriend?"

"Yes!" she cried. The tears she had been holding back started to fall. "It was about something called *Hero's Knot,* but it's such a far-fetched story that I can't understand why it would even be classified. It has to be fiction."

The detective tapped his fingertips against his knee. "Tell me what you know about it," he said in a calm, measured tone.

Aislinn told Molyneaux everything she had learned from Tray's aunt. The detective's eyes widened, and his jaw gaped as she recounted the information.

"Miss Gilchrist, you do know that giving false information to the police is a criminal offense?"

"I'm not lying," she said with conviction. "Aunt Jane said she got the information from her contact at the Egyptian National Library. Just because you don't believe it doesn't mean it's not what somebody told us."

"I'll check with NYPD to see if their search of Lennox's apartment uncovered this file you allegedly saw. I'm also going to contact the Egyptian National Library. Now, if you would kindly give me," he made finger quotes, "*Aunt Jane's* contact information, I'd like to speak to her as well."

As soon as Molyneaux departed, Aislinn called Jane to warn her that the detective planned to question her about Hero's Knot.

Mark Allen, aka Pete Majewski, hated to go off-script. In the past, loosening a valve in the tank room had proved to be the way to keep Achille happy, and with Carey Lennox supposedly out of the picture, Allen saw no need to do things differently.

His biggest difficulty would be getting rid of the decontamination suit he needed to wear to enter the tank room. It wasn't something he could easily do unnoticed, especially if he ventured into the area alone. He would have to double up with someone else doing maintenance and mess with the valve when the guy wasn't watching.

His visit to the Comanche Peak Nuclear Plant proceeded like clockwork. *No one suspects a thing.* It would take a while before anyone noticed an issue with the radiation levels, and they'd be hard-pressed to pin it on him.

That evening, he called Achille, telling him he could check another plant off his list.

"Are you sure no one can trace this back to you?"

"Yes, and just to be safe, when I first arrived and cleared security, I signed in as Carey Lennox. They never check your signature once they've cleared you. Now they can't even be sure I was here."

"Cameras, damn it. Security. They scanned your badge. You're playing with fire."

"No. *You're* playing with fire. You and the *Anti-Nuke Senator*. He's the one who wants the nuclear reactors decommissioned. I'm just doing your bidding, so protect me. Even if you need to hire a hacker to break into each power plant server and erase all evidence of my visiting there."

"You're being handsomely compensated to cover your own tracks."

"Maybe so. But the way I look at it, you and the senator have more to lose."

Achille kept most of his conversation with Pete Majewski to himself when he called the senator. He just said their man in the field had confirmed another nuclear problem when visiting the Comanche Peak power plant. "That's another piece of ammunition we can add to our arsenal."

UNLIKE MANY OTHER staffers working on Capitol Hill, Achille didn't have an Ivy League education or parents working in politics, but he had a sharp intellect. He didn't mind taking risks. He equated money to power, so he always tried to earn more. When he first graduated college, he'd worked two jobs, one to pay the bills and the other to make investments. His investing skills had helped him buy his first home, a small condo in an outlying Washington suburb. Three years later, he traded up to a small condo inside the District. But it took another five years before he could buy his townhouse on Capitol Hill. He loved that townhouse. It had a yard that allowed him to rescue Hercule from the pound. Hercule was an adult black lab who had a habit of gnawing on wood furniture. Lucky for Achille, most of his furniture was a mix of industrial and mid-century modern and had metal legs. Still, he and Hercule took training classes together, so Hercule would learn which one of them was the master and which one of them was not allowed to chew on the woodwork.

Early on, Achille had found that the excitement of a campaign, combined with his competitive spirit, created a kind of nirvana. When he received an opportunity to work on a campaign, he jumped at it. By the time he moved into his Capitol Hill home, he had scored a job with Senator Phineas Paige and felt it was time to establish a base and branch out into additional money-making interests, like arms trafficking.

SENATOR PAIGE'S EYES gleamed with satisfaction. He wasn't happy that there was a problem at a nuclear plant. However, he was delighted that he was one step closer to slamming the lid on nuclear power—a war he'd been waging since college.

HARVARD UNIVERSITY– SPRING – 1986

In his sophomore year at Harvard, Phin Paige met the love of his life. Valentina Kushnir had long, honey-hued hair, darker brows and lashes, and eyes the color of a brilliant summer sky. From the first moment he saw her, he thought she was the most beautiful girl in the world. Phin caught sight of her every day, sitting under the same tree as he walked between classes in Harvard Yard. One day, he finally found the courage to talk to her. "Don't you ever go to class?"

She looked him over for several seconds before answering with a heavy Ukrainian accent, "No. You confuse me with my father. He is student here."

He crouched, so he would be on eye level with her. "But what are you doing here?"

"I make English better reading book and talking to schoolboys like you."

"Tomorrow. We'll have coffee together." He didn't voice it as a request; it was more of a demand. Then he hurried away, praying she would be there the following day.

She was.

As the days passed, Valentina told Phin that her father was a Ukrainian diplomat enrolled in post-doctoral courses. Her mother had chosen not to make the trip because she was going through a difficult pregnancy. Valentina's one older and two younger sisters were all with her mother to ensure she wouldn't be alone in case of complications. She confided that her father always wanted a son, and after four daughters, her mother was determined to try 'just once more.'

Soon, Phin was stealing kisses from Valentina each time he saw her. It didn't take long for the kisses to escalate into something more heartfelt. He had stars in his eyes from their growing romance.

One beautiful April day, as they walked beneath a row of blossoming cherry trees, Phin confessed to Valentina that he loved her.

For the next week, they discussed how they might continue their relationship once her father had to return to the USSR. Phin knew his parents would never allow him to marry. He was only twenty and still had his college career ahead of him. "Perhaps your family will allow you to attend college here in the US," he told her.

"I do not know," she answered. "I think is time you meet my father."

"Right now?" Phin's nerves danced unpleasantly. He had only seen her father from a distance. He wasn't sure he was ready to meet him. Why is he even here? *he wondered.* Aren't we in the middle of a cold war with the USSR?

"Not this minute. You meet him Sunday. I cook dinner."

Phin did his best to prepare himself—after all, he was a political science major, and Valentina's father was a diplomat. This meeting could be a good opportunity to call on the skills he had hoped to acquire here at Harvard.

He took a deep breath before ringing the buzzer for the Kushnir apartment. The following two minutes were the longest in history.

Valentina pulled the door open a moment later, tears streaming down her face.

He immediately pulled her to him, not caring what her father might think. "What is it?"

"*Something happened at home. They say is fine, but Tato has friend—say is bad. We go home now.*"

"*What do you mean, now?*"

"*My mother, my sisters. If as bad as Tato's friend say, we must pack. We must move someplace else.*"

Valentina's father entered the room, speaking to his daughter in Ukrainian. He stopped when he saw the stricken look on Phin's face. He nodded at Phin, said a few more words, and left the room.

"*Our plane leaves in few hours. Tato say he's sorry. I must go away.*"

"*But I love you,*" *Phin said, pulling her back into his arms.*

"*I love you,*" *she replied. "I come back for you." She grabbed a paper and pencil and scribbled her address in Pripyat. "You write me here. If I move, I write you. You must go." She stood up on her toes and kissed him one last time. "Always, I love you."*

She pushed him out the door and closed it without saying another word.

Phin ran. He had no destination in mind. He just needed to move. To run. To spend all the negative energy he felt building in his body. What could have gone so terribly wrong?

In the days and weeks to come, Phin heard about the Chernobyl Nuclear Power Plant disaster and knew instinctively it was the reason for Valentina's sudden departure. A single reactor in the plant had turned spring into an endless winter for tens of thousands of people. Radioactivity killed or incapacitated residents hundreds of miles away. Moscow kept saying the accident was "under control." The dead couldn't say otherwise.

He received a single postcard from Valentina. It simply said I love you. *It was postmarked in Ukraine. It gave him hope.*

False hope, as it turned out.

He never heard from Valentina again.

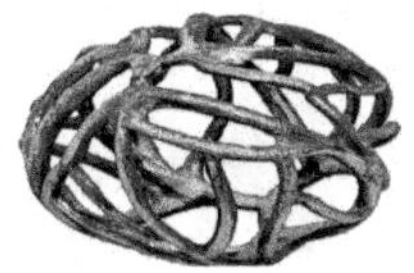

CHAPTER THIRTEEN

Jane Deveraux felt fully prepared when she received a knock on her door later that day. She had a list with the names, professional titles, and contact information of all the people she had spoken with while gathering information on Hero's Knot. She'd also made a list of bullet points detailing all the salient facts about the artifact.

"Good afternoon, I'm—"

She nodded and pulled the door wide open. "Detective Molyneaux. I know. Come on in. I'm Dr. Jane Deveraux, an archeology professor and lecturer on antiquities. You're here about my nephew Tray's death and what its connection might be to an artifact known as Hero's Knot. Have a seat." A high-pitched whistling sound came from the kitchen. "You're just in time for tea." She handed him the contact list and led him to the dining room table. "Look this over while I get it ready. These experts can verify everything I tell you."

A few minutes later, she returned with a tea tray and scones.

He handed her his card as she sat across from him.

Jane studied the name on his card. "Molyneaux. Are your people from Normandy?"

"They might have been a long time ago. Now, the few relatives I have left all hail from Lancashire. In the UK."

Jane handed the detective a cup of tea from across the table. "Aislinn says you didn't believe what she told you about Hero's Knot."

"It is a very implausible story."

"Perhaps, yet there are many independent reports of a strange metal object—attributed to Hero of Alexandria—that coincide directly with several devastating earthquakes. I've been told credible scientists are now studying the claim that—when exposed to the sun near a volcano—the artifact triangulates with both, supposedly intensifying the sun's energy until it causes the volcano to erupt. Most likely, it's responsible for the big one in 79 CE that destroyed Pompeii. But it doesn't stop there."

"I'm going to need to check your story out."

"Please do. That's why I gave you that contact list." She nodded toward the page he had laid on the table. "I want to know why my nephew is dead. And who killed him. And if it was over some ancient artifact that I wish had been destroyed when Vesuvius erupted."

Molyneaux sipped his tea. "Do you or any of your associates know, or have they alluded to knowing, where this magical object is currently located?"

Jane squinted. "I'm sure I don't know, Detective. And no one I spoke with gave me any indication that they know where it is." The sun's rays through the window blinded her, making her feel like a character being grilled by the cops in a low-budget movie. She got up to adjust the blinds.

"Someone, somewhere, has got to know where this thing is," Molyneaux said, more to himself than Jane, "if it actually exists."

"You may be right," she answered. "But is your job to recover a *magical object*," she wriggled her hands—to mock the detective's words, "or is it to solve my nephew's murder?"

THE FOLLOWING DAY, Aislinn begged her cousin Jude to take her to Chapter One on Main for lunch.

"Why would you ever want to return there?" he asked. "Doesn't it make you relive all the bad memories associated with Tray's death?"

"I'm trying to find out why he was killed. I owe him that much."

"Why do you owe him anything?"

She sighed. "Because I loved him."

Jude allowed her to drag him off the couch in the den and push him toward the door. "Okay. But only because my stomach is already rumbling, and I was just about to go down to Bostwick's Chowder House for a lobster roll."

"It has to be Chapter One on Main."

"Then it's your treat. And tomorrow, you're taking me to Bostwick's. Your treat again."

"Fine. Let's go."

They settled in at a table where they could see everyone who walked in, not to mention most of the people who were already there. They placed their orders, and Aislinn gasped when the waiter moved away, revealing someone walking in the door. She had seen the young woman here at the restaurant on the day of the murder. She nudged Jude, whispering, "Do you see that girl over there?"

"She's kind of cute," he replied. "Are you thinking of setting us up?"

"She was here the day Tray died."

"So, what do you want to do?"

"Talk to her," Aislinn replied, pushing back from the table.

"Do you want me to come with you?"

"No. I wouldn't want to scare her away."

He scowled. "Thanks for the vote of confidence."

"I didn't mean anything against you. I just meant she might feel like we're ganging up on her if there are two of us."

"Go."

Aislinn crossed the room, sitting next to the woman who was nursing a drink at the bar. "Do you mind if I sit down?"

Jin looked shocked that someone would intrude on her solitude. She was doubly surprised when she recognized Aislinn. "What can I do for you?"

"I believe you were here the day a man was killed behind the restaurant. When I came back to talk to the detectives, I saw you. I assume you were here while they were questioning diners. I had to leave the restaurant for a while after the murder and was wondering if you had heard anything interesting that day." She stuck out her hand. "I'm Aislinn Gilchrist, by the way, but everyone calls me Ash."

Jin shook her hand. "My friends call me … Jen." She purposefully changed the sound of the vowel in her name. She didn't think East Hampton police knew who she was, even if the NYPD did. But the fewer people who knew her actual name, the better. "I only know that someone was killed out back, but I have no idea who that was or what kind of information the police were after. They seemed to ask everyone basic stuff, people's names and addresses, and what they saw. I really didn't hear anything interesting."

"You didn't see anything suspicious?"

"No, I was more interested in the omelet I was eating, and the guy who was supposed to meet me here but never showed up."

"Sorry to bother you, but it was worth a try—in case you saw something important."

"I understand completely." Jin nodded. "I think it may have been a tough day for police," she added, studying Aislinn closely, "because I heard there was a second murder in Room 2 at The Old Salt House. Can you imagine that? Two murders in one day. I wonder if they're connected?"

Aislinn paled a little. "I heard about that, but I'm more concerned about the shooting behind this restaurant." She focused on Jin's face. "Did you know either of the victims?"

Jin hesitated a split second too long before saying, "No. I just find the coincidence interesting."

Aislinn noted the hesitation but let it pass. "Thank you for speaking with me." She got up and returned to her cousin's table.

"What was that all about?" Jude asked.

"Like I said, she was here the day of Tray's murder. She just mentioned the murder at The Old Salt House as well. The one in the room Tray and I had stayed in. She said she finds the coincidence interesting. There's something about her I don't trust."

"Just because she finds the coincidence interesting?"

"No, because she mentioned the room number at the

inn where the murder took place. Who does that? Plus, she was sitting nearby on the day of the murder when I told police what room we had been staying in. I felt like she was mocking me by saying she knew nothing about it."

IT'S TIME TO *be more proactive,* Aislinn decided after Jude took her back to Thorne House. She drove herself to the East Hampton Village Police Department. "I'm here to see Detective Molyneaux."

"Is he expecting you?" the officer manning the front lobby asked. "He may temporarily utilize one of our desks, but his office is in Yaphank."

"I'm a suspect in his murder investigation, and I have fresh information for him." It was a simple, declaratory sentence.

"Wait here," he said, walking into a back office.

A moment later, Molyneaux came out and beckoned Aislinn to follow him. "Walk with me." He led her outside. "As I've previously informed you, you are no longer a suspect in this case. However, Ms. Gilchrist, I would like to know what your 'fresh information' is."

"I met a small Asian woman named Jen, whom I'm sure was in Chapter One on Main on the day of the murder."

Molyneaux's eyebrows rose a bit. He assumed she meant *Jin* and was surprised Aislinn knew anything about her. "How do you know her?"

Aislinn recounted their conversation and explained why it put her on edge.

"Thank you for the information. We'll look into it. Is there anything else?"

"No."

"Then let me see you to your car." She walked ahead

of him, leading the way. He found himself mesmerized by the sway of her hips.

Another officer, just arriving, cleared his throat and caught Molyneaux's eye when the detective looked up.

Molyneaux turned red, realizing he'd been caught staring at Aislinn's rump. *Okay, Aislinn Gilchrist is a looker. But she's more than a pretty package. She's classy, yet vulnerable and down to earth at the same time. Maybe she needs a sympathetic shoulder to cry on.* If Molyneaux were ready to settle down, he thought Aislinn would be perfect for him. Then again, she was in mourning and might not think it suitable for him to ask her out. *Neither would headquarters.*

Maybe, after the case closed, he'd invite her to dinner—giving him more reason to wrap up the case quickly.

NEARLY FOUR THOUSAND miles away, Zander Bakker popped another Xanax in his mouth. He washed it down with a generous amount of cognac. His tension was palpable—the tic in his eye apparent. He stared out the window at Lake Zurich. Usually, the tranquil water and the mountains in the distance had a calming effect on him. But not today. Even Adolfus appeared wary of his master, studying Bakker from the corner of the room rather than sitting at his side.

What is the point of having big plans if they're all based on half-truths, myths, and unknown variables, and they are being carried out by bumbling idiots? Still, the speculation on Hero's Knot had come from some of the world's most educated and respected experts. For the past few years, he'd had teams of archaeologists searching for the ancient object. They had last seen it at an auction house in Bakker's home city of Zurich, but someone apparently stole it out from under him.

Bakker felt the magnetism of the artifact even before learning about its incredible history. It promised great potential. When he heard it was up for sale, he put people in place with instructions that they bid to win, even if the price rose dramatically.

However, the object never came up for bid. Bakker's people inquired why, and they learned someone had broken into the secure facility and had liberated that one item. Nothing else. And then, someone stole the item from the thief.

International officials became interested in the theft and requested that Interpol help recover it.

The network of law enforcement agencies' involvement made Bakker even more incensed. There were now too many eyes on an artifact he desired. It made operating under the radar next to impossible.

At least now, he had a picture of Hero's Knot that the auction house had taken. After what he'd learned about it, he felt sure the markings on it could be "adjusted" to suit a particular need. If the object could induce volcanic eruptions, why not other types of energy? Bakker was interested in *adjusting* the artifact to triangulate the sun's power with a focus on triggering nuclear warheads rather than volcanoes. He already had a doctor in Tehran working on how to adapt the relic. For that reason, he did not want to draw undue attention to himself.

What's the use of paying large salaries to the people surrounding me if they can't provide the services I need—like finding out who else is interested in the artifact? And why?

Jin hated driving, especially in New York City traffic. It wasn't that she didn't know how to drive. Her brother had taught her before he moved back to Japan. However, working for Godfrey Munk meant she always had to be on the lookout for possible threats. Driving took too much concentration away from staying alert to the possibility of outside interference, so Munk's honchos always drove, and she had fallen out of practice.

Regrettably, cars were apparently good for stakeouts. And so, Jin found herself in a rented Cadillac XT4 with a navigation system set to take her to 'her grandmother's house' in Scarsdale. The rental agent gladly showed her how to set the seat height and mirrors and adjust the radio. Unfortunately, he forgot to tell her what side of the vehicle the gas tank was on or how to open the cap. So, after pulling into a self-service gas station to top off the half-full tank, she was at odds with what to do next.

"You're facing the wrong way."

She stared at the stranger outside her window. "What?"

"The gas tank is on the other side. You pulled up on the wrong side."

"Right." She looked around. It was a busy station. She knew as soon as she pulled away to change sides, another car would take her spot, and she would be forced to double around. She got out and walked around to the other side of the car, studying the gas cap.

"Pull up a few feet."

She turned and glared at the same guy, placing her hands on her hips. "Why?"

"Because if we pull the hose across the back, it may fit. Pull up."

We? Jin wasn't sure she trusted the guy—but it sounded logical—so she did as he said.

When she got out of the car, he was holding the nozzle.

"Put your credit card in the machine."

"I've never done this before."

"It's intuitive. Put your credit card in the machine and answer the questions on the little screen."

She followed the instructions with help from her new friend, and gas flowed into the vehicle a minute later. "Thank you," she said.

His eyes narrowed. "You have driven before, haven't you?"

"Yes. I have a license. I just don't drive very often, and this is a rental."

"Be safe out there."

On the road to Scarsdale, she hoped her stakeout would be worth it. She couldn't think of anything more boring than staring at someone's home and hoping they'd come out and go someplace important. She wasn't sure what she was looking for, but with Traynor Lennox dead, she needed to find that artifact. Her job depended on it.

The woman who had arranged his funeral apparently lived inside a large co-op complex. That would make keeping an eye on her a little more complicated. Jin had no idea if she would be able to park close enough to keep tabs on Jane Deveraux or if the woman would come out of the front door or use a different entrance. Not to mention, other people would be walking in and out of the building all day, distracting her.

She got out of the car and walked around the complex. Jane lived in a large building—among many similar large buildings. Jin wished she had paid closer attention to the type of car Jane had driven on the day of the funeral.

Back in her rental car, she finally saw her mark heading out. Jane had empty canvas grocery bags slung over her arms. Jin watched as she got into a blue Volvo and pulled away. Rather than following her to the grocery store, Jin hung out by the door to the building, waiting for someone else to leave so she could let herself into the lobby. A bank of mailboxes helped her determine which unit Jane lived in.

It didn't take her long to pick the lock. She entered Jane's apartment and worked quickly, planting listening devices near a kitchen cabinet and under the dining room table. Upon further inspection, she discovered that Jane used her second bedroom as an office and planted another device there. Jin only had one small camera with her and hoped Jane would be most likely to talk with other people at the dining room table. She placed the camera in an inconspicuous spot that would capture any action in the living room or dining room.

Leaving the apartment, she casually walked back to her car. *I hope she doesn't take too long. I want to see how well this equipment works.*

TRAY REMAINED HOLED up in his brother's condo, using his twin's computer to hack into the digital back door of his FBI work account. He needed information he had requested before Carey's murder. The results described how the sun's fusion process not only created a nucleus containing a deuterium, a positron, and a neutrino but also liberated mega electron volts that formed neutrons. According to the physicist he'd contacted, if Hero's Knot was strong enough to use the sun's energy to force a volcanic eruption, it could also be strong enough to redirect free neutrons toward nuclear warheads, causing a quick fission reaction.

CHAPTER FOURTEEN

BACK IN HER apartment, Jane shuddered at the thought of calling Carey, not worried that he might answer but fearing he would not. Once again, she left a message on his machine saying she needed to speak with him urgently. "Where have you been, Carey? You missed something significant. It's not like you, and now I'm worried."

She paced back and forth in her apartment. *Where can he be? Maybe I should call the NRC rather than just take the medical examiner's word for it that Carey is supposedly 'out of town.'*

FROM HER CAR, Jin had a clear view of Jane pacing. Both the camera and the microphones worked as well as she expected. Jin wasn't sure who 'Carey' was, nor did she care. She simply wanted to stay on top of whether Jane mentioned Hero's Knot or made any move to retrieve it.

Uncomfortable, Jin shifted her weight. *I should have thought this through more clearly. There are empty apartments in that building.* She had seen real estate listings posted by the mailboxes in the lobby. *I could camp in one of them if I had an air mattress and a blanket.* She considered whether she should leave or not. She could probably get what she needed and return in less than an hour, but she might miss something.

She suddenly felt the urge to pee. *Well, that seals the deal.* She looked up the nearest discount store on her phone. It was sure to have a restroom.

As predicted, Jin was back within an hour, and as luck would have it, she found a better parking space. Not that she needed it anymore.

She headed into the building, hurrying to catch the door before it locked behind another resident. The listing of available apartments included one down the hall from Jane. Jin only had to pick the lock and remove the realtor's lockbox. *Wouldn't want anyone barging in on me.* Before long, she'd made herself comfortable on the air mattress and waited for something to happen.

TRAY WANTED TO kick himself. Carey's voicemail had run out of space. It wouldn't have if Tray had checked it more often. He wanted to ensure he heard all his brother's messages so he could determine if any of them sounded shady. Carey's voicemail box was a testament to his popularity, considering it always seemed to be full. The only reason their Aunt Jane had been able to leave a message was because Tray had erased all the previous messages after listening to them for clues about what was going on in his brother's life.

He closed his eyes, remembering Carey's last call to him. His voice had been full of fear. Tray knew his twin was working on something complicated that could be linked to nuclear terrorism. *I should be doing more for Carey instead of protecting my own hide, squirreled away here in his apartment. Meanwhile, poor Jane is going out of her mind. It's time to break the silence.*

He got up and jammed some of Carey's clothing into his backpack. *Transportation will be a bitch.* He wasn't sure of the train schedule but didn't think anyone would look for him at the Arlington station, so it might not be so bad if he had to wait around. Then, a light bulb lit up inside his brain. He looked around for his brother's spare keys. The key to Carey's Cadillac Eldorado Biarritz, Elbi, was easy to spot. It had the Cadillac crest right on it.

Tray headed down to the garage, looking forward to driving the car. He searched for his twin's usual parking space, and his jaw dropped when he spotted the Cadillac.

It's a boat. A tanker. A freaking aircraft carrier.

Elbi was an enormous, shiny, hard-to-miss, bright turquoise *stunner* with whitewall tires and a big-ass chrome grill.

Well, there goes incognito. At least it has a rag roof. That should offer some protection from prying eyes. Besides, who would ever expect to see me driving this colossal tribute to the 1950s?

THE DRIVE FROM Arlington to Scarsdale wasn't too bad. There was a bit of rush hour traffic near DC, but the roads were not nearly as congested as they would have been during the fall and winter months. And even though the Cadillac was well over a half-century old, the ride was spectacular. *No wonder Carey wanted this car.* Tray had thought it was a ridiculous purchase when he first heard about it, but not anymore.

A wave of melancholy rolled over him. Carey would never enjoy driving this car again.

Tray looked toward the horizon. "Don't worry, bro," he said aloud. "I'll take care of Elbi for you. And Joey Sam."

He suddenly thought of Caterina and wondered if she knew Carey was dead.

Probably not. No one knows. Except me. Another wave of sadness rolled over Tray. *I need to get to the bottom of this. And soon.*

During much of the trip, he argued with himself about whether to call Jane ahead of time and warn her that he was on his way. Hearing from the dead over the phone was a sure-fire way to spook someone. He decided against it. It would still be a traumatic reunion, but at least he would be there to catch her if she fainted.

It WAS LATE by the time Tray reached Scarsdale. He knew his aunt was a night owl because she always told him the best time to write and research was late at night when there were no interruptions from the visitors, phone calls, and the minutiae of daytime living. He buzzed her unit. "Aunt Jane, it's me."

"Oh my God! Come up." She buzzed him in.

Jane was waiting at her open door when Tray arrived. She abruptly took a step back. Jane studied his face, looking confused. "Carey? What happened to you?"

He didn't look anything like she expected. He had shorn his head, leaving only uneven stubble. He had a week's worth of facial hair on his cheeks and chin in an unkempt beard.

"What happened to your hair? And how did you get so tan? You could never stay in the sun long because your skin always burned and freckled." He was also wearing contacts. She stepped forward, looking more closely. "Your eyes are brown."

He took a deep breath to steady himself after feeling an uncomfortable prickling in his nose. "Aunt Jane, I'm not Carey. It's me, Tray."

The blood drained away from Jane's face, turning her complexion the color of uncooked dough. She swayed. Tray grabbed her elbow and led her back into the apartment. He bypassed the couch—strewn with books and notes—and showed her into the dining room, seating her at the table. He spotted the tea kettle on the stove. "I'll make you some tea."

Jane barely moved for several minutes, trying to absorb the information. "You're dead." Her voice registered somewhere between a rasp and a squeak. Tears rolled down her cheeks.

Tray put two mugs of green tea on the table before pulling a chair close and taking her hands. "Carey's dead, Aunt Jane. The day he died, he called me on the phone and said someone was following him." Tray sucked in a breath, trying to put a lid on his emotions. "I tried to get to him— to help him—but by the time I did, they'd already shot him. I was trying to stop the bleeding when he passed."

Jane couldn't bottle her emotions as easily. Tears ran freely down her face. "Why would anybody want to harm dear, sweet Carey?"

They both sat in silence, pondering the answer to that question.

156

Tray felt the room closing in on him. *I need fresh air.* He crossed the room and opened the window, praying a breeze would clear his mind. "Carey may have been working on something sensitive for the NRC. I don't know. Maybe he heard or saw something that someone else wanted to keep secret. I've been thinking about it for days, but I'm not any closer to knowing why someone would want him dead."

Jane rubbed behind her left ear, which she often did when she felt perplexed. "Why did they say it was you who died?"

Tray hesitated. He wasn't sure exactly how much to tell Jane. He tried to keep his reason vague yet help her understand why he had resorted to subterfuge. "I don't know why anyone would want Carey dead, but there is a reason someone might target me. A couple of years ago, I came into possession of a valuable, ancient artifact. Some people would stop at nothing to obtain it. Switching identities with Carey was a last-minute decision that I consciously made. I didn't think it mattered if the people who were after him thought he was still alive. They would continue trying to flush him out, making it easier for me to catch them. It also wouldn't hurt me if the people after the artifact thought I was dead. I hope they give up looking for it and crawl back into whatever hole they came out of."

Jane sobbed openly. "You have no idea all the terrible things I thought about your brother when he didn't get back to me after you'd died. I was so angry with him for missing your funeral."

Tray grabbed his chair and pulled it over to her. He squeezed her hand after he sat down. "About the funeral. I was astonished when I heard about it. I didn't think you would do anything without hearing from me or Carey first."

"You can blame that on the Suffolk County Medical Examiner's office. They couldn't reach you. They said they were done examining the body and wanted to get it out of there. I had a local funeral director pick it up, but then there was an explosion at a tire factory, and bodies flooded all the funeral parlors. They refused to freeze you until I heard from your brother. I wanted you to rest in peace, so I took the only memorial service they had available."

"I'm surprised you didn't recognize Carey when you identified the body."

"You're identical twins, Tray. And I didn't look closely. I was too busy crying. Not to mention, I identified him over the phone."

Tray's mouth opened, but no words came out. A look of confusion contorted his features. It took him a few moments to speak. "Over the phone? Why would they do that?"

"I have no idea. And then the funeral director called me to say that the casket would remain sealed during the service due to time constraints."

"Well, that explains that."

Jane took a sip of tea. "Can I ask you something, Traynor?"

One side of his mouth almost pulled up in an involuntary smirk. "Uh-oh, it must be serious if you're using my full name."

"That artifact you were talking about. It's not Hero's Knot, is it?"

It was Tray's turn to be stunned. "What makes you ask that?"

"Your girlfriend was asking about it. Then the detective assigned to your murder came up here, asking about it.

Suddenly, it's a hot topic. Is that what everyone is after? I was just talking to one of my contacts in the Egyptian National Library, and she heard a 'rumor' that Hero's Knot will be used in what she called a 'test situation' on a small nuke."

Tray went cold. *How can they use Hero's Knot? Unless they found it at the cabin?*

He stood suddenly, pulling Jane onto her feet. "Aunt Jane . . . Jane. I have to go." He pulled her in for a fast hug. "Be very careful about whom you let in or talk to."

She clutched his arm. "Why? What's the matter?"

"Until now, I thought I was the only person who knew the location of Hero's Knot. If I'm wrong, if it's missing, someone on the wrong side of the law has taken possession of a powerful weapon."

"You're scaring me."

"Go to bed. Get some sleep." He grabbed a scrap of paper and wrote down a new cell phone number. "This is temporary, a number where you can reach me, but you shouldn't need it. I'll be back in time for breakfast."

Down the hall, Jin watched and listened in on Tray and Jane's conversation using the devices she had planted in the apartment. *Pay dirt.* She was surprised Munk's 'rumor' idea had worked. However, if it led her to the artifact so she could complete her assignment, that's all she cared about.

She followed Tray out of the building and tailed him. *His car is so huge. And distinctive. Following him should be a piece of cake.*

CHAPTER FIFTEEN

TRAY FLOORED ELBI, afraid that someone had discovered the artifact and had stolen it. He hadn't seen it since he hid it in the root cellar of the Roscoe fishing cabin. *How could anyone have found it there unless they were tailing me when I first hid it?*

In his haste to get to the cabin, he didn't notice someone following him. Unlike his brother, he had seen the headlights behind him but surmised they could belong to almost anyone. Why would somebody follow him now? Surely, they all thought he was dead.

The fishing cabin reeked of disuse. Tray rummaged around a drawer for the key to the root cellar and headed out back. Unlocking the door, he held it open for a minute to allow some of the musty odor to dissipate. *It doesn't look like it's been disturbed.* He pulled out his phone and used the flashlight app to illuminate the far corner. He kicked at it with his foot and connected with the bag containing the artifact, sighing with relief as he turned off the phone—*no need to call attention to myself.*

Whack!

Tray never saw it coming. His phone flew out of his hand, landing several feet away in a pile of muck. He went down, his world going dark before he hit the floor.

Jin used the shovel she'd hit Tray with to root around, looking for the object she saw fly out of his hand. The space was dark and filled with cobwebs and debris, not to mention several decomposing rodents. The stench of rot and death was overwhelming. She wasn't even sure he'd had a phone. All she'd seen was a light, which could have been a flashlight. She needed to get out of there.

She crept into the far corner, using the shovel to find the bundle Tray had kicked, but disturbed a mouse instead. It ran up the handle and, by extension, Jin's arm. She screamed, throwing the shovel to the side and swatting at the rodent until it fell off. *To hell with his phone.* She grabbed the artifact and rushed out of the root cellar, only stopping to lock Tray inside. She didn't relax until she was miles away.

I need to find another line of work.

HOURS LATER, TRAY struggled to embrace consciousness. His head felt like an anvil in a busy blacksmith's shop. The pounding was nasty, the pain intense. When he tried to move, a wave of nausea stopped him. He instinctively knew he was lying on a pillow of rodent waste and again struggled to sit up. However, the effort overwhelmed him. He passed out again, and for the next twenty-four hours, he drifted in and out of consciousness.

*

Jane couldn't sit still. It was lunchtime, and Tray still hadn't returned. She'd tried calling the phone number he'd given her, but there was no answer, no message, no mailbox. His words, 'I'll be back in time for breakfast,' echoed through her brain. She wasn't sure what to do. She could always call the state police and ask them to check the fishing cabin, but how was she supposed to explain she was looking for her *dead* nephew. *Is switching identities with someone who's dead a crime? Fraud? It must be something.* She held off on calling the police but kept trying Tray's number every half hour.

Her nerves were beyond frayed. She jumped every time her phone rang. More often than not, it was a colleague wanting to share their research with her or former students asking her to write letters of recommendation. A couple of calls were from telemarketers. She slammed down the receiver on those, wishing there was some way she could spike their phones.

By dinnertime, her stomach was signaling its discontent by grumbling loudly. In her worry, she had skipped lunch. She took a few minutes to heat a can of soup and make a slice of toast before continuing her trek back and forth across the living room floor. The last vestiges of sunlight had vanished, and the old grandfather clock that her great-grandparents had given her grandparents as a wedding gift struck ten. She picked up her phone and called Tray's number again, listening as it rang incessantly.

Tray could hear a phone ringing. It sounded fuzzy. *Is it mine?* He could barely lift his head, but he had to contact someone and tell them he needed help. He reached out in

162

the direction of the ringing and tried inching toward the sound.

He'd moved less than a foot before the ringing stopped.

JANE SLAMMED DOWN the phone. It was becoming an ugly habit. She didn't want to lose another nephew. If Tray didn't answer soon, she would take matters into her own hands.

By midnight, she was a nervous wreck. Her former students would have called her *certifiable* if they could see her. She grabbed her phone and again punched in Tray's number, listening to it ring.

TRAY HEARD THE phone. He stretched toward it, his fingers touching something that wasn't mulch or animal feces. He grasped it and brought it closer. He stared at it, trying to decipher if the caller's number belonged to Jane, but his eyes wouldn't focus. *It's now or never.* He accepted the call with a weak "Yeah."

His aunt sounded frantic. "Tray, is that you?"

"Someone … attacked me. Cabin … Roscoe. Root … cellar. Can't… focus … need … help."

BACK IN BEECHHURST, Jin threw the artifact on Munk's desk. "You have what you want. Now, I'm going after what I want—a quiet, meditative life. When you promoted me to be your bodyguard, I thought I had it made. The extra money was a blessing. Working for you in that capacity allowed me to keep my skills sharp. I felt useful, but you hired me as a protector, not as an instrument to hurt people and perform petty crimes. Agreeing to the Hamptons job seemed like fun. Calam and I were simply going to find something and hand it off to you. No one was supposed to die. Calam was not supposed to die."

She fought tears. "I loved him. Now he's gone forever because of some stupid artifact, and you wouldn't even let me try to find him because you didn't want officials to trace his shooting back to us. How am I supposed to get any closure? I want out, Mr. Munk. I can't do this anymore. Your secret is safe with me. Lord knows you have enough on me to send me to jail for a very long time. And I wouldn't like that at all."

Munk shook his head. "You can't quit, Jin. I need you now more than ever. Especially with the artifact in our possession." He opened the plastic bag she had dumped Hero's Knot in and made a face of disgust. "Where'd you find this, in a sewer?"

"I found it hidden in a shed with dead rodents. I had to pick through their carcasses to locate it. I also had to injure someone who may very well be dead. Although, I don't care about that guy. I think he may have killed Calam. If he did, then he deserves to die. But that's it, Mr. Munk. No more killing. Consider this my formal notice."

"Don't be so hasty. Why don't you take a vacation first? Clear your mind. You're always talking about your brother in Japan. Why don't you visit him? I'll pay for the trip. Take a month. Relax. Let's not make any final decisions now. You just need a little time to reset your priorities. When you return, you'll need a job, and finding one may be difficult. I'm just saying to keep your options open. And if you do choose to come back, it will strictly be as a bodyguard. No side jobs. Okay? Just think about it."

THERE WAS NO way Mark Allen could loosen a valve without being noticed inside the tank room at the Diablo Canyon Nuclear Power Plant in Avila Beach, California.

The people here had their backs up after reports of sabotage at other nuclear facilities. He had to decide whether to take an enormous risk or face his boss's ire.

That night, he called Achille. "The security at Diablo Canyon is tight. There's no way I can do a little damage without being seen. We can either give up on this plant or go full bore and trigger the alarm, which would not be that difficult. Then everyone will start putting on radiation suits, and I could mask myself underneath, becoming one among the many. With so many people in identical decontamination suits looking for problems, I'd be able to hide in plain sight and pretend I'm tightening when I'm actually loosening."

"Sounds risky."

"It's that or abort."

Achille paused for a long moment, thinking about how to extract himself and the senator if everything went belly-up. *There's no real connection between us and Allen, at least, nothing that would stand up in court. I could blame it all on detractors putting him up to it.* Having convinced himself, he told Allen, "Do it."

Jane put on jeans and flat boots and pulled on a windbreaker. It didn't matter that it was the middle of summer. It could get cool in the Catskills at night. She packed a thermos of hot tea and bottles of cold water and stuffed a sandwich and chocolate bars in a bag.

By the time she had located the largest flashlight she owned, it was already closing in on two a.m. She sighed, wishing Tray had answered the phone while it was still daylight. *Being up at the cabin in the middle of the night gives me the creeps.* However, it didn't stop her from making the journey. *Tray needs me.*

The navigation system in Jane's car guided her to where she needed to go. Unfortunately, there were no streetlights on the roads leading out to the lake, and because she drove slowly, it took Jane longer than expected to find the cabin. She was only sure she was in the right place because of the huge Cadillac in the driveway. *Carey's Eldorado Biarritz.*

She tried the front door. It was locked. She pounded on it, not really expecting anyone to answer. After a minute, she moved on. She tried the door to the screened porch, but it only gave her access to the porch and not the cabin's interior. *Tray's not inside the house. Where is the root cellar?*

She walked around to the far side, looking for another door, and found one. It was sturdy and made of metal, although it appeared to have rusted over. She pounded on it. "Tray. Are you in there?"

INSIDE THE ROOT cellar, Tray opened his eyes. His pounding head felt ready to explode. He squeezed his eyes shut to block out the noise but continued to hear hammering. *Did someone just mention my name?* He swallowed—or at least tried to. His mouth was so dry he felt like the skin on the roof of his mouth would rip off and stick to his tongue if he tried opening it.

Thump. Thump. Thump.

The hammering sounded again. He moaned in frustration.

JANE STOPPED BANGING on the door. *I'm sure I heard something inside.* She aimed the flashlight at the door handle. *Maybe if I bash it with a rock.*

A twig snapped behind her, and she froze.

*

TRAY TRIED TO take a deep breath. The rancid air stung the inside of his nostrils, making them prickle. *At least the hammering stopped.* He vaguely remembered talking to someone on the phone. His eyes popped open. *What if it was Jane?* He tried to move. To roll over. To sit up. Anything. He needed to bang on the door so she would know he was in there.

JANE SQUINTED AT the bright light shining directly in her eyes. The high-wattage torch blinded her. She would have complained, but she was too scared to speak.

"Can I ask you what you're doing here?" a deep voice said. It didn't sound friendly.

Jane wished to hell that she had waited for daylight, though she couldn't afford to do that with Tray's life hanging in the balance. "I think somebody's trapped inside."

The beam of the stranger's torch traveled from her to the door handle. She used her flashlight to see who had interrupted her but suddenly stopped. *No, idiot. It's best not to know. If you can identify him, he might kill you. But now it's too late!*

The state trooper banged on the door. *Thump. Thump. Thump.*

"Tray, are you in there?" Jane yelled.

"Do you have a key?" the trooper asked.

"No, but the man trapped inside is the owner."

"I'll be right back."

"Tray, we're going to get you out of there. Just hold on a little longer."

The state trooper returned a minute later with a pry bar and went to work on the entry. Though the door appeared rusted, it was solid. Fortunately, the wood frame around it was old and rotted. It splintered, and then the frame gave way. The trooper wrenched the door open, directing the powerful torch beam inside.

Tray groaned when the light hit his eyes.

The trooper tried to help him up but had to settle on dragging him outside. "How'd you get locked up in there?"

"Someone ... wanted ... something ... I ... had. Followed ... me. Attacked ... me." Tray's voice sounded as rusty as the door to the root cellar.

"Did they take anything?"

While the trooper asked the question, Jane gave Tray a sip of water.

Tray didn't answer right away. His brain was still fuzzy, but he knew he had to temper his answer. "I'm an ... antiques appraiser ... in possession of ... a valuable object I ... needed to ... hold for safekeeping." He stopped for another sip of water. "I hid it ... out here because ... I figured nobody ... would bother it ... in the root cellar." He looked longingly at the water bottle, and Jane gave him more. "No one did ... until tonight ... when I led them ... straight to it ... like an idiot."

"Last night." Jane emphatically corrected him. "You've been missing for more than twenty-four hours." She handed him the bottle to finish drinking on his own. He took another sip, followed by several more rapid ones. "Take it easy," she said. "You don't want to choke."

"Wouldn't being stored inside a root cellar damage an antique?" the trooper asked. "This place seems like nothing more than a burial ground for wildlife and rusting tools."

"It doesn't matter now. It's gone."

"You'll need to file a report."

"Not until I take him to an emergency room," Jane said. "He's dehydrated. And his head has been bashed in."

The trooper aimed the torch at the back of Tray's head, which was caked with clotted blood and dirt. "Damn. Let me get an ambulance out here."

"Jane can take me," Tray said.

"No. Jane can follow the ambulance." The trooper looked at her. "Is that your Caddy in the driveway?"

"No," Tray answered. "It's mine. Or my brother's. But he died … so I'm taking care of it … for him."

"Leave it to you in his will, did he?"

"I don't even know … if he had a will." Tray looked at Jane.

"Don't look at me," she said. "Until last night, I didn't even know he was dead."

Out on the east end of Long Island, Aislinn lay in bed, struggling over what to do next. Ever since talking to Jin in Chapter One on Main, she had the distinct feeling that "Jen" knew much more than she was saying and might be connected to what had happened to Tray.

The police must have questioned her. Why don't they see what I see? Or maybe they do.

She made up her mind. First thing tomorrow, she'd find Detective Molyneaux and tell him her observations about Jen.

She felt a tiny frisson of electricity thinking about the detective. Something about his dark, brooding looks played in her mind. The first time she had met him, his eyes had flashed with mistrust, and he'd been gruff in the way he asked questions. However, the last time they spoke, she'd noticed a gentleness in his eyes and more deference in his manner.

He's really quite good-looking. Perhaps I should fix him up with my cousin Bryn. She felt jealous as soon as she thought about Bryn and Molyneaux together.

Aislinn and Molyneaux guided their kayak through Sag Harbor Cove, looking for clues. "Tray and I never spent time together out here," she told the detective. "What makes you think we'll find something?"

"The dead body we found in your room was wearing boat shoes."

She stopped paddling. "But what does that have to do with anything?"

"Let's pull up there," Molyneaux said, pointing toward a wooded area near North Haven. They guided the kayak to the beachfront and pulled it onto the sand. They sat at the water's edge, watching the lights come on in the buildings across the way.

"Why are we here?" she asked.

At first, the detective didn't speak, although crickets chirping their late afternoon mating calls over the sounds of the water gently lapping against the shore, broke the silence. "Why didn't you and your boyfriend spend any time out here? It's a very romantic place for young lovers."

"We'd only known each other a couple of weeks," she said. "And sometimes I feel like we hardly knew each other at all."

"What was his favorite color?"

"I don't know."

170

"Mine is navy blue. Where was he born?"

"I don't know?"

"I was born and raised in Patchogue. Where did he go to college?"

"I don't remember."

"I graduated from Stony Brook University and went to Touro Law School for a while. There. You now know more about me than you do about him. What's your favorite color?"

She looked into his eyes. "Pale yellow, like the first light of the morning sun."

"Spoken like an artist. Where were you born?"

"East Hampton."

"And college?"

"I graduated from the Rhode Island School of ..."

Before Aislinn could finish, Molyneaux's hand cupped her face, and his lips brushed hers. Heat rushed through her body, like tiny electrical impulses tingling all over. She couldn't help but return his level of ardor. She wanted to get closer to him—to become part of him. Molyneaux gently pushed her flat on the sand and covered her with kisses as she tried to catch her breath. The light, butterfly kisses he pressed all over her skin made her shudder.

Heat built inside her body, and she had to have more. She arched her back, pulling him against her until she could wrap her legs around him to hold him in place. She could feel his responding desire pressing against her. It only made the passion coursing through her more intense. "Make love to me," she whispered.

Aislinn woke in a sweat, her heart beating wildly. It took her a moment to realize she was at Thorne House. Alone. She felt like she had betrayed Tray in her dream, yet she couldn't help thinking about Molyneaux: how he had tried to get to know her, asking her the questions Tray had never asked; how Molyneaux took his time with her while showering her with kisses. Her lovemaking with Tray had been pure energy and lust. She wondered if making love to the detective would be a replay of what she had experienced with Tray or more of what she'd felt in her dream. She could see stability in Molyneaux's serious brown eyes compared to the capriciousness she always saw in Tray's.

It was only a dream, she told herself. But she tossed and turned for the rest of the night, thinking of Molyneaux.

BACK IN THE Catskills, an alert came in over the police scanner regarding a multi-vehicle crash with severe injuries on NY 17 in Monticello.

The trooper stared at Tray, wondering if he had stolen his brother's car before the will could go through probate. *Maybe the whole story is a line of codswallop,* he thought. However, after seeing Tray secured in an ambulance, the trooper decided to give him the benefit of the doubt and rushed off to the accident on NY 17.

Jane followed the ambulance to the nearest regional hospital, where everyone not assigned to Tray gave him a wide berth because he smelled so bad.

A single state trooper may have known that his name was *Tray*, but that man had departed for Monticello. Tray told everyone else that he, *Carey Lennox*, had fallen down the steps of an old root cellar, and his aunt found him the following day, some of which was close to the truth.

A doctor not assigned to *Carey's* injury observed him being admitted and overheard bits and pieces of his medical examination. She didn't believe the patient's head injury had occurred, falling down the steps of a root cellar. She took the bull by the horns when no one else was nearby. She strolled over, looked at his chart, and after reading his patient information, she asked, "What did you say made you fall down those stairs?"

Tray immediately sensed skepticism in the doctor's tone. "I'm not sure, but considering my headache, I'd say I was helped by an overzealous neighbor with a big stick."

The doctor would have liked to examine Tray's injury, but it was already dressed and bandaged. She studied the file. "More like a shovel," she replied, looking at the X-ray. "That would be more consistent with the shape of your wound."

"That makes sense," Tray replied. "There was more than one shovel near the door of the root cellar."

The doctor pressed on. "Why would a neighbor do you harm?"

"I've only owned the property for a few years, and I've had little time to use it. I'd say my neighbors probably don't even know who I am. Maybe the guy who hit me was on neighborhood watch patrol. Maybe he saw a man he didn't recognize and decided to protect his community and my property. Little did he know I belonged there."

"So, you're labeling your concussion—among other ailments—a housewarming gift?"

Tray gave her a crooked smile. "I wish he would have asked first. I'd rather have a toaster."

A nurse interrupted with the necessary paperwork to admit *Carey* Lennox for observation.

Afterward, as Tray lay in bed, he wondered what Aislinn was doing. He hadn't seen her for weeks. *She'll probably hate me for pretending to be dead and not telling her I'm still alive. But how could I?*

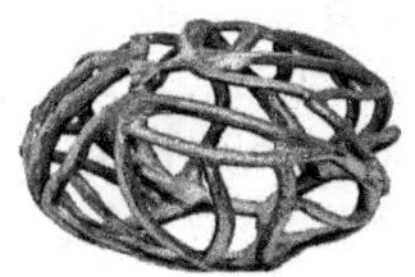

CHAPTER SIXTEEN

GODFREY MUNK LOOKED at the chunk of twisted metal lying on a towel on his desk. It made him shiver. Not because it was ancient or allegedly powerful, but because it looked like it was writhing—even though he didn't see any actual movement. It also smelled foul. At least the wrapping it came in did. He held his breath as he looked closer. There were markings on the long strings of metal that crisscrossed each other.

This hunk of junk is what everyone is going crazy about? They can keep it. He steeled himself in preparation to place a call. When he felt ready, he dialed Zander Bakker. He wanted to tell him he finally had possession of Hero's Knot, but Bakker's flunky took his time putting the call through. He asked Munk to hold, and he did, for forty-five minutes before Bakker got on the line.

"Why should I believe you have the artifact when you so completely bungled buying it at auction?"

Munk's nerves tightened. "I didn't bungle anything. They didn't put it up for sale at the auction. But if you don't want this, I'm sure I can find another buyer."

"Not so fast, Mr. Munk. You are on *my* payroll, and finding another buyer for whatever you have is above your pay grade. It already belongs to me. Unless you wish to terminate our agreement?" Bakker's voice was cold enough to freeze the Caribbean Sea.

Munk shuddered, trying to keep the fear out of his voice. He knew when Bakker terminated an agreement, it usually meant he terminated the life of his *business partner,* as well. "That won't be necessary. I will bring the artifact to Zurich and personally hand it to you."

"Monday morning," Bakker stated before hanging up the phone.

OVER THE COURSE of the day, Tray tried to make every test the hospital staff threw at him look effortless. He refused to show them how much being bashed over the head still affected him. He didn't see double anymore, nor did he feel as queasy as he had the night before. As far as he was concerned, it was time to get on with his life. He could take aspirin for the pain, and they had already given him antibiotics for the wound.

He worked all day on wearing down the staff, trying to convince them to send him home. But he couldn't hide the slight fever he was running. In the end, the hospital decided to keep him for another night in case the wound was infected.

*

Mark Allen told his supervisor at Diablo Canyon he could only work a half-day. He followed his usual daily routine until he saw no one paying attention, then suited up for a visit to the tank room. He triggered the alarm before descending into the tank. Everyone else was so busy scrambling for contamination suits or evacuating that he loosened a valve without a hitch. By the time everyone else started searching for the problem, he had already removed his suit and decontaminated.

"You're leaving?" a security guard asked. "I'm surprised you're taking off in the middle of a crisis."

Mark shrugged. "I didn't come in anticipating a problem. My four-year-old's birthday party is today, so I only planned to work half a day. I promised her I would be on time. I would have stayed otherwise, but the other workers here have the expertise to fix whatever is wrong." He signed out, adding, "Not to mention, our kids grow up so quickly. I already feel like I've missed out on a lot of her life. You know?"

"Yeah. I know what you mean. I've got a six-year-old." The guard smiled. "Have a good time at the party."

Mark drove away and kept on going, far up into the redwood forests of Northern California and beyond. Maybe he'd find a lazy little town in Oregon to hide out in. He had caused a problem at every plant on Achille's list. Now, he needed to make one last call. "It's done. Triggering the alarm turned this into an incident you can point a finger at. Wire the money you owe me into my account. I'm lying low for a while."

"Good," Achille replied. "That's just what I was going to suggest."

*

AT THE FBI's Long Island Field Office, officials spent more than an hour on the phone, bringing Special Agent Sam Flores into the loop on a Hamptons murder involving a member of the Art Crime Team.

"This incident happened a week ago," Flores said.

"Why are you only calling us in on it now?"

"It's the middle of the summer. Staff is light. There was no apparent connection between the murder and the victim's position in the agency, so we took a *wait and see* attitude. However, things are now getting dicey. Someone burglarized the victim's apartment, and that put his death on our radar. Hearing his twin brother was admitted to an upstate hospital after being attacked, sealed the deal. It's time to insert ourselves and make sure the locals don't fuck up the investigation. Just don't make a big thing of it. Tread lightly. We're still not sure why our guy got whacked."

"What's his name?"

"Traynor Lennox. Suffolk County Homicide Squad will have more detailed information."

AISLINN DROVE TO her Sag Harbor apartment to pick up her mail. Among the bills and junk, she discovered a letter from Guild Hall. She ripped it open and found an invitation to display some of her art at the upcoming exposition. She felt her heart lighten. *At least now I have something to look forward to.*

MUNK SETTLED INTO the plush leather seat of the private jet he'd hired to take him to Switzerland. He planned to hand off the artifact and get paid his 'finder's fee.' Only then would he feel all was right with the world. He was reluctant to admit that Bakker scared him. *Some of those*

Swiss types claim they're neutral, but they're a little too Aryan for me.

He looked at the leather bowling ball bag strapped into the seat across from him. He doubted anyone could find a more perfect way to carry this particular prize. This job had been worth a pretty penny, and he expected Bakker to compensate him handsomely. That payoff would go a long way, as far as Munk was concerned. He just wanted his money. He would steer clear of Bakker in the future. *That guy gives me the creeps.*

Bakker's people monitored Munk's progress and kept their employer informed about the American crime lord's ETA. Bakker had them bring his car around, and he and his right-hand man, Krieg, made what he hoped would be a quick trip to the airport.

As soon as Munk's jet taxied to a stop, Bakker's Rolls Royce pulled close to it.

Munk stepped out of the aircraft, and a tall, dark-haired man in aviator sunglasses greeted him. "Mr. Munk. Mr. Bakker is ready to conclude your business transaction."

"And you are?"

"Krieg." He led Munk to the car, opened the back door, and closed it as soon as the American climbed inside. Krieg walked to the aircraft to ask the pilot to wait. "Mr. Munk will be returning home directly. We will pay you double your fee to facilitate the return trip."

"Of course," the pilot replied.

Krieg opened a messenger bag and handed the man several stacks containing €500 notes, each bundle worth fifty thousand euros.

The pilot smiled, shaking Krieg's hand before re-entering the plane.

Munk shrank into a corner of the car when a wolf dog in the front seat began howling and barking, launching itself at the plexiglass barrier separating him from the rear occupants.

Bakker ignored the animal's antics, more interested in examining the artifact. It was exactly what he expected, right down to the undulating look of the metal. *You, my little beauty, are about to make me richer than Croesus.* He placed it back in the bowling bag. By then, Krieg had returned and had removed a large suitcase from the back of the vehicle.

Bakker lowered the window and nodded.

Krieg opened the door. "Slide over, Mr. Munk."

Munk tried to leave as much space as possible between himself and Bakker, not to mention the animal in the front.

Krieg heaved the suitcase onto the seat and opened it, facing Munk. It was stuffed with stacks of €500 bills. Munk dug his hand into the middle of the neatly piled bills, grabbing a package at random. He went through it, making sure it contained currency and not blanks. He did the same thing a few times before he shut the suitcase and smiled at Bakker, sticking out his hand. "Pleasure doing business with you."

Bakker did not take Munk's hand. "Yes, Mr. Munk, I'm sure it was. If you'll excuse me, I have an appointment to keep."

Krieg helped Munk out of the vehicle. "Mr. Munk, we have arranged for your jet to return you to New York. Mr. Bakker has taken care of the charge as a personal thank you for your service."

Munk had thought he might spend a few days in Switzerland, living the high life. However, having Bakker pay for his return trip home by private jet presented him with an option he couldn't refuse.

"Thank you." Munk rolled the suitcase to the jet, where an attendant carried it onboard. He turned to say goodbye to Krieg, but Bakker's man was already inside the Rolls, and the car was pulling away.

Just like I thought, these people are rude.

Munk sat back in the same seat he had arrived in and asked the flight attendant for a glass of champagne, which she served him immediately. Ten minutes later, they were wheels up, and he felt like the king of the world.

BAKKER ASKED KRIEG if everything had gone smoothly.

"Yes, sir."

"Excellent."

The Rolls Royce pulled up in front of a nearby hangar. The hangar door slid open, and a small plane pulled out, stopping near the Rolls. Krieg transferred the artifact to the plane, which took off for Tehran. Krieg took a deep breath and relaxed. Everything had gone smoothly. *That should keep Mr. Bakker's blood pressure down.* Krieg hated when Mr. Bakker's blood pressure went up precipitously. Everybody did. Bakker's high blood pressure could prove deadly—to nearly everyone around him.

EVERY DAILY NEWSPAPER and media outlet carried the story: *Near Meltdown at California Nuclear Plant.* It didn't matter that an actual meltdown hadn't occurred. The scrambled workers had discovered the leaking valve only minutes after Mark Allen had departed the facility. However, protocol required them to report the incident, which immediately ignited headlines.

The media would point fingers at figures from the highest levels of government to the lowest civilian workers at the plant. They would want to know what went wrong. Was it an equipment malfunction? Was it a worker error? Or was it sabotage? If so, who would deliberately damage a nuclear power plant? And why? The op-ed pages would soon be filled with discussions like *When is 'dangerous' too dangerous?* And *Nuclear power: Why good ideas are not always good for humanity.*

In the background of finger-pointers and nuclear naysayers stood Senator Phineas Paige, who for years had said the government should outlaw all nuclear facilities. Now, he intended to use the 'California incident' to propel himself to a position of power—*the* position of power—in the White House.

SOPHIA BRODEUR CLOSED her eyes, just for a second, enjoying the sun's warmth on her shoulders. It was a perfect day for outdoor surveillance work in Zurich.

She stepped away from a telephoto camera. The transaction she'd just recorded had ended, and she quickly took apart the parabolic microphone she had set up to record any conversation. She had been following Zander Bakker all day but had pulled off in a secluded spot once she realized the road he traveled led only to a private airfield. Bakker would have to return in this direction, where she could quickly tail him again.

She'd taken video of a man named *Munk* carrying a roundish bag to Bakker's vehicle. When Munk departed, he lugged an enormous suitcase behind him. The only thing larger than the suitcase was his smile. A lot of "lost" conversation had occurred inside Bakker's car, but what Sophia had observed had convinced her a sale had taken place. Besides, the man called 'Krieg' had said enough outside the vehicle to give her the impression that money was no object.

She slid behind the wheel of her rental vehicle and waited for Bakker and Krieg to hit the road. She did not find this part of her job exciting. It was slow and performed from a distance. Sophia was more of a hands-on operative, which is why she had refused a job as a pencil pusher for MI6. She easily gravitated toward Special Forces, knowing that's where all the action occurred. She would never have referred to herself as an adrenaline junkie, but that's what drove her.

She saw Bakker's Rolls Royce coming, and she deliberately pulled out in front of him, going as slowly as she dared. Within moments, his driver gunned the engine. As he passed her, she noticed what appeared to be a wolf's head hanging out of an open window. The animal stared at her, and she shivered. She allowed the vehicle to proceed a small distance before speeding up so she wouldn't lose it.

Now, if they notice a car behind them, they'll see it as the woman driver they passed, not a potential threat.

Dr. Zana Ahmadi, an Iranian physicist at the University of Tehran, carefully unwrapped an artifact delivered to his lab by a special courier. A university benefactor had promised to give the school a sizable endowment in Dr. Ahmadi's name, if the physicist could 'successfully' modify the engravings on the artifact to the philanthropist's specifications.

The benefactor chose Dr. Ahmadi because he was both a mathematician and an archaeologist and should understand the markings on the item. He had also sworn the matter to secrecy. The university was not to learn anything about the object known as *Hero's Knot*. Dr. Ahmadi didn't mind that stipulation. As he saw it, his standing at the university would increase once the school received the donation, and the less anyone else knew about it, the better. Leaving Bakker's name out of it would make him—Zana Ahmadi—appear much more generous.

He slipped on a pair of eyeglasses to study the writing. He had previously read all the research notes and heard the rumors about the ancient piece. Now, he mentally prepared himself to engage with it. The directive required him to separate the strands of the knot and change one formula carved into it. It should be easy to find. Some experts rumored that it had been changed once before, so he hoped it would look cruder than the other notations etched into the metal.

He adjusted his lighted magnifier and stared at the object. *Is it moving?* He stuck his fingers under his glasses and rubbed his eyes. *It's a trick of the light. It must be.*

Settling his glasses back on the bridge of his nose, he picked up a small saw and tried cutting a strand in an area with less writing. It was a slow process. He had to be careful not to change any written notations except the one someone had previously modified. The undulating appearance of the metal distracted him. It sickened him. He placed the saw on the work surface.

I'll stop for my midday meal and come back to it—when I'm fortified—for a fresh start.

When Zana returned thirty minutes later, he sat at the worktable and picked up the saw. He looked for the area where he had already started a cut and gasped, surprised to see it had healed. There was no sign that he had used a saw on the surface. *The object must have gotten turned around.* He examined the artifact for the cut but could find no evidence of it. *What is this thing?*

He went back to his notes, rechecking them carefully. *Perhaps heat.* He searched for a small torch. He hated the idea of using heat because it might melt the engraving.

He locked away the artifact and left his lab again. This time, he visited a local jeweler who was also a close friend.

"This is a surprise." His friend, Hassan, carefully laid aside a necklace. "I doubt you're here to buy jewelry. Or are you?"

"I'm here because I've seen you use a small torch—the size of a pencil—to weld my mother's broken chain. I'd like to borrow it."

"Thinking of going into jewelry repair?" His friend laughed. "I hope our friendship can stand up to the competition."

"I need it for a delicate experiment in the lab. I'll even buy it from you if you're afraid I might ruin it."

"Pencil torches are not that precious." His friend took one out of a drawer and filled it with fuel, showing Zana how to adjust the flame. "You can have this. Consider it a gift."

"Thank you."

Back in his lab, Zana found an area on the artifact with a space separating Hero's various formulas. He lit the torch and lightly placed it near the metal, severing the knot. He pulled the strands apart, looking for the theorem he'd been tasked with adjusting.

On closer inspection, many of the inscriptions in the metal looked more like notes than theorems, but Zana was concerned with only one, and he searched for the exact formula he needed to adjust. He found what appeared to be a heavier gash and set to work with a diamond knife and the small torch, melting and inscribing the necessary adjustment.

So, you won't let me cut you, but you'll let me change an inscription. What are you, alive?

After revising the formula, Zana paged through his notes, looking for a schematic that showed how to reform the knot. There was none. He spent several hours and made dozens of attempts, plus a few frantic phone calls, trying to recreate Hero's Knot—to no avail.

Shoulders slumped, he logged off the computer. None of his colleagues had been able to help him. He leaned his head against the back of the chair, telling himself he would only close his eyes for a few minutes.

Zana awakened hours later, surprised to find Hero's Knot had reformed on its own, except for the two ends sticking out of the top.

His mouth still agape, he grabbed the pencil torch and fused the loose ends back together. *I hope this works.*

He placed a call to Zander Bakker's office. "It's done," he said, not quite triumphantly. His voice didn't quiver, but a bead of sweat chose that moment to roll down his brow.

Krieg told him he would come to the lab the following day to pick up the artifact. "Here's to a successful conclusion," he said before hanging up.

Zana's forehead continued to sweat. Bakker had voiced a previous warning that still haunted him. *"Failure is unacceptable."*

*

MILES AND MILES of ocean lay beneath the plane carrying Godfrey Munk back to New York. Not that he was in any position to appreciate it. The hum of the engines droned hypnotically, and Munk had fallen asleep, the sound of his snores dampened by the plush interior of the jet.

They had been aloft about three hours, during which time the crime lord had downed several glasses of champagne and eaten a full meal. It didn't take long for him to drift off, dreaming of everything he could do with his money.

BOOM!

Godfrey Munk and his suitcase, filled with cash, littered the sky.

The explosion over the Atlantic Ocean was unexpected. No warning lights. No mayday calls. No survivors. No time to wonder what the hell had happened. All that remained was the flaming debris of a private plane en route from Zurich to New York. Who knew if anyone would ever discover the remnants? Or even look for it? Krieg had made sure its flight plan had been deleted within minutes of the plane leaving the ground.

It was just as well the money disintegrated upon detonation, that way, no one would ever know Bakker's organization had printed it. It was worthless, but it didn't matter. Bakker's people were the only ones who might put two and two together, and they had a good reason to keep his secret. Bakker could be a very vindictive man.

Godfrey Munk had been a loose cannon. The plane crash erased any chance Munk would speak of Hero's Knot in the future. And that alone made Zander Bakker a very happy man.

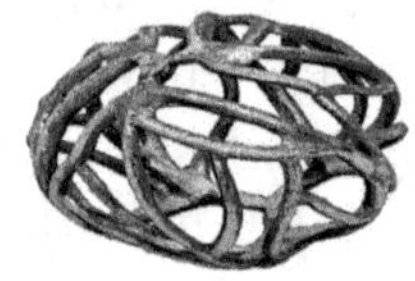

CHAPTER SEVENTEEN

Detective Molyneaux walked into the East Hampton Police Department, clutching a container of coffee. He sat at the desk he'd been using while working the Lennox and Fergus cases and stared at the files. Would going through them again bring him any closer to a conclusion? He'd been staying in East Hampton since the investigation had begun, wondering if anyone would care if he took a day off, so he could drive home and catch up on sleep in his own bed.

"Ahem!"

Molyneaux looked up at the sound, startled to see Suffolk County Chief of Detectives, Liam O'Meara, making a surprise appearance. "Chief, why aren't you at headquarters? You're the last person I expected to see here."

The chief of detectives grabbed a metal chair from an unoccupied desk and dragged it near Molyneaux. "I brought the DNA results for the murder at The Old Salt

House that you've been begging me to expedite. I thought you'd want to see them as soon as possible. In a nutshell, most of the blood in the room belonged to Calam Fergus. However, a tiny flake of it belongs to someone else. At first, I thought it was our other victim, but it doesn't match Traynor Lennox. It is, however, genetically close. *Extremely* genetically close."

"What's that supposed to mean?"

The chief grinned. "The victim has a twin brother, Carey Lennox."

Molyneaux leaned back in his desk chair until it squealed its need for oil. "So, you think the twin brother murdered Fergus in retaliation?"

"It sounds like a possibility to me."

"Then I guess I should track down Carey Lennox."

The chief wagged his index finger at the detective. "We've been told not to. Not *asked.* Told. Carey Lennox works for the government."

"In what capacity?"

"He's a nuclear inspector for the NRC, and he's— you didn't hear this from me—currently on the trail of a possible saboteur."

"A saboteur of what?"

"I don't know. We're talking NRC. Nuclear reactors, perhaps?"

Molyneaux raised a brow. "Well then, I'm more than happy to let the feds handle that one."

"Right."

"So, tell me how you got the DNA results back so soon. It's only been a week."

The chief pulled his chair closer to Molyneaux. "It seems our victim *also* worked for the federal government."

Molyneaux's eyes narrowed. "In what capacity?"

"Special agent for the FBI."

"Well, that explains the classified file." His gaze became unfocused as he sipped his coffee—the wheels of deduction churning in his brain. He zeroed in on his superior officer. "Why haven't the feds swooped in to relieve us of this entire investigation?"

"It's not like they haven't. They just don't want it to *appear* like they have. The twins are, or were, apparently each enmeshed in separate high-priority investigations that the government doesn't want to draw attention to. So, the FBI is covertly calling the shots from its Melville office. I'll handle them. You just continue doing what you're doing."

"I hate jurisdictions. I hate when people in one agency or department hide information from people in another agency or department. I hate politics and power plays and posturing."

"Then why'd you go to law school?"

"To put the bad guys behind bars."

"And why didn't you ever finish?"

"My grandfather was paying my tuition. He died intestate during my last year. By the time the family finished fighting over his money and the attorneys were paid, there was no tuition money left for me."

"Your folks didn't get any money?"

"They did. They put it all toward a bigger house. They said doing that would benefit *everybody* instead of just me."

"How close were you to getting your degree?"

"Nine credits away."

O'Meara shook his head as he threw the file on Molyneaux's desk. "You really should finish law school."

"Not in the cards. Besides, I was already on the force by then." He shrugged. "Anyway, I'd better get back to work. If I don't pick away at it, we'll never unravel who did what to whom. Thanks for the information."

Molyneaux was glad to see the chief walk away. He had put law school out of his mind for years. *What am I supposed to do, upend my life?* He could take courses part-time, but his job schedule would only get in the way. *Stop thinking about it,* he admonished himself. *That ship has sailed.*

Tray felt like the medical center in the Catskills should be re-designated as a *prison*. "Why am I still hospitalized?" he asked the doctor as she examined the wound on the back of his head.

"It's healing nicely," she replied.

"But that doesn't answer my question."

The doctor looked at the patient's file. "I see your fever has finally gone away."

"And I'd like to go away with it."

"If you play nice today, we may make your wish come true. But first, I'm ordering an MRI. I want to ensure your brain is intact under that mess on the back of your head. If there's no further swelling and the wound isn't excessively weeping, you can go home."

"I'll be the one excessively weeping if you don't let me out of here."

"Trust me, we don't want to keep you here any longer than we have to. Although the more your fake tan fades, the sicker the nurses will think you are."

"How do you know it's a fake tan?"

"I'm a physician. We're rigorously trained in medical

school to recognize the fading orange edges of a tan that suddenly stops in a zigzag on your chest. Not to mention, you missed a patch behind your right ear."

Tray's hand immediately went up to his ear. "You're kidding, right?"

The doctor smirked as she shook her head. "See you after the MRI."

TRAY EXPECTED EVERYTHING to be done in a *New York minute,* but in the Catskills, the minutes apparently lasted much longer. His doctor ordered the MRI the first thing that morning. However, Tray didn't get his wheelchair ride to the radiology department until well after noon.

As he lay inside the tube, thinking of all the things he needed to do, he felt fidgety. He had to keep reminding himself not to move, or they'd never let him leave. *I hope it doesn't take them as long to read the results of this damn test as it took for me to get it.*

ALMOST HALFWAY AROUND the world, in the Sistan and Baluchestan Province on the southern coast of Iran, Sophia Brodeur hid behind a pair of dark sunglasses and a royal blue hijab.

As luck would have it, the winds kicked up, carrying a fair amount of dry sand with them. She wrapped the trailing portion of her scarf around her face to cover her nose and mouth. She relished this opportunity to hide in plain sight, so whomever she ended up tailing wouldn't easily recognize her when or if he saw her again.

A private security force closely guarded the gathering on the beach, but Sophia was well dressed and fit the part of a wife or girlfriend. She'd snuck in among several small groups who had all ended up simultaneously at the entrance. When asked for her credentials, Sophia explained in perfect Arabic that she was with the General, who had gone ahead without her while she was talking with someone. She appeared flustered. "He probably doesn't even know I'm missing."

The guard waved her through.

She worked her way into the crowd, occasionally brushing up against women and apologizing for it. If anyone were watching from afar, she would appear to be talking to people she knew.

THE ECLECTIC GROUP of investors eagerly anticipated a demonstration of the abilities of a weapon being touted as the *Artifact*. Their host's minions had hurriedly put together a small test targeting an old American warhead known as a Davy Crockett.

A spokesperson introduced Zander Bakker, who boasted how the Americans had gifted a vast quantity of these "sub-standard" warheads to their allies. He joked about how the ordnance, known for its inaccuracy, was later dumped on the black market. "They tried to turn trash into cash, and we have benefited from it. Even though their cast-offs are of laughable accuracy, they still make enough noise to attract attention.

"However, you're not here to see the warhead per se, but the controller that will detonate it. The Artifact. It is one of a kind and will be auctioned off immediately following the demonstration. Please direct your attention to the horizon of the water."

The Davy Crockett—weighed down by an anchor— floated below the surface of the Gulf of Oman about three kilometers off Bandar-E Tang. "We will not physically detonate the bomb. It does not have to be fired; it needs merely to react."

Some invited guests took advantage of the bleachers hastily erected the previous afternoon for this occasion. Various tactical vehicles surrounded the immediate area, ensuring privacy.

One young man had no shortage of women clustered around him. Celebrity and gossip magazines described Deepak Bhatti, the son of billionaire industrialist Palanivel Bhatti, as a smoldering chick magnet with deep pockets and more sexual prowess in his scant twenty-nine years than most men could hope for after many lifetimes of female companionship.

It was just as well the young stud kept most of the women busy. It gave their husbands and boyfriends more time to show off in front of their friends and associates and perhaps bid higher than they may have planned on what was sure to be a coveted item.

Once the crowd had settled, Bakker pressed a button, sending a remotely controlled watercraft out into the water. It stopped a half-kilometer away from the shoreline, directly between the people who had gathered and the nuclear weapon.

"That's your device," someone called out, laughing. "A toy boat?"

The others waited patiently. They had dealt with Bakker in the past and knew he had no tolerance for detractors.

Bakker put on a pair of protective lenses and advised the crowd to don the safety goggles his employees had handed out or, at the very least, to wear sunglasses to protect their eyes from the glare.

Nothing happened for several minutes. The crowd grew restless, and a nerve in Bakker's forehead began to throb.

Suddenly, the ground vibrated, signaling that something wasn't quite right. A high-pitched squeal followed. People twisted around to see what caused the noise and witnessed a plume of mud and liquid shooting from the Tang Mud Volcano. That alone astounded them because the volcano was almost fourteen kilometers away and rarely erupted with such ferocity. Men argued about how many tons of mud would probably be released by the volcanic aberration and started placing bets.

Then, a pop of sound diverted their attention, and they turned in unison toward the water. The surface of the gulf shuddered as the Davy Crockett detonated. A plume of water, vapor, and smoke shot upward as the crowd erupted into applause.

The artifact worked.

Interested parties immediately bid on its purchase. Bakker shook his head. The bidding was way too low in his estimation, and he threw his hands up, pretending to leave.

A voice in the crowd called out, "Five hundred million Kuwaiti dinars."

"Ah, finally," Bakker exclaimed, "we have a viable bid."

Jane stayed at the hospital with Tray for most of the day, happy to support him in any way possible, although she felt uncomfortable calling him 'Carey.' Doing so—so casually—made her feel like Carey's life didn't really matter, and they could take advantage of his identity as a means to an end. She felt like they were diminishing his memory even though, deep down, she knew they were trying to solve his murder.

She had brought all her notes pertaining to Hero's Knot, so she and Tray could discuss them and reason out what to do next.

"Mr. Lennox," the doctor said as she walked into the room carrying a printout. "The good news is your head is harder than whatever it came into contact with over the weekend."

Tray narrowed his eyes. "Is there bad news?"

The doctor laid the printout on the edge of the bed and looked at Tray's file. "The bad news is, you'll have to pay the bill before we let you out of here."

Tray stilled for a moment. "You have my insurance information," he said tentatively. In reality, they had Carey's info, but Tray hoped that would be enough to get him out the door since no one knew Carey was dead— well, except for him, Jane, and a state trooper whom Tray had no control over. He felt himself break out into a sweat.

The doctor didn't notice. "Then, I'll let them know at the nurses' station that they can process you out of here."

As the doctor walked out, another man walked in. He looked directly at Tray. "Carey Lennox?"

Tray's internal self-preservation mode kicked into gear, but before he could speak, Jane said, "Detective Molyneaux."

Molyneaux flashed his badge. "Ms. Deveraux. I'm here to talk to your nephew. Would you mind stepping outside? I know that sounds like a question, but it's not."

Jane cocked an eyebrow. She considered her options for several moments before grabbing her bag. "I'm going for a cup of coffee," she told her nephew. "Would you like one?"

"No, I'm good," he replied, before she left the room.

"Now, Mr. Lennox, why don't you tell me what the hell is going on?"

Tray made a point of looking at the IV that was still attached to his arm and the EKG machine, quietly beeping next to his bed. He took a deep breath before finally speaking. "I got smacked in the head and was left to die in a root cellar. Thank you for asking."

"I'm more interested in why you got smacked in the head."

"As I told the doctor, it was probably an overly vigilant neighbor who didn't know I owned the property and thought he was protecting his community."

"So, you don't think it has anything to do with your brother's murder?"

"I doubt it. Except for my Aunt Jane, we have very few connections in common."

"What do you know about your brother's work for the FBI?"

If Tray was shocked by Molyneaux's knowledge of his ties to the FBI, he hid it well. "Tray appraises … appraised art and antiquities at an import-export company in Manhattan. When he came across counterfeits or stolen items, arrests were made."

"Did he talk about anyone being after him?"

"Not to me, but considering what happened, I'd say someone was definitely after somebody."

"We found your DNA at the crime scene."

Tray could not school his face quickly enough for Molyneaux not to see his surprise. "How is that possible?"

"We believe you saw Calam Fergus kill your brother. You followed him to your brother's hotel and killed him."

"I did not see who killed my brother—well, maybe

his back as he ran around the side of a building—but I wouldn't be able to identify him, except to say I got the distinct impression it was a male. I was more interested in trying to prevent my brother from bleeding to death. He died in my arms."

"What were you doing on Long Island? According to the NRC, you had been exposed to a high dose of radiation the previous evening."

"Someone was after me," Tray said, remembering what Carey had told him. "I needed my brother's help."

"He's your identical twin, right?"

"Yes."

Molyneaux paced the room before coming to rest in the chair vacated by Jane. "Could your assailants have mistaken him for you and killed him?"

Tray remained quiet for a moment, closing his eyes while he thought over the detective's words. "It's possible," he finally said.

"So, would you like to tell me how your DNA got inside your brother's hotel room?"

"As I've just confirmed, we were identical twins. It's probably my brother's DNA."

"Not according to the crime lab."

Tray could feel his stomach flip, but he was saved from responding when a nurse walked into the room and interrupted them. "Okay, Mr. Lennox,' she said. "I have your discharge papers here." She turned to the detective. "Are you his caregiver?"

"No."

"That would be me," Jane said from the doorway.

"Okay. If you would come in, and sir," she addressed Molyneaux, "because of privacy laws, I need to ask you to leave while I go over these papers with my patient." She stared at Molyneaux, waiting for him to depart.

"We'll be in touch," the detective said as he walked toward the door. He turned. "Where will you be staying?"

"He's staying with me," Jane said. "I *am* his caregiver, as I just told the nurse."

"Make sure he stays where I can find him."

Molyneaux punched the steering wheel of his car. He'd made the trip upstate—against orders—and it seemed like a colossal waste of time. He was no closer to the answers he needed to solve an extremely convoluted case.

Jane pulled her car in front of the hospital, and once Tray sat safely beside her, she breathed a sigh of relief. "I'm glad that's over."

"I need you to take me back to the cabin."

"What?" The car jerked as she pulled away from the curb. "No."

"I need to pick up Carey's car."

"You're in no condition to drive," she argued. "Besides, you heard the detective. You need to stay with me."

"Jane. We're playing with fire here. You already know how dangerous the artifact can be, and now it's fallen into the wrong hands. I need to find out what happened to it. And what happened to Carey."

"You don't have to do that," she stated emphatically. "It sounds more like a job for the FBI."

Tray sighed. "I *am* the FBI. I'd show you my badge, but I didn't have it with me when this whole fiasco began. And since I haven't returned to my apartment—" he paused a second, "for the most part, I don't have it to show you.

But I'm a special agent for the FBI Art Crime Team, and antiquities come under our purview."

She slammed her fist against the steering wheel. "No wonder you had that folder."

Tray felt the hairs on the back of his neck prickle. "What folder?"

"The one marked *Classified* that contained restricted data about Hero's Knot."

"Where is it now?"

"Aislinn has it. She was trying to find out what happened to you and brought it up to me to ask if I knew anything about it. I told her what I know."

Tray did his best to quell a number of curses that sprang to mind. "I sure hope Aislinn is working for our side because I'd hate to think she was a spy for the enemy."

Jane paled. "Good God."

Jane accompanied Tray inside the fishing cabin, even though he told her he was fine on his own and that she should go home.

"We both know what happened the last time you came here alone." She looked around before grabbing a fireplace poker and standing with her back to the wall. She wanted to see in all directions while having her back protected. "Go do what you've got to do."

One side of Tray's mouth lifted in a smile. "I would, but you're standing right where I need to do it."

She narrowed her eyes in what she hoped was a menacing look before moving to her right.

Tray slid a hidden panel in the living room wall, unlocking a gun safe. He pulled out a go-bag stuffed with cash and passports. He returned several passports and most of the currency to the safe, but he kept a Ukrainian passport for Nikola Bondarenko and a mix of euros, rials, and hryvnia. He also removed a bag containing a camera before locking the safe and sliding the panel back in place.

Jane's eyes were huge. "That's handy. What do you intend to do with all that Monopoly money?"

"It's best if you don't know." He walked across the room. "Wait here. I need to change my clothes."

He disappeared into a bedroom and quickly changed into a linen shirt and khaki pants under a distressed brown leather vest. He secured the money and passport inside the vest's hidden pockets. After sticking his feet inside a pair of sturdy boots, he grabbed a tan Panama hat and rejoined Jane.

Tray searched through a drawer, removing a business card and writing some information on it. "We can leave now. Drive straight home." He handed her the card. "Tomorrow, call the number I wrote on the back and speak to Paul. Tell him you're my aunt and believe your home has been compromised. I'm not sure how anyone knew to follow me unless your apartment is bugged. Paul will sweep the interior, and if it has any listening devices, he'll remove them. Tell him to bill the Bureau. I may not be able to contact you for a while, and I'm sorry. But I need to nail these bastards, and I have to do it anonymously."

A HOSPITAL ORDERLY IN the Catskills stuffed dirty sheets in a hamper after cleaning a room.

"Is that room vacant now?" a newly hired nurse asked.

The orderly nodded.

She said aloud to no one in particular, "I guess I can submit this paperwork now that the patient's been discharged." She immediately sent a digital copy of the "Carey Lennox" file to accounting, so the hospital could submit an insurance claim.

MANY AMERICAN MEDIA outlets embraced the mantra *if it bleeds, it leads,* which might explain why the detonation of a tiny bomb off the coast of Iran, involving no loss of life or property damage, did not immediately make local headlines. However, considering the detonation was accompanied by a mushroom cloud and coincided with an unusual mud volcano eruption a dozen kilometers away, it stirred international interest.

The initial source of information came from bidders who had attended the auction of an artifact.

An Iranian military representative, careful to mention only an "odd" explosion of water on the gulf's surface, said it immediately followed the unusually explosive eruption of the Tang mud volcano.

Others who had been on the beach that day more clearly described the mushroom cloud that formed over the Gulf of Oman, following the detonation of a warhead.

BBC—and then NPR—both picked up the story. It soon spread like wildfire.

CHAPTER EIGHTEEN

Tray headed directly to the John F. Kennedy International Airport on Long Island.

He turned on the radio and tuned it to NPR, suddenly going cold when he heard a report about a mushroom cloud over Iran that coincided with a mud volcano eruption.

That explains what happened to Hero's Knot. This is all my fault. I fell for their ruse, and now a powerful weapon is in the wrong hands. I wonder how effective a dead man can be at recovering stolen goods.

He left Carey's car in long-term parking and found his way to Terminal 8. The Passenger Service Agent didn't even blink when he paid cash for a ticket on the next flight to Imam Khomeini International Airport. All he had with him was his camera case strapped around his neck.

He handed his camera case to the guard when he reached the security checkpoint. "Do you think you can hand-inspect this? It's old and has film in it instead of a digital card. I'd hate for it to get ruined by the X-ray machine."

The security officer took the case and gave the items inside a cursory inspection while Tray walked through the body scanner. The guard returned the case to Tray—or Nikola Bondarenko—Tray's newly assumed identity.

Tray put on his belt and shoes and turned to walk away when the guard stopped him. "I need to see the inside pockets of your vest."

Tray schooled his features into a look of confusion. "The inside pockets?" he repeated.

"Yes, the *carry* pockets for handguns that the vest you're wearing is known for."

"Right." Tray reluctantly opened his vest.

"The inspector checked the pockets, which proved to be empty. "Humph." He nodded at Tray. You're free to go."

Too many members of the DC media insisted on cramming themselves into a small conference room in the Dirksen Senate Office Building. They were there for a press conference by Senator Paige regarding the near meltdown at a California nuclear facility.

Paige would be the first US Senator to address the issue. Assignment editors couldn't scramble their crews fast enough.

High school juniors in the Senate Page Program, searched for a larger conference room while Phineas Paige worked on perfecting his talking points. His message called for safety first. His political agenda required the decommissioning of all nuclear power plants across the country.

Paige kept his introduction brief, more intent on launching into the main message of his press conference.

204

"In light of recent events in California, I'm asking you, the people, to write to your government representatives today. Tell them the only way they'll earn your vote is by rallying to decommission all nuclear facilities. We have lived in the shadows of a potential nuclear meltdown for far too long. Let's not forget the partial core meltdown at Three Mile Island in Pennsylvania. Or the David-Besse Nuclear Power Plant incidents in Ohio. Or the four deaths at the Surry Nuclear Power Plant in Virginia. And now a near meltdown at Diablo Canyon in California. Nuclear inspectors discovered these problems in time to prevent a major loss of life. But when does 'in time' become 'too late?' Do we need to have a Chernobyl or Fukushima Daiichi-level incident before we recognize nuclear reactors are dangerous? I've spoken to the president about this issue on numerous occasions, but he has always brushed me aside like I'm some kind of conspiracy theorist or charlatan.

"Don't let your elected officials play with your children's and grandchildren's health and safety. Today, I am questioning whether the current administration is strong enough to handle this issue. If they don't step up to the plate, I may have to consider running for higher office, if only to make our homeland less dangerous. It's time to make our well-being a priority. For all our sakes. For your children's health. For your grandchildren and great-grandchildren's futures. Repeat after me: *Safety over politics.*"

IT TOOK A WHILE to clear customs in Tehran, but *Nikola Bondarenko* did not encounter any problems and was ready to move at Mach speed.

He visited a men's restroom, where he splashed water on his face to revive himself. Once he determined no one was watching, he slipped into a stall.

He worked quickly, opening the camera case and bypassing the larger DSLR to grab what appeared to be a smaller point-and-click camera. Nikola twisted it in half and attached the lower chamber to a detachable camera grip. He plucked a ballpoint pen from his shirt pocket and unscrewed it, removing the spring. He slipped it into the chamber, where it would act as a firing pin.

Some part of his subconscious registered the *plink* of water dripping nearby. He looked down to remind himself not to accidentally step into the squat toilet built flush into the floor. He berated himself for losing his concentration as he grasped a quick-release tripod plate adapter. He snapped the section holding the lever—which would act as a trigger—into the chamber of his newly formed gun. *This is taking shape nicely.* He grabbed a metal film canister and twisted the container, allowing the interior to telescope outward, turning it into a muzzle. Inside another canister, nestled beneath a fake film insert, Nikola removed several .22 caliber bullets suspended in cotton fibers and loaded them into the gun. He slipped the pistol into one of the inside pockets of his vest. It was time to find a taxi.

He had already decided his best contact would be Bijan Isaak, a Mossad agent currently working in Iran.

Tray avoided contacting CIA or MI6 operatives, working in the area. He didn't want to tip anyone off to the fact that he was still alive. He knew the Israeli agent would be discreet and that he could quickly be in and out of Iran with the information he needed.

He found Isaak sitting alone in the courtyard that encircled a fountain at the Baccara Café. The air was thick with turmeric, saffron, and a hint of rose water. Tray slid into the empty chair across from Isaak. Before the Mossad agent could say a word, Tray spoke. "You look confused. I hope you remember me—Nikola Bondarenko? We met at university."

Isaak studied Tray's face. "Mr. Bondarenko."

"It's Dr. Bondarenko now." Tray broke into a wide smile. "But you can still call me Nikola."

"Of course." Isaak lowered his voice, his lip curling into a smirk. "I see reports of your death have been greatly exaggerated."

"I need to stay dead if it's all the same to you." He gestured toward Isaak's lunch. "How is that?"

"You can never go wrong with the crispy filet. It's perfect."

Tray ordered lunch, allowing Isaak to finish his own before bringing up the explosion on the coast.

"It wasn't much," Isaak said. "A small warhead detonated in the water. It may have killed a few fish, nothing more."

"I heard that a mud volcano erupted with some force right around the same time."

"Quite true."

"I wonder why?"

Isaak smiled. "Now we're getting somewhere," he muttered under his breath. "Rumor has it the mud volcano entertained the participants at an auction taking place on a beach about fourteen kilometers away. They had gathered for the sale of an ancient artifact. Egyptian, I'm told."

"Hmmm … I wonder how much it went for?" Tray mused, taking a sip of his drink.

"Five billion Kuwaiti dinar."

Tray choked, much to Isaak's amusement. It took a few minutes for Tray to stop coughing. "I guess the auction was a success."

"I'm sure the seller thinks so. The buyer probably does as well." Isaak lowered his voice so only Tray could hear him. "I had considered going after it but was told to stand down by my superiors."

"They're not interested?"

"An 'ally' apparently has someone trailing the buyer. They want me to concentrate on the seller."

"And who might that be?"

"The power broker *du jour*, Zander Bakker."

Tray merely nodded. "I wonder who's trailing the buyer."

"Someone you may want to get in bed with again. Literally."

Tray's jaw dropped. "Sophia is here?"

"Was here. Now she's tracking the buyer."

"You have any idea where?"

"I wouldn't do this for anyone else. But since you saved my life by digging a bullet out of my back a few years ago, I'll make an exception. As of this morning, she was in France, splashing money around the Club Barrière Paris. I'm guessing that's where the buyer is, and she's trying to make an impression."

Tray sighed. "If there's one thing Sophia is good at, it's making an impression."

When Tray arrived in Paris, he headed to the hotel and casino, where Sophia was busy getting noticed.

"Mr. Bondarenko," the front desk clerk said, "welcome to the Hôtel Barrière Le Fouquet's Paris. Is this your first time at the hotel?"

"Yes." *Unless you count when I previously stayed here under my real name.*

"It's a pleasure to have you with us. We have delivered the items you ordered to your room."

"Thank you very much."

Inside the suite, he walked over to a window, smiling at the view of the Champs-Élysées. He nodded ever so slightly. *This will do nicely.* In the back of his mind, he knew Sophia would love this room, but he couldn't allow himself to dwell on her. He needed to find the artifact first, and then his next priority would be to find Carey's killer.

A large, gold-colored upholstered headboard dominated the creamy-white bedroom. Tray opened the wardrobe and found a dark business suit, dress shirt, and shoes, as well as casual clothing, underwear, and toiletries. Other items he had purchased were laid out nearby.

There's nothing like using cryptocurrency to buy everything you need from the comfort of your airplane seat.

He hopped into the shower before preparing for an evening at the casino.

Standing in front of the steamy mirror, wearing only a towel, he critically studied his image. He no longer had a full head of hair, nor did he have a bald head, except for a large section in the back, covered by a surgical dressing. He hadn't shaved the rest of his head since the funeral, and it now looked more like a butchered buzz cut than the hastily created chrome dome he had given himself after the murder.

He'd developed deeper color on top of his out-of-a-can man tan, though he'd only spent one day in Iran inspecting the area where the demonstration of the artifact had taken place.

He picked up the phone and called the concierge. "*Bonjour.* This is Nikola Bondarenko. Is it possible to have a barber, *le coiffeur,* attend to me in my suite?"

"Nous sommes heureux de vous aider." We are happy to help you.

"I also need a black *shemagh* or scarf. Can someone obtain one for me quickly?"

"Oui. We can do that for you as well."

"Merci."

A half-hour later, Sergei arrived and looked Tray over. "How can I help you?"

"I've been on the road, so to speak, traveling for work and unable to attend to my grooming. I don't know what you can do with my hair, but the rest of my face could use some care."

"Remove the beard?"

"Improve the beard."

Sergei pulled over a chair and instructed Tray to sit. The barber opened a leather pouch and removed a tube of dark beard filler. "This will help." He used it to make Tray's beard look more filled-in and defined. "It looks good, no?"

Tray studied his face in a mirror. "Where can I get one of these?" he asked, taking the tube from Sergei and opening it.

Sergei rummaged among the supplies in his satchel and handed Tray an unopened tube. "I will put it on your tab."

"Excellent," Tray answered, handing back the opened tube.

There was a knock at the door.

"Stay," Sergei said, answering the door. A woman handed him a package that he gave to Tray. Inside was a very fine, black pashmina headscarf.

Tray held it out to Sergei. "Do you know how to form a *shemagh* out of this? Or a turban?"

Sergei stared at the bandage on the back of Tray's head and nodded. "I can see how this could make you look much more dashing than the puny head covering you are now wearing." Within minutes, Sergei had expertly twisted and tied the scarf around Tray's head, hiding the bandage and his uneven hair growth. He studied his handiwork, using the beard filler to make Tray's eyebrows thicker and darker. "A nice look for you, no?"

Tray looked more exotic than scruffy. His two-week-old beard growth was well-manicured, and the *shemagh* hid his recent injury and his self-inflicted scalping.

After complimenting Sergei profusely and showing him out the door, Tray finished dressing. He inserted a pair of brown contact lenses as his last bit of preparation and smiled. *I doubt even Sophia could identify me now.* If she did, he hoped she'd realize he didn't want to be recognized and wouldn't give him away.

Sophia Brodeur practically sizzled in her one-shoulder cocktail dress. The deep emerald color brought out the green in her eyes, and though the dress ended below her knee, an almost-indecent thigh-high slit showed off her very alluring assets. It was off-the-rack but fit like a glove. She'd complemented it with a pair of very well-cut *faux* emerald earrings that only a jeweler would catch, and she wore strawberry red lipstick to balance the intensity of the color.

She allowed herself to lose heavily at the blackjack table. *Thank you, John Bull,* she thought, referencing Britain's version of 'Uncle Sam.' She left looking downcast, but she didn't go quietly. She was looking for a very particular man to console her—the new owner of Hero's

Knot—and wanted to make sure that he believed her to be a damsel in distress.

Deepak Bhatti had just taken the first sip of his single malt whisky. He turned to observe the players on the gaming floor and leaned against the bar. He soon lost interest in the players as he caught sight of a long-legged beauty in emerald green.

Sophia approached the bar with a pout on her lips. "They've taken all my money," she said with a heavy French accent. "I think they cheated me because I am a woman alone." She moved close to Deepak until their arms brushed but did not look directly at him. Instead, she addressed the bartender. "They didn't even leave me with enough money to buy a drink." She coughed before throwing her hands upward. "And now I am choking."

Deepak threw a fifty Euro note on the bar. "Give the lady a drink."

Sophia looked him in the eye and smiled. "*Merci beaucoup!* You are much more of a gentleman than anyone who runs this," she made a sweeping motion with her arm, "road to poverty." She turned to the bartender. "*Soixante Quinze, s'il vous plaît.*"

"What is that?" Deepak asked as he watched her take a long sip.

"It is French lemonade, helped by the addition of gin and champagne." She linked the arm, not holding a drink through Deepak's, and gave him a dazzling smile. *I am going to enjoy this,* she thought. *It's always much nicer to reel in a young, handsome man than an old, trouty one.*

Tray arrived in time to watch Sophia flirt with a man at the bar. He hoped his new look was different enough to keep her from recognizing him too quickly. He preferred to remain incognito.

He needn't have worried. Neither Sophia nor Deepak appeared to be interested in any of the people around them, nor were they in much of a hurry. Tray slowly worked his way over in their direction, getting reasonably close to them at the bar. He faced away so they wouldn't see his face.

"Why is it I have not seen you here before?" Sophia asked Deepak. "Are you a tourist?"

"I'm more of a businessman than a tourist. My father owns a home in Paris, although I'm staying here at the Hôtel Barrière Le Fouquet's Paris. I only arrived today. I had business elsewhere to attend to first."

"Business is so tedious," she said with a frown. "I prefer fun. And buying beautiful things. Or at least intriguing ones."

Deepak ordered another round.

Sophia ran the tip of her index finger around the rim of her half-finished drink. "I recently tried to buy a lovely Monet painting at auction, but a pesky little man from Bruges kept bidding it up. I had to drop out. It made me so mad I tried to trip him when he left the salon, but he just walked around my leg."

Deepak laughed. "It's much more fun to win."

"Do you win?" she asked.

"I make a point of it."

She pretended to brush lint from his lapel. "So where was this business of yours? Was it very boring?"

"It was not boring at all. It was actually quite exciting. And I got to see an unusual phenomenon."

"What phenomenon?" She slowly ran her hand up and down his arm.

"An unexpected volcanic eruption."

Her eyes widened. "A volcano! Not here in France, I hope."

"No. Far away."

"But now you are here on holiday?" She leaned against him, caressing his cheek.

"After the weekend, I can think about being on holiday," he said. "First, I have a couple more business items on my agenda."

"That sounds stuffy."

"They will create a lot of excitement, I can assure you. And it should be extremely lucrative."

"In that case, we should celebrate. I'm told your hotel is very luxurious." She rubbed the front of her body against him. "You can ply me with champagne, and I will tell you all my secrets."

"I wouldn't think of inconveniencing you. We should go to your hotel. Or perhaps you live nearby?"

That would most definitely inconvenience me, she thought. Sophia needed to search Deepak's hotel room. "I'm staying with *ma mère* in her bed-sit."

Deepak jerked back and stared at her, unsure he had heard correctly. *What is this ravishing minx talking about?* "You bid on a Monet painting, yet you are living with your mummy in a one-room flat?"

Sophia scowled. "*Ma maison,* my house is being renovated, and I rarely get to spend time with *Mamam,* if you must know." She dipped her finger in her drink and seductively sucked off the alcohol.

She's harmless enough. "All right," Deepak said, placing his hand on the small of her back and leading her out of the casino. "How can I possibly say no to someone as lovely as you?"

214

*

"I'LL BE RIGHT back," Deepak said, leaving Sophia in the middle of the Hôtel Barrière Le Fouquet's Paris lobby. He approached the reception desk to ask if he'd received any messages. It took a minute because there were people ahead of him.

The clerk handed him an envelope, and he immediately read the message inside. He returned it, saying, "Here's something to feed your shredder." The clerk laughed and tossed the note away.

Deepak rejoined Sophia, taking her arm and leading her toward the elevators.

TRAY FORCED HIMSELF to walk calmly into the lobby—even though he felt like rushing—afraid he'd lost the buyer and Sophia. He wasn't paying attention and bumped into an older woman. *"Pardonnez vous,"* he said, realizing he'd bungled the words when the woman slapped him.

Sophia witnessed the exchange and recognized the odd turn of phrase. She looked at the man more closely. *Is that Tray in disguise?* He didn't look like Tray. His coloring was darker, and he appeared Middle Eastern, although he had the right height and build. They made eye contact, and Tray quickly looked away.

She looked up adoringly at Deepak as he took her arm. "Important business?" she inquired in a joking manner.

Deepak laughed. "My father wants to meet me for breakfast so he can poke his nose into my personal affairs. I guess he thinks it's important."

Once again, she pouted. "But then, who will I have breakfast with?"

"Mamam?" Deepak laughed when Sophia smacked his arm.

*

TRAY HAD SEEN the recognition on Sophia's face, even though it was subtle. He removed his watch before dashing for the same elevator and looked down continuously while playing with the timepiece as if it had a problem. He got off right after Deepak and Sophia on the same floor, which was one floor below his own. While they walked away, he hesitated, playing with his watch. He pretended to go in the opposite direction, discretely doubling back to ensure he saw which room they disappeared into. It annoyed him that Sophia would seduce the man who now owned Hero's Knot, but Tray had no right to stop her. He was merely there to recover the artifact and disappear with it before it could do any more damage.

ONCE DEEPAK AND Sophia were inside Bhatti's suite, Tray quietly made his way to the room across the hall from them. Looking around to make sure he was alone, he pulled a tiny camera from his pocket and stuck it on the upper part of the door frame. The miniature lens was capable of wide-angle video and would capture anyone entering or leaving Deepak's room.

Tray wondered if he should commandeer a room service cart just to make sure it would work. Instead, he walked to their door and lifted his hand to knock but suddenly thought better of it and headed to the stairwell. He'd be able to see any action from his room upstairs. Unfortunately, he would probably be too far away if he needed to apprehend someone quickly, but he had no intention of hanging out in the stairwell all night.

*

DEEPAK ORDERED CHAMPAGNE for Sophia.

"That is perfect," she said. "You are perfect." She planted a kiss on his lips, parting them with her tongue. When he reacted, she pulled back and laughed and told him she needed to visit the powder room. She searched the powder room and adjoining wardrobe but found nothing. She quickly removed her dress and put on a hotel robe, tying it tightly.

"Sophia?"

"I'll be a minute," she said. *I need to search your bedroom first.* She waited a few seconds before opening the door and poking her head into the bedroom. He wasn't there, so she searched through the drawers and under the mattress. His suitcase was under the bed. She opened it, searching hurriedly, but it was empty. She heard a door open and, shoving the suitcase back under the bed, opened the bedroom door just in time to see Deepak hand a package about the size of Hero's Knot to some unknown person out in the hallway. *Damn.*

Deepak turned suddenly, seeing her. "There you are. The champagne should be here any minute."

"I cannot stay," she said, forcing a tear down her cheek. "*Mamam* just called me. She is having one of her attacks. I must go home."

"I'll take you immediately," he answered.

"No," she replied too suddenly and with more force than she'd planned. "She doesn't like anyone to see her when she has an attack. It's ugly. I must go alone."

She grabbed her purse and walked toward the front door. Deepak smiled. "Shouldn't you get dressed first?"

"Oh!" She looked down and blushed. *"Oui.* I suppose I should."

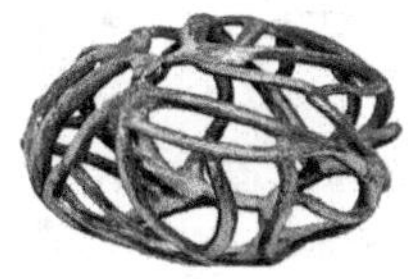

CHAPTER NINETEEN

AFTER DITCHING DEEPAK at the Hôtel Barrière Le Fouquet's Paris, Sophia employed all her skills to find Tray. She asked around the hotel, contacted people they both knew and even tried her last phone number for him, which didn't go through. Frustrated, she knew someone on Earth had to know how to reach him, and an image of Bijan Isaak flashed before her. She returned to the privacy of her hotel room before calling him.

The Mossad agent didn't sound surprised to hear from her. "To what do I owe the honor?"

"Have you seen Tray lately?"

"I have seen no one named Tray."

She slumped back into the sofa cushions. *That's unexpected.* Then she realized Tray would probably be traveling under an assumed name. Once again, she sat up straight. "In that case, have you recently seen an American trying to blend in as a Middle Easterner?"

"Ah. The questions become more pointed."

"Ah," she mimicked. "You didn't answer the question."

"I haven't seen any Americans looking particularly Middle Eastern."

She squeezed her eyes shut and leaned forward while she thought. Her right knee bobbed up and down rapidly. "Have you recently seen an American who once dug a bullet out of your back and saved your life?"

Isaak laughed. "I may have."

Now we're getting somewhere. Sophia's bouncing knee stilled. "I saw Tray in Paris, but I couldn't speak with him in front of my target. I need to connect with him. It's important."

"I can confirm that he did say he was leaving for Paris when I saw him."

She explained her dilemma in more detail and promised to assist Bijan in a future matter—no questions asked—before he passed on Tray's contact number. "I can't guarantee you'll reach him at that cell number," he said. "I know he planned to buy a couple more burner phones before leaving Tehran. So, if you're going to contact him, act fast."

TRAY WATCHED AS a woman carrying a large canvas market bag knocked on Deepak Bhatti's hotel room door. When Bhatti pulled the door open, neither he nor the woman spoke, she simply placed the bundle he handed her into her market bag and departed.

Tray followed her to an apartment overlooking the Rue de Furstemberg, where she handed the parcel to the gentleman who answered the door.

Who are you? Tray needed answers, but the only

people—aside from his aunt—who knew he was alive were Bijan and, perhaps, Sophia. He called Bijan, explaining why he needed a favor.

"Do you know what time it is?"

"I'm helping you get an early start on your day."

"It must be my lucky day. I already earned a *no-questions-asked* favor from your former paramour, and now you will also be in my debt. Same conditions. You must assist me—without question—at some future time. No excuses."

A half-hour later, Tray received a call, identifying the property owner on Rue de Furstemberg as Palanivel Bhatti. "Is he related to Deepak Bhatti?" he asked.

"Indeed," Bijan answered. "He's his father."

"What does Daddy do for a living?"

"I guess you'd call him a billionaire industrialist. He's had his hand in many pots and has dipped deeply into each one. He's beyond uber-wealthy."

"Just the kind of man who would buy or steal an ancient artifact—"

"—so he can extort even more money using it," Bijan confirmed before saying goodbye.

Tray didn't want to stay out on the street all night, but he had to monitor Bhatti's movements. He looked around and spotted a discreet sign about a rental apartment across the way. The sign was in the front window of a first-floor flat. He prayed it was empty. He pressed all the buzzers until someone let him into the building and knocked on the apartment door.

When no one answered, he picked the lock and entered. His sigh of relief was audible. The apartment looked vacant, even though several pieces of furniture remained—most of them large and probably too heavy to move easily. A decent-looking *bergère* chair in the corner appeared to have been overlooked. He quietly moved it to the window and sat. A spring poked him in the butt. Grimacing, he moved gingerly to find a decent position. *At least I won't get comfortable enough to fall asleep.* Still, he dozed off twice during the night, but never for more than a few minutes. He hoped he hadn't missed anything important.

WHILE MOST OF Paris slept, Palanivel Bhatti arranged to have ten twenty-ton nuclear devices planted near a London landmark.

The group he hired to set them in position complained that security was high and the timing too tight to do what he wanted.

"If I double my offer, will you be able to do it?"

"It remains a very rushed and dangerous job."

"I will triple my offer. That is as high as I will go. If you don't take the job, I'm sure there are others who will."

"It will only make up for the obstacles we must face in a small part. But I can see your need to get the job done. We need full payment upfront."

Bhatti tensed. He hated it when someone put him on the spot, but he had little time left. He agreed to the payment terms, electronically transferring the sum into the bank account number they gave him. It would still be a couple of hours before he arrived in England, and he wanted them to start moving everything into place immediately.

Although he hated placing his trust in mercenaries, he had faith they would do the job. So much faith, in fact, that he had Jagan place a call to the British Prime Minister.

That should shake things up.

Bhatti didn't suffer fools lightly—not that he took the time to form any particular opinions about people he considered beneath him. Instead, he simply blocked out all sentiment, having learned as a four-year-old child that emotions can lead to agony.

His birth father had died of a Krait bite while on a tiger safari. His grandfather quickly arranged for Palanivel's mother to remarry what amounted to the highest bidder—a man who went on to make both his new wife and her son miserable. That resulted in two crucial life lessons. Feelings could be painful, and he should block them at all costs. And money equals power. Those two precepts became ingrained within him, and he found that being cold and calculating made him rich and influential.

SOPHIA DIDN'T GET the chance to call Tray. As soon as she hung up with Bijan, her superiors in the SRR contacted her and ordered her to return to headquarters.

"Why am I being diverted?" she asked in a crisp British accent. "I'm so close."

"Not close enough, or you'd know the person in possession of the artifact has just threatened to use it to detonate a nuclear warhead in London." Director of Special Forces George Andrew Michaelson cleared his throat. "We need you here, now."

AISLINN LINED UP her paintings against the side of her bed. Studying them from a distance was difficult because her studio apartment in Sag Harbor was small. However, if she opened the door and stood outside, she could get the perspective she wanted.

She had five paintings and only needed four for the exhibit at Guild Hall. Unfortunately, one of them was too small to make an impact, and she felt another—an impressionist painting of her parents—was far too personal. Besides, she painted that for herself, not for someone to buy at an exhibit. *I need another painting.* She took the ones she had and placed them in a corner out of harm's way.

She hummed to herself as she rummaged through the art supplies she kept in a nineteenth-century camphorwood sea captain's chest. She had purchased it at a small antique shop in New England and had gotten a great deal on it. Any similar chest sold here in the Hamptons would have cost ten times the amount. The rich patina of the wooden exterior was wonderful, even with its scratches, and the brass fittings that held it together—although pitted and dented—added to its character. It was one of her most prized possessions. Most people would expect her to store items that she cherished inside—and she did. It held her art supplies. The interior wood was raw and untreated, and she took care to make sure she didn't smear it with paint or solvents. However, she wouldn't be inconsolable if she happened to stain the interior of the chest, after all, wasn't that what life is all about—making your mark on the world?

She took a quick inventory. *No titanium white. No stretcher bars.* She grabbed her car keys and headed out. She needed to get to the art supply store before it closed.

As soon as Senator Paige's press conference aired, phones rang off the hook at the Dirksen Senate Office Building. Americans wanted to show their support for Paige's message of *safety over politics,* and they were doing it through cash contributions to his campaign coffers.

"At this rate," one of his office staffers said, "he'll have his next election all sewn up. These people adore him."

Paige had seemingly transformed from a lukewarm career politician to a hot American hero overnight.

TRAY GLANCED AT his watch. It was 6:00 a.m. in Paris. He wondered if Bhatti was an early riser. His question was answered almost immediately when a flashy sports car slid to a halt in front of the industrialist's premises.

The ultramodern Ferrari 296 GTN looked almost anachronistic in this chic, left-bank enclave of beautiful old buildings that seemed to belong to another era. No one immediately exited the vehicle. However, the residence's front door opened a few minutes later, and Palanivel Bhatti walked out carrying what appeared to be a doctor's satchel. A man followed him, carrying an overnight bag.

Deepak emerged from the vehicle's driver's door and opened the passenger door for his father and the boot for the valet.

Tray noted the license plate number before father and son took off.

SOPHIA STRODE INTO SRR headquarters, located just outside of Hereford, England. It made her proud to think she had qualified as a member of the military's elite—yet not very well-publicized—*Special Reconnaissance Regiment*. The SRR recruited Sophia after the government awarded her a Distinguished Flying Cross for protecting highly placed UK Service personnel, cut off and isolated by Taliban insurgents.

Within minutes of the incident report, the military scrambled nearby air force personnel to engage with various enemy aircraft—deployed within a fifty-mile radius. However, Sophia stayed with the ambushed troops. Flying an A10 Thunderbolt, she single-handedly protected the British service members for more than an hour before additional air support arrived to take over. She thought nothing of it until her superiors later told her she had saved "royal" skin.

She laughed, thinking about her latest mission as she walked alone down the hallway, the click of her heels echoing on the tiled floor. *If ma mère really had been French, or my father Iranian, I wouldn't be here.* Smiling, she knocked on the door before entering.

"Ah, Sophia, go right through. You're the last to arrive."

Inside, several service personnel sat around an oval table helmed by their boss, his second-in-command, and, astonishingly, the prime minister. Large flat-panel monitors—spread across the room's longest wall—showed a satellite overview of the City of London and multiple live feeds from the Downing Street Situation Centre and other strategic offices and news organizations.

"Let's begin. Some of you already know about Hero's Knot. Others may not have heard of it yet. To be brief, Hero's Knot is an ancient artifact believed to have been created, in part, by Hero of Alexandria in the first century AD. It is notable because highly regarded experts previously speculated that it could triangulate with the sun's power to activate volcanoes. Unfortunately, it doesn't stop there. There is chatter that the relic has been tampered with, and new reports say it can now incite fission in nuclear devices." The noise level in the room suddenly ratcheted up. "Sophia, I believe you saw a demonstration of that in Iran?"

"Yes, sir." She stood. "It appeared to be a non-military demonstration on the south coast of Iran. First, a mud volcano more than a dozen kilometers away threw up an impressive display of mud and water that could be seen by anyone as far away as the coast. The detonation of a small nuclear weapon about three kilometers offshore immediately followed. They both happened within a few minutes of uncovering the artifact."

"What does the artifact look like?" someone asked.

"I couldn't see it from my location. However," Sophia pointed the fingertips of both hands toward each other and bent them to form a circular shape, "it's believed to be a little smaller than the size of a football."

"But you haven't seen it," Chauncey Llewellyn Pike, one of her male colleagues, repeated.

Sophia stared at him with a look of cool resolve. Her face showed absolutely no emotion, although inside, her temper roiled. "No, but I saw a package about that size passed from the man who purchased it in Iran, to another unidentified person."

"How far away were you when that happened?" the PM asked.

"Three meters," she guessed.

"You were that close, and you let it get away," Pike said with a sneer.

"I can see the word *covert* is not part of your vocabulary," she said under her breath, although everyone in the room clearly heard her.

The prime minister cleared his throat. "How can we be sure the package contained the artifact?"

"I trailed the buyer from the auction in Iran to his hotel in Paris. He was only out of my sight in the time it took me to change into something appropriate for the casino. I'd heard him mention it to the desk clerk when he walked in. I kept watch over him until he left for the evening—without the package. There were too many people around to break into his room at that time. Instead, I changed quickly and went to the casino, where I found him firmly ensconced at the blackjack table. Later, when he took me back to his room for a nightcap, I searched everywhere except the living room, where he must have stashed it. I was just in time to see him hand it off to someone when I exited the bedroom. In my estimation, the package *had* to have been Hero's Knot."

Pike shook his head. "You were in his room with him."

"Yes. I didn't want to lose track of the artifact."

"And yet he still managed to hand it off. You certainly botched that mission," he declared derisively.

"Where is Deepak Bhatti now?" Director Michaelson asked.

"I left after he gave away the package. I wanted to stay on its trail, but it was no use. The hotel said no cars had arrived or departed the premises during the time frame I gave them. I've requested more information from the three primary taxi companies in Paris but have not heard back. All I know for certain is he's up to no good."

The prime minister shifted in his chair. "'No good' doesn't begin to describe what the Bhattis have planned for the artifact. We were informed this morning at 0700 hours that there will be a nuclear detonation in London today if we do not pay a fifty-million-dollar ransom in crypto-currency by noon."

Sophia stiffened. "Are we paying it?"

The PM opened his mouth to answer, but Pike couldn't

stop himself. "Well, what do you think, *Miss I-speak-six-languages-and-have-a-140-IQ?* You let it get away."

"It's 157, you jackhole," she muttered under her breath.

One of the other operatives in the room looked up, intrigued. "What languages do you speak?"

"English, French, Spanish, Arabic, German, and Mandarin," Sophia rattled off.

"You mean you can't speak Russian?" Pike sneered.

"Отвяжись!" she answered.

Pike narrowed his eyes as another operative laughed.

"I speak Russian," Art Davies said, "and she just told you to fuck off."

Laughter erupted. Michaelson banged the flat of his hand against the tabletop. "This is not a free-for-all." He turned to the PM. "You were about to say something, sir?"

"I was just going to say, threats like this are why there are no nuclear plants in or around London."

"Unfortunately," Michaelson replied, "small nuclear ordnance is available on the dark web. And anyone with half a brain and the necessary funds can use an anonymous browser to access it and buy what they want."

Pike stood. "Would you like me to search for a link, sir?"

"No," Michaelson answered. "That ship has sailed."

The PM leaned back in his chair. "I would like Miss Brodeur to reconnect with Mr. Bhatti as soon as possible."

"I will do so immediately, sir," Sophia answered. "If you'll excuse me."

The PM nodded, taking his leave as well.

The remaining operatives looked at Michaelson. "What should we be doing in the meantime?" one asked.

"Contact every applicable asset you've developed and milk them for information. There must be some way to stop this nonsense."

Sophia called Deepak at the Hôtel Barrière Le Fouquet's Paris, but the receptionist said Monsieur Bhatti had checked out at dawn, leaving no forwarding address.

She paced. The steady rhythm of walking helped her think. It wasn't long before she remembered a friend at MI5 mentioning a program he had worked on that simultaneously accessed databases at multiple hotels within a defined geographic area using digital records. The program would spit out a list of everyone who had checked into or out of the designated properties during a specified time frame.

Within the hour, her friend sent her an encrypted list of guests coming and going at London hotels that morning. She complained that Bhatti wasn't on it.

"All of these hotels have cameras. Do you want to see images of the men who checked in?"

"Yes," she answered.

Minutes later, she received an encrypted folder filled with images.

She found Bhatti among the photos. He had made a reservation at The Winslow under the name Geoffrey Havisham. The Winslow was a quirky hotel encompassing various smaller properties that prided itself on anonymity and discretion.

She hoped the fact he was staying in London meant the warhead would have a contained blast radius.

*

THE MERCENARIES HIRED by Palanivel Bhatti planted the first four devices without issue. However, one of the men noticed a marine policing unit heading straight toward their boat—which was moored in the Thames near Traitor's Gate—just as they were about to sink the fifth warhead. They let it drop immediately without taking the time to release the coiled line that would allow the nuclear device to float just below the surface. They could not afford to let anyone see it. The remaining devices lay beneath a tarp on the deck, partially obscured by a bench built into the back of the boat. They kicked some fishing gear into a more prominent position.

"You're out early, gents. What's your business out here?" an inspector asked.

One of them answered that they were looking for a good place to fish but didn't think they had found the right spot yet.

"It's too busy here," the inspector told them. "Try further west, near Putney."

"Ta," one of them called out, while another started the motor and slowly pulled away—leaving the area. Four bombs would definitely explode, maybe five. They didn't care how much Bhatti had paid them. They couldn't afford to stick around and place the rest of the bombs now that officials had spotted them.

Besides, they were using old, leftover American ordnance. They could always blame a less-than-spectacular explosion on the age of the merchandise Bhatti told them to procure.

CHAPTER TWENTY

How can you use resources to track someone when you're dead?

Tray had remained dead too long. It severely limited him, especially now with the race to prevent Hero's Knot from activating. However, placing the call to his superior and admitting the deception made him feel like an eight-year-old who had gotten caught with his hand in the cookie jar. He needed to give himself a half-hour pep talk before contacting his boss at the FBI. He knew he could be fired on the spot. He wondered if he could also be charged with a crime.

It took Deneil Abernathy—the Special Agent in charge of the Art Crime Team—a minute to process the information. "Not dead?"

"Not dead."

"Where are you?"

Tray looked around the busy airport. His fellow

passengers in the waiting area were mostly older couples who appeared to be part of a tour group. He could see a plane taxiing toward the gate and hoped it was his. "Charles-de-Gaulle Airport in Paris, waiting for a flight to London."

"And you're going to London because …?"

"I believe Hero's Knot is headed there right now."

"We have agents there who will follow up. I need you to return to the US right away."

Tray felt his adrenaline plummet while his frustration skyrocketed. He stood up and walked toward the window, where he watched the plane inch its way toward the terminal. "I have had my eyes on this thing since it left Iran."

"Your designation at the Bureau is *inactive* because we all believed you were dead. I need you here. Now. Do not, I repeat, do not go to London.

"Masters," Abernathy shouted. "I need you to book the next flight out of CDG to DCA for Tray Lennox right away."

Administrative assistant Tanya Masters walked to Abernathy's door and just stood there, staring at her boss. Her face turned ashen and her eyes glassy as she almost imperceptibly shook her head.

"What are you waiting for?" Abernathy pounded his fist against his desk, causing a glass of water to wobble. "I'd like to give him that information while I still have him on the phone."

Her voice sounded raspy. "Tray Lennox … is dead."

"If he were, he wouldn't be on the other end of this phone line, turning my life into hell on earth." Abernathy spoke into the phone, "How *did* you pull that off?"

"Someone killed my brother."

"Your brother who's been undercover, tracking down a nuclear saboteur for the NRC? That brother?"

Tray stiffened. "You know about that?"

"Of course, I know about it. It's a big fucking deal over at the NRC. How did they mix him up with you?"

"We're twins."

"Why did he have your ID?"

"That's a long story."

"I can't wait to hear all about it." Abernathy drummed his fingers against his desk. "What name are you traveling under?" He listened for a moment before turning back to Masters. "I need that ticket booked for Nikola Bondarenko ASAP. Move!"

ONCE SOPHIA REPORTED her findings to the Director of Special Forces, she immediately helicoptered from HQ to the London Heliport. Time was evaporating. While in the air, she'd arranged for car service to The Winslow. She disconnected the call, trying to collect her thoughts, but felt restless. She borrowed a pair of binoculars to keep herself busy and scanned her destination. As the helicopter descended toward the landing pad, Sophia swore under her breath. Not thirty meters away, she could see Deepak Bhatti boarding another helicopter parked at the facility.

By the time Sophia was safely on the ground, the other helicopter had taken off. She turned to her pilot. "How can I find out where that aircraft is going?"

"Check the office."

A fat lot of good that did her. "Helicopters aren't required to file flight plans," the dispatcher said.

"Can you tell me who owns it?" Sophia asked.

"All I know is the landing fee was charged to a company called Jaitra Global Pvt. Ltd."

"Damn."

She got into the car and instructed the driver to take her to The Winslow. "Wait for me," she said, once they reached the hotel. It didn't take long.

"Mr. Havisham had a change of heart and checked out an hour after checking in," the desk clerk told her. There is no forwarding address."

She contacted Michaelson from the car and told him what she knew.

"Head back to the heliport. I'm instructing the helicopter to return for you. I don't know what you can pick up in London without Bhatti, and since we don't know where they're setting off nukes, it's better if you return here."

"But what if I'm needed in the city?"

"Don't worry about London. I want you here."

SOPHIA WALKED INTO the command center at SRR headquarters just in time to see the live stream on the largest screen—flash white. The flash made her blink. The image dissolved into static. Another smaller screen showed a distant shot of a plume rising above the Thames.

"Oh my God," the prime minister exclaimed, rising abruptly from his chair. "They actually did it."

"Did we pay the ransom?" Sophia asked.

"No," Michaelson answered. "The demonstration of the device to buyers in Iran, while credible, appeared too small to worry about. All smoke and mirrors, as it were."

"We raised the terrorism threat level to *imminent*," the PM added, "and had extra patrols investigating potential target areas, but we had little to go on. The attack had a tight timeline—almost as if the terrorists didn't want us to negotiate to stop them."

A soldier wearing headphones turned to the PM. "Sir, multiple detonations, concentrated in the same area, damaged Tower Bridge and the Tower of London."

"Have we received any communication since the initial demand for money?" the director asked.

"No one has contacted us yet, but estimates of casualty counts are coming in. Considering the location and the size of the detonation, they'll add up quickly and could climb into the thousands. We are warning Londoners to seek shelter indoors and to seal all doors and windows."

"Isn't it a little too late for that?" Pike asked. "They weren't given any warning. Would they even have the supplies on hand to seal everything off?"

"Not helping," Sophia muttered under her breath.

Another operative spoke up. "There are reports that the south side of the White Tower is badly damaged, with smaller structures along the southern perimeter obliterated." He paused before grimacing. "Good God. Part of the Tower Bridge span just dropped into the Thames."

As the afternoon shadows grew, a steady stream of reports from the field filtered in.

"We're being asked if emergency personnel should respond immediately or wait for radiation levels to decrease?"

"There are multiple fires surrounding the explosion. Also reports that streets in the immediate area are impassible."

"Cameras and communications in the area have been knocked out. We're doing our best to establish satellite coverage."

"Most of the hospitals are on the south side of the river. With Tower Bridge impassible, everyone is diverting to Bart's Health, which says it's overwhelmed by walk-ins."

"The Ministry of Defense is sending RFA Argus to help with the casualties."

One of the soldiers monitoring communications took off his headset and rubbed his eyes. "Sir, we're receiving calls asking where to take the bodies."

The PM sighed. "Do we have any better idea of the number of casualties we're talking about?"

A minute passed before a marine answered the PM's question. "We don't have exact numbers, sir, but we do have an expert's estimate that we will probably see close to four thousand deaths with well over thirteen thousand injuries."

The prime minister's chief of staff walked in with a satellite phone. "The American president, sir."

The PM greeted his counterpart and then closed his eyes as he listened. After a minute, he concisely outlined what he knew of the bombing and the casualties.

"No, we did not," he replied to an unheard question.

He nodded. "We can do that."

After a few more seconds, he said, "God be with you," before hanging up.

"Are the Americans sending aid?" Michaelson asked.

"No. They're asking for it. They've been given until Sunday to pay a one-trillion-dollar ransom, or Washington, DC, will cease to exist."

Aislinn studied the canvas in front of her. She had sketched out a rudimentary outline of Tray as he stooped down at the shoreline and examined a shell in the sand. The image was etched in her memory from their walk along Main Beach on the morning he died. *Painting Tray is one way I can respect his memory. But I'd better make sure everyone knows this painting will not be for sale.*

She grabbed a small tub of modeling paste and used her palette knife to scrape some onto the canvas where she wanted extra depth and texture.

She ate an omelet while it dried but jumped back into creative mode after finishing her lunch.

Ready to commit her memories to canvas, she grabbed her favorite palette and squeezed out generous blobs of ultramarine blue, phthalo green, burnt umber, and cadmium yellow. She added the white and cobalt paints she had picked up at the art store the day before and selected the perfect brush to create the desired effect.

Aislinn began layering paint and slipped into a state of nirvana, where nothing else could penetrate the bubble of creativity that overtook her. It wasn't until the sun set and she could no longer see—that she stopped for the day.

She had worked long and hard and liked what she produced. She noted a few changes she wanted to make and where to add some gloss over the color. *Not bad for a day's work.*

THE INCIDENT AT Diablo Canyon may have pushed Phineas Paige into the media spotlight. However, the near meltdown at the Comanche Peak Nuclear Power Plant in Glen Rose, Texas, sealed the deal on the senator's burgeoning popularity.

His rise to fame wasn't lost on political party bosses who bandied his name about for higher office. Indeed, a

Paige presidential run looked likely. The time had come to groom him, solidify his platform, and design a media blitz that would propel him higher into the stratosphere.

Phineas Paige, the anti-nuke president.
Phineas Paige, making America safe again.
Phineas Paige, no nukes, no kidding!

Paige was telegenic, well-spoken, and had attended Harvard, which appealed to Republicans and Conservatives. His push for safety over politics made him popular with Democrats and Liberals. And his votes on centrist legislation made him well-liked on both sides of the aisle. He was a negotiator. People felt they could work with him. But he also appeared low-key. People thought they could *sway* him.

Paige had grown very popular, seemingly overnight. It was obvious, considering all the *Paige for President* bobblehead dolls that suddenly appeared for sale on Amazon.

ARLINGTON, VIRGINIA, is not too far from Washington, in fact, two hundred years ago, it had been ceded to the federal government to become part of the District of Columbia. However, due to popular demand by its residents, the suburban-feeling Arlington County was given back to Virginia less than a half-century later. And why not? It was on the opposite side of the river from DC. The residents were more family-oriented, giving them a different mindset. And the pace was not nearly as hectic. Arlington was not *The District*.

That did not mean it wasn't conveniently located.

Locked inside a large safe deposit box at Arlington's Bank of America Financial Center, sat several ledgers and notebooks, each filled with cramped—yet meticulous—hand-printed notes identifying problems at several nuclear power plants across the country. It listed the employees and plant visitors to each site, along with everyone's credentials and, if applicable, police records.

Carey Lennox had gathered a vast amount of data, some minutiae and some pointing to serious breaks in oversight. He'd delved into how the information led to the formulation of a hypothesis predicting a massive grid failure, designed to originate in Washington, DC.

He had planned to release the information at a nuclear power summit scheduled for the last day of July. He had confirmed his speaking slot two nights before the East Hampton shooting. Without his information—*without him*—the sabotage may very well continue unchecked.

There were also files with damning evidence against specific individuals—including captains of industry and high-level politicians. Lists of offshore accounts, proof of money laundering, and substantiation of weapons dealing were all accompanied by written testimony, detailing a plot to shut down the electrical power grid in the forty-eight contiguous states.

Carey only needed one more piece of information to make his evidence airtight: background reports on Senator Phineas Paige and his campaign manager and fixer, Achille Pasquarelli.

Knowing the danger associated with his findings, Carey had added an addendum to his will containing the Bank of America rental agreement for the safe deposit box. That way, if something happened to him, others would learn about what was going on. However, he hadn't included the key to the box. He had worn that on an adjustable silk cord around his neck. He'd felt it was the best way to keep the evidence safe.

Lawmakers in Washington, DC, scrambled to put together a response to the ransom demand, even though the Pentagon argued the US should not deal with terrorists.

On the positive side, Congress found that pooling money from several sources could scrape together enough cryptocurrency to pay the trillion-dollar ransom. On the negative side, there would be no way to prevent terrorists from regularly asking for more money.

"Where the hell is Carey Lennox?" Vernon Cruikshank, Chairman of the National Security Council, asked. "I need his intel. I want to know if this ransom demand is tied to the sabotage at our nuclear power plants."

"We're working on it, sir," his aide replied. "We have calls, emails, texts, and telegrams sent to all his known addresses and members of his family. We'll track him down."

Not ten feet away, Senator Paige and Achille Pasquarelli stilled as they strained to listen.

"Why is this Carey Lennox person so important?" someone asked.

"Because he's been covertly tracking a suspected nuclear terrorist, and I need to know what he's learned so far."

"What if this threat is only a coincidence?" the aide asked.

Pasquarelli took a deep breath. *That's exactly the question I'd like answered.*

The general raised an eyebrow and waved him off. "If you believe in coincidences, you shouldn't be working in this department."

HAD AMERICAN CITIZENS known about the threat to their capital, they might have clamored for Senator Paige's opinion on nuclear weapons. Sure, they knew he was against nuclear power plants, but how did he feel about warheads?

Fortunately for the senator, the question didn't come up because many Americans didn't know about the impending danger. However, Paige did, and it wasn't from a terrorist threat. It was in having heard that Carey Lennox's twin brother had been killed in his place, meaning Carey was still out there, amassing evidence of sabotage against nuclear facilities.

That was enough to make Paige sweat in his lightweight Armani silk suit.

THE DIRECTOR OF Special Forces led Sophia away from the hubbub. "I'm sending you to the States. Washington, DC. They will need whatever intel we have, and while we can give them our *locked-in at HQ* observations, you were boots on the ground in Iran and Paris. You know the players better."

His assistant walked in. He nodded at Sophia but spoke to the director. "I've booked Colonel Brodeur on the next commercial flight out of Heathrow to Dulles International Airport. There's a helicopter outside, waiting to transport her. I had the go-kit she brought with her from Paris stowed onboard." He turned to Sophia. "Do you have your passport on you?"

She patted the cross-body bag she had been wearing since her return.

"Hand it over."

Her eyes flashed. "Why?"

He held up an envelope but didn't hand it to her. "I need it."

She reluctantly fished for it in her bag and gave it to him.

He handed her the envelope. "You have been authorized to carry a diplomatic passport, and we've included some American currency in case you need it."

"Oh." She rolled her shoulders to get them to relax. "Thank you."

"Go, Sophia," the director said. "The Americans will need all the help they can get."

Tray's flight forced him to change planes at Heathrow Airport. Everyone in the terminal was panicking over the Tower explosion. He gleaned as much information as he could from people milling about before boarding a commercial flight. He stowed his carry-on bag and sat in the back row of the first-class section, waiting for his fellow passengers to settle in. He felt chills when he heard Sophia Brodeur's voice speaking to the flight attendant. She couldn't be more than a few feet away, asking for champagne. He waited for the commotion to die down and the plane to pull away from the gate before saying, "I hope we don't *fall out* in Washington."

The term "fallout" caused Sophia to freeze momentarily before standing up to see who had said it.

Tray slid open the privacy screen that separated their seats. "You can sit down," he said quietly. "We're row-mates."

Sophia placed her jacket in the overhead bin to disguise why she stood, then lowered herself back into the seat. She stared at him, looking for signs of the Tray she remembered. She stared into his eyes as memories overtook her but shook them off.

Tray watched her carefully. "It's been a long time."

"Yes, but we can talk about that later," she whispered. "Do you know where the artifact is?"

"The last I knew, it was on its way to London. I would have followed it but got called back to DC. I'm glad I did, or I might have ended up in the middle of the explosion."

"I almost did, but I was also called back."

He massaged the bridge of his nose. "And now you're on your way to Washington. Why?"

She looked around the plane before continuing to whisper. "For the next threat."

"What's the next threat?"

"You don't know?" She bent her head past the perimeter of the privacy screen so only Tray would hear. "The Bhattis have apparently demanded a one-trillion-dollar ransom from the US government, or they're going to bomb Washington, DC, off the face of the earth."

Outwardly, Tray neither moved nor responded. His thoughts had taken off in a hundred different directions as he processed what she had said.

While she waited for him to speak, Sophia inspected the armrests on her seat and the wings around the headrest that would ensure she wouldn't find a fellow passenger sleeping on her shoulder. Not that it was possible—the seats were spaced too far apart. *This is nice. I didn't expect John Bull to spring for first-class. It's certainly a step up from my usual travel arrangements.*

The cabin was only a little roomier than business class and had less privacy than expected. Still, it was a definite step up from traveling economy or being on a military flight. "I wonder what we're doing in first class?" Sophia said aloud. She sniffed a deodorant stick she found inside the amenities bag next to her seat.

"I know my ticket was a very last-minute decision," Tray said. "This was probably the only seat left."

Sophia sighed. "Same here." She stuffed the amenities kit back where she found it. "What's wrong with us?"

"You mean, why haven't we stopped them yet?"

"No. Why do we keep running into the face of danger? Do people like you and I have a death wish?"

"I doubt it."

She pursed her lips for a second while she thought. "You're right. It's more of an *anti-death wish*. We're trying to prevent other people from dying needlessly."

"So, we're heroes."

"Don't say, 'Hero.' He's the one that got us into this predicament." She took a sip of her champagne. "Did you ever think our lives would get this complicated?"

"I hadn't actually thought about it."

"There were times, back at Balliol, when I imagined you might one day pop the question and marry me. I thought we'd live in a nice little cottage and have two perfect children. You would consult on archaeological artifacts and write articles about them for prestigious journals. I would translate those articles so they could be published in even more prestigious journals around the world."

"You never told me you felt that way."

"It was my most precious daydream." She sighed. "What happened to us, Tray?"

"My grandparents were murdered in their beds."

"I'm sorry. When you walked out of my life to return to America, it never occurred to me that you wouldn't come back. But then, you never responded to my emails. Texts. Letters. Nothing. For all I knew, someone may have murdered you as well."

"I wasn't murdered. I was recruited. A notorious group of thieves killed my grandparents for their art collection. It was worth millions. The FBI initially suspected me because I was an art history major. But then, the information I gave them helped them catch the killers. They told me I was an asset and offered me a job. I took it."

"I know. I saw you in Morocco. I would have approached you, but a Mossad agent named Bijan Isaak held me back. He told me you were in the middle of an op for the Americans and handling a delicate negotiation. I realized that you probably didn't know that I also worked for the government. My government. I thought I might see you again when it was over, but I got diverted to another mission."

She paused when the flight attendant stopped by her seat to refresh her champagne. She waited until Tray was served before continuing.

He looked at her through the partition, staring into her eyes. "I saw you in Morocco. I was on the trail of a Van Gogh painting that hadn't been seen since the Nazis confiscated it during the Second World War. I wanted the person I was dealing with to believe I was ready to pay a king's ransom for it. Unfortunately, he disappeared before we could make a deal.

"I looked for you after that, but you had already left Morocco."

"That's what happens when you work for the government. They call it 'following orders.' Besides, I figured by then, all the feelings you once had for me had probably faded away."

"That's where you're wrong. I still had very definite feelings for you. Unfortunately for Bijan, I unleashed my tale of woe on him." Tray paused, looking abashed. "He knows a lot about us."

"I am well aware of how good a confidant Bijan Isaak is. I poured out my heart to him—all about you—one night in a drunken stupor. He later remarked about you and I having been intimate, and I punched him. I couldn't fathom why he would say such a thing. Then he revealed that I was the one who told him. In my defense, I don't remember that conversation. But apparently, you and I both have loose lips."

"So, Mossad knows all about our youthful indiscretions."

"Yes. But I don't think we need to get fired up over it. Why would Mossad use it against us if we're on the same side? At least, for now."

"On the same side . . . "Tray's voice trailed off as the plane's engines began to thrum. The captain announced that air traffic control had cleared the plane for take-off, and the aircraft lurched as it pulled away from the gate.

Tray sat back, fastening his seatbelt. He closed his eyes as he thought about everything Sophia had said. Exhaustion overwhelmed him, and he instantly dozed off.

Sophia leaned back as well, but rather than sleep, she soon became lost in her memories.

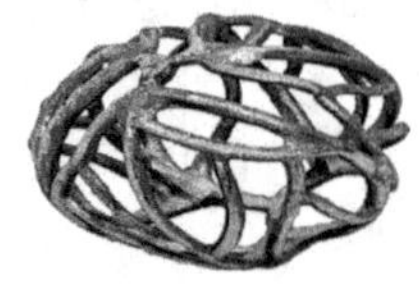

CHAPTER TWENTY-ONE

THE PLANE TOUCHED down in Washington, DC, without incident, and aside from small talk while gathering their possessions to disembark, Tray and Sophia kept their own counsel.

After clearing customs, Tray picked out special agent Miller Jean from the Art Crime Team, holding a sign that said *Lennox.* "I've got to leave," he told Sophia. "But the way things are going, I'll probably see you again. Soon." He handed her a card with a cell phone number scribbled on the back. "You can reach me at this number for now."

Miller escorted him to a black Chevy Suburban and opened the front seat passenger door.

"I don't get to sit in the back and pretend you're my personal chauffeur?"

"Nope. You're just a peon on this trip."

Miller got into the driver's seat, and they both buckled up, then sat there.

"What are you waiting for?" Tray asked. "Aren't we under a time constraint?"

The back door opened, and two more people slid in—special agent Kai Yamamoto and SRR operative Sophia Brodeur. "I can't seem to get rid of you," Sophia said to Tray.

Kai put on her seat belt. "You two know each other?"

"Didn't anyone ever tell you?" Miller replied. "Tray knows all the beautiful women."

TRAY AND SOPHIA followed Miller and Kai into FBI Headquarters, separating after going through security. Sophia and Kai headed in one direction, Tray and Miller in another.

The men proceeded through a door marked *Art Crime Team,* their appearance almost instantly causing the decibel level among the agents inside to peter out.

Tray's co-workers couldn't help but gape at him. It wasn't that they were surprised to see him. News of him joining the ranks of the "undead" had spread like an unchecked virus. It was more that they were stunned to see what he looked like. He had dressed in the same outfit he had flown to Iran in, with the addition of the *shemagh* and brown contacts. Plus, he sported a dark beard, a heavy tan, and an earring. His colleagues expected the Tray Lennox, who looked like he'd just stepped off the cover of GQ. Instead, they found Nikola Bondarenko. He removed the *shemagh*, revealing a whopping white gauze pad stuck to the back of a badly buzzed head, covered in uneven stubble.

Tray and Miller ignored the gawking and continued to Program Manager Deneil Abernathy's office. Abernathy already stood at the open door and stared as Tray approached.

"Until now, I never thought I'd see a 'dead man walking' outside of cable TV. You have a lot of explaining to do." He closed the door, ensuring their privacy.

Tray took a seat in front of Abernathy's desk. The program manager made himself comfortable behind it. Miller remained standing, next to the door.

Abernathy voiced a succinct command. "Start talking."

Tray explained how he'd been a guest at a weekend society wedding and how the next day, when he had attended brunch with his girlfriend's family, he had received a call from his brother, Carey, saying someone was after him. "I thought it was odd that someone would follow Carey when I was the FBI agent connected to Hero's Knot. I honestly believed it was a case of mistaken identity."

"Did your brother know about your investigation?"

"I may have mentioned it in passing, but we never really discussed it."

"Are you aware that your brother was recruited by the Bureau once his investigation involving nuclear reactors was re-designated a suspected terrorist plot?"

Tray leaned forward. "Excuse me?"

"Carey discovered a number of incidents of sabotage at some of the plants he inspected and brought it to our attention."

"I know he was concerned about the problems he found and got some guy fired a while back, but I didn't know he contacted the FBI about it."

Abernathy opened his desk drawer and removed a file. He shuffled through some papers and took a moment to read them, before returning the file to his drawer. "His investigation had progressed since the last time you spoke with him. His superiors contacted our counterterrorism division, and we asked him to continue reporting anything unusual that he found during his inspections—directly to us. The NRC told me your brother developed intel on each suspect in the various cases. I know some names popped up more than once, but no one has ever seen his files. He stopped contacting us about ten days ago. Everyone believed he had gone off the rails following your death. But you're alive."

Tray did his best to mask the sting of impending tears. "And Carey is dead."

"What makes you say that?"

"Because he died in my arms. I thought someone mistook him for me, and that's why they killed him. I switched wallets with him after that. Since I thought I was the target, I wanted people to think I was dead so they would leave me alone while I followed up on Carey's killer. The impact my actions would have on people who knew or worked with Carey never occurred to me. And I certainly didn't know the FBI had recruited him."

"What made you think someone was after you?"

"Because the chatter on Hero's Knot suddenly increased, and I had possession of it."

Abernathy stood so quickly his chair banged into the credenza behind his desk. "*You* had possession of Hero's Knot?"

"Yes."

"How?"

"I stole it from a thief who stole it from the *Galerie Blanc* in Zurich three years ago."

Abernathy appeared to be completely stunned. He paced for a minute, the Moroccan rug muffling the sounds of his footfalls. His thoughts momentarily caused a range of emotions to flash across his face, but he quickly composed himself. Finally, he lowered himself back into the chair and asked in a very calm, controlled voice, "Why didn't you return here and relinquish it to the team?"

"Because of possible reprisals. I didn't want to be the target of an unsub with vast influence in Europe. I chose to play it close to the vest, hiding the artifact instead. That way, there would be no chatter, and no one would know what I had done. It felt like the safest plan."

"The 'safest plan' would have been to place the artifact in the US government's possession."

"I disagree. It happened around the same time a former president"—Tray made air quotes—"declared war on the FBI. How could I hand in a potentially dangerous object and possibly watch it be used as a political football by the administration? I hid it well. I never thought anyone would find it."

Abernathy's voice increased in volume. "In Iran?"

Tray's brow furrowed. "No. In Roscoe, New York."

Several moments passed before the program director spoke again. "How did it get to Iran?"

It was Tray's turn to stand up and pace. "Someone sussed out that I had it. They must have followed me upstate when I went to check on it. They attacked me from behind—you can see the evidence of that on the back of my skull—and they snatched it."

"And you didn't think that, maybe, you should have reported it then?"

"By then, I was supposed to be dead. And it was a *stolen* artifact, smuggled into this country from Europe. Who was I supposed to report that to? Besides, I would have risked losing its trail."

"I'm pretty sure everyone knows where it was yesterday. And where's it's going to be on Sunday."

"I'd stake my life that the people behind this are Palanivel and Deepak Bhatti."

"Who are …"

"Palanivel Bhatti is a billionaire industrialist in India who owns Jaitra Global Limited, a private company. And Deepak is his son and heir apparent."

"What makes you so sure it's them?"

"Because Sophia Brodeur of the SRR and I have been following the artifact since Deepak Bhatti purchased it at auction in Iran."

"It's time we get the counterterrorism division in on this." Abernathy picked up the phone and explained the essentials to the assistant director. He listened intently for a moment before asking, "Your place or mine?" He hung up the phone. "OP-2 is in the middle of questioning your friend, the SRR agent. We're meeting them there."

AISLINN RECEIVED A CALL asking her to come down to the East Hampton Police Station. She hated leaving her painting but knew she couldn't refuse. She washed the splatter off her hands, pulled herself together, and jumped into her Miata for the fifteen-minute trip.

She made a face when a police officer showed her into an interrogation room. "Why am I here?"

"Detective Molyneaux will be right with you."

She walked around the room while she waited, forming an opinion on how utilitarian it was: all hard surfaces, very little color, absolutely no decoration. She wasn't looking for pictures or ornamentation, but there wasn't even a memo taped to the wall that she could read to pass the time.

Twenty minutes later, Molyneaux walked into the room followed by FBI Special Agent Sam Flores. "Good morning, Miss Gilchrist. Thank you for coming. Have you met Special Agent Flores from the FBI's Long Island Bureau?"

"No, I haven't."

"He has a few questions for you concerning your boyfriend."

Flores gestured for Aislinn to take a seat before sitting down across from her. "How long have you known Traynor Lennox?"

"Since the second Friday of June. I don't remember the exact date."

"But you know it was the second Friday? What year was that?"

"This year. Last month. I met Tray at a party in honor of my cousin and her fiancé—a couple of weeks before they tied the knot."

"And what do you know about him?"

"He's an art appraiser for an import-export business in Manhattan. He must do well because he has an incredibly posh apartment. And he's very, very sexy."

"What do you know about his family?" Flores continued.

"I know his parents are dead." She nervously picked at the edge of the table. "He said he had a brother, but I never met him. He didn't even show up for Tray's funeral." Her face softened with the hint of a smile. "And, of course, there's his Aunt Jane, who is the sweetest woman." She paused again. "I don't know if there's anybody else."

"Did he ever tell you he loved you?"

Aislinn reddened as her facial muscles tensed. "I think that's a highly personal question, and I refuse to answer it."

254

"We believe it's pertinent and important to the investigation."

Her eyes clouded up as she stared at nothing. "No," she whispered after a long silence.

"Excuse me," Flores said. "I didn't hear you."

Aislinn looked at him, trying to hold back a tear she felt welling in her eye. "No," she said, her volume growing as she leaned forward, no longer calm. "He never told me he loved me." She slumped back into the chair.

Molyneaux, who had been watching her, stared more intently.

"What would you say if we told you Traynor Lennox is not dead?"

Gravity claimed the tear. "I'd say you're wrong. We were together that morning. He went outside to take a call, and when I went to find him a little while later, I saw police standing over him, saying he was dead." She turned her attention to Molyneaux. "Why would they do that? Why would someone say he was dead if he wasn't?"

"Because the driver's license in his wallet identified him as Traynor Lennox, and the picture matched."

Flores put up his hand to silence Molyneaux. "The victim was Carey Lennox, your boyfriend's twin brother."

Her mouth opened and closed silently for a moment before she began speaking. "Do you mean the man I was dating was actually Carey Lennox? Why would he lie about his name?"

It was Flores's turn to pause. "I can't say definitively. I only know that Traynor Lennox is being escorted right now into the DC offices of the FBI—alive and well."

Aislinn visibly shivered as she stared down at the table. When she lifted her head, new tears threatened to spill onto her cheeks. "I don't understand."

"Neither do we, Miss Gilchrist, but we intend to." Flores's cell phone rang, and he excused himself to take the call. "You're free to go," he said with a wave of his hand.

Aislinn took a tissue from her handbag and wiped her face.

Molyneaux took a step toward her. "Are you okay?"

She appeared to be overwhelmed by sadness. "I don't know. Was it all a sham?"

"I wish we could tell you." He took her arm and helped her up. "I'll walk you to your car." He could feel her tremble as she leaned against him. "I'm sorry you're so upset."

Her step faltered. She hesitated. "I guess I never really knew him. I'm a fool to think I loved him."

"Sometimes, we have no control over the people we're attracted to." *Like right now.* Molyneaux felt an inexplicable magnetic pull as if he were being drawn to Aislinn like a compass needle.

"I guess it's time for me to stop mourning Tray, especially considering he's not dead. For all I know, I've never even met the real Tray Lennox."

Molyneaux cupped her elbow with his hand as he guided her out of the building. "Getting over your sense of loss may be easier said than done."

"I was asked to display some artwork in a show this weekend. I was excited about it. I even painted a picture of Tray for it. But now I think I'll call them and tell them I changed my mind." She lifted her face to look at Molyneaux. "It will be too hard to face people I know. There's no way I can explain any of this." She sighed. "Canceling it will give me something to do when I get home. Then I can wallow in self-pity."

He tightened his grip on her elbow and gently pulled her to a stop. "Where's the show?"

"Guild Hall."

"That's a pretty prestigious venue to be invited to show your work at. I think you should still do it."

She looked down at the pavement. "Everyone will talk about me."

"They won't know anything more than they did yesterday. The FBI is keeping a tight lid on this case for now. And you did nothing wrong. Don't sacrifice your self-confidence and future because of some guy who isn't trustworthy."

As they crossed the street to her car, she thought about the potential boost to her career. "I really do want to do that show. Are you sure the public won't know anything? I don't know how I could face them if they did."

"I'm sure no one will know unless you tell them, and please don't. At least, not until the investigation is over." He rubbed the stubble on his face. "Is this art exhibit by invitation only, or are off-duty police detectives allowed to attend?"

A hint of a smile touched Aislinn's face. "Would you come? I can give your name to the people at the door."

"What time does it start?"

"There's a cocktail reception at eight p.m. on Friday, but the show runs all weekend."

"I can't promise I'll be there all weekend, but I can be there Friday night."

Her face brightened. "Thank you, Detective Molyneaux. I'll see you then."

"Call me Miles."

"First name basis." Her smile widened. "I'm going to

have to put you on my *family and friends* list now, Miles," she said as she got into her car.

He watched her drive away until her car disappeared around a corner. Whether he realized it or not, his grin was even wider than hers had been.

Sophia did not seem surprised when Tray and his boss entered the office of FBI Assistant Director for National Security Therese Vasko.

"Well, now," AD Vasko said, "let's see if we can put our respective puzzle pieces together and make some sense out of what's going on."

Abernathy looked at Tray. "You'd better start with Hero's Knot."

A lot of what Tray said over the next hour correlated directly with what SRR squadron leader Sophia Brodeur had said. He had more details about the artifact up until the auction. Her information was more detailed following the auction. "We'll put out warrants for the Bhattis."

"What if they don't come to this country?" Sophia asked.

"This is too big an operation to leave to chance. At least one of them will be here to supervise. I'll let Interpol know what's going on as well."

Abernathy and Vasko's eyes met. "If I were Palanivel Bhatti," Abernathy said, "I'd make sure I was doing something very public this Sunday, far away from Washington, and send my young pup to do my bidding. If Deepak wants to inherit the family business, he's going to have to earn it by dirtying his hands and then saving himself."

"We need to apprehend them both." Vasko told her administrative assistant to set up secure calls with Interpol and the British Director of Special Forces. "ASAP."

"I guess the big question," Tray said, "is where are the nukes?"

"What do you mean?"

"From what we've seen and heard, Hero's Knot is going to triangulate with the sun's fusion process, directing the resulting neutrons into a focused beam strong enough to make a warhead explode."

"Any warheads currently in or around DC are deep underground," Abernathy replied. "I doubt sunbeams can affect them."

"Neutrons can travel through almost anything, and these aren't ordinary neutrons. They've been transmuted by Hero's Knot. They are blamed for the bombing of the Tower of London and Tower Bridge. They've been linked to some of the earth's major earthquakes over the past two millennia."

Abernathy rubbed his temple. "So, we're not talking about apprehending people? We're after rogue neutrons?"

"The people in control of Hero's Knot control those neutrons."

"And what's preventing the artifact from working wherever it is right now?" AD Vasko asked. "Why aren't nukes exploding as we speak?"

Tray gave it some thought. "They must be shielding it somehow, maybe inside a lead case, which would be sufficiently dense and have a high enough number of electrons to scatter any energy. Or they may just be keeping it indoors. If it can't triangulate with the sun, maybe it can't do any damage."

*

DEEPAK BHATTI THREW his bag on the long sectional sofa, inside his suite at the MGM National Harbor Hotel in Forest Heights, Maryland. He opened his oversized leather duffel to remove his laptop and stared at the bowling bag taking up a quarter of the interior. He hadn't been exactly sure how to get Hero's Knot into the US, but all it had taken was a private jet. TSA security checks were apparently more stringent for passengers on commercial flights.

Now, he merely had to hook up with his father's band of merry men, who were responsible for putting everything into place. He stared at the bag. There was nothing special about it, nothing to protect its contents from interacting with the sun, except the leather exterior. The artifact itself was wrapped in a quilted drawstring bag inside the carrier, if only because it smelled better than the liner it replaced. Deepak's only job would be to remove the artifact and expose it to the sun within reasonable proximity to the warheads—a mile or two away.

He sank onto the couch and looked at the floor-to-ceiling windows that lined the entire wall. Outside was an incredible panoramic view. The hotel had even supplied a telescope, so occupants could bring distant sights into focus. *Once I trigger the box, I can come down here and watch everything.* His eyes narrowed. *That can't be right.* He called his father on a secure phone.

Palanivel Bhatti tossed back the remaining whiskey in his Baccarat Harmonie tumbler and slammed the glass on his polished ebony desk, after Jagan informed him that Deepak was on the line. He modulated his voice to show no emotion. "Is everything in place, my son?"

"I texted your contact that I have arrived, but I haven't heard back from him."

"I'm positive he is hard at work, ensuring everything is ready for you. He will contact you when it is appropriate."

"I saw the artifact work in Iran. It only takes a minute or two. If I'm a mile from a nuclear blast that's expected to decimate an entire city, won't I be killed in the explosion?"

There was silence on the other end of the phone.

"Father?"

"Of course. You are correct. I need to contact the engineer working on the mechanized system that will open at the appropriate time, exposing the artifact. I thought you already had it. I will make sure you receive it well in advance. It will give you approximately twenty minutes to get away—"

Deepak's voice rose. "I can't get far enough away from a nuclear explosion in twenty minutes!"

Another long pause ensued, during which Palanivel smashed his crystal glass against the window. A single drop of alcohol slowly dripped out of sight. "You did not allow me to finish. I am arranging to ship a Mosquito ML two-seater helicopter to my man in the States. He will pick you up once the box is set in place and will take you to an airport a safe distance away, where a plane will be waiting to fly you back to Mumbai."

"What if the Americans agree to pay?"

"Then you will leave with the artifact and return home."

After disconnecting from his father, Deepak poured himself a double shot of fifty-year-old scotch. Something seemed off. Maybe it was his father's hesitation when Deepak first voiced his concern—as if *dear old dad* needed a moment to make up a plausible excuse. *He's given this artifact more consideration than he's ever given me.*

He and his father had never been particularly close. Now, he had the distinct impression that if he had never questioned his own safety, his father would have written him off as collateral damage.

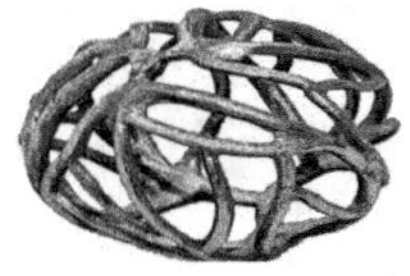

CHAPTER TWENTY-TWO

Palanivel Bhatti's *'man in the States'* tested the box again at his garage workshop on the outskirts of New York City. Jaitra Global had promised him a tremendous amount of money to design this device in an unbelievably short amount of time. It hadn't taken long to cut and weld. He already had the tools and materials available in his workshop. The tricky part was adding a timer that would remove the pins holding the lead plates together. It required the precision of a finely tuned Swiss watch movement. That was more difficult to pull off. Not that he couldn't do it, but his client wanted him to rush through a task he hadn't already mastered.

After two previous failures, he was ready to try again. He set the timer, inserted the pin through the lid, and waited. Twenty minutes later, the lid popped open, and the sides fell away, exposing whatever would be inside.

He released a breath. He was ready to proclaim success

but knew he should test it again. And he did, three more times, before finally calling his contact in India. "It is done."

Jagan noted the information on his computer. "Deepak Bhatti needs it as soon as possible. You must personally deliver it to him at the MGM National Harbor Hotel in," he took a moment to click through to the correct page, "Forest Heights, Maryland. How long will it take you to get there?"

"At least five and a half to six hours."

"Do it now. Things are moving quickly, and he needs to have it as soon as possible."

At FBI Headquarters, AD Vasko had assembled a small team of experts, including the Under Secretary for Nuclear Security, Pete Pettigrew. They met in a Strategic Information & Operations conference room to discuss possibilities and probabilities.

Vasko and Abernathy brought everybody up to speed. "Assuming this is going to happen," Vasko said, "where do you think terrorists are most likely to strike, Mr. Pettigrew?"

"I can't see them getting access to our nuclear warheads."

"They don't need access," Abernathy replied. "Tray, will you explain?"

Tray reiterated the scientific theory behind the artifact and asked Sophia to describe what happened in Iran.

She finished by saying, "So, sir, they only had to be within a kilometer or two for the warhead's detonation. The mud volcano was much farther away."

"What you're describing," the undersecretary said, "are warheads that were close to the surface, volcanoes that are exposed. To foment devastation on a scale to obliterate

DC, they would have to detonate a nuclear arsenal bunker located a hundred feet beneath the Potomac. That would take out the entire city. No other devices in the vicinity could do that kind of damage."

"How deep is the Potomac in that area?" Tray asked.

"Maybe twenty-five feet. It varies."

"So, less than a mile underground," he stated.

The undersecretary stared at Tray for a moment. "Yes."

"That means anybody on a boat, anybody on the shore, anybody on I-495 could expose the artifact to the sun and cause detonation."

"And they would be killed in the blast."

"There's no global limit on suicide bombers."

"But so many other people would die," Sophia said. "And hundreds of thousands would be injured."

"How do you propose we prevent it?" the undersecretary asked. "And that question is open to the floor."

Deputy Assistant Secretary of Defense for Nuclear Matters, Marshall Aguta, cleared his throat. "Our specific problem, in this case, is fission. It sounds like we need to slow down the means leading to fission, which are neutrons. They don't live very long, perhaps fifteen minutes, and more than half of that would be spent traveling from the sun to the earth. We just need to impede their progress long enough, so they'll die before reaching the warheads."

"And just how do we do that?" the undersecretary asked.

"Hmmm." Aguta paused. "I need to make some phone calls. Talk to a few scientists and engineers. If you'll excuse me, I'll do my best to find the answers you need as quickly as possible."

"Why don't we all take a break for a short while,"

Vasko said, "and contact any experts we have access to. Let's reconvene here in an hour to establish a plan."

Everyone agreed, immediately pulling out cells and tablets to arm themselves with information.

Jagan hung up the phone in his office in Mumbai. *That's one fire out. I'd better track down the helicopter.* He called Jaitra Global's Transportation Department.

Someone picked up on the fifth ring. "Transportation."

"It took you long enough. It's Jagan. What's the status of the Mosquito ML?"

"It's en route. The pilot will collect it, assemble it at the hangar he works out of, then contact Deepak about where to pick him up."

"Call him. Tell him to contact Deepak now and set up a schedule with an approximate time frame."

"Will do."

Jagan checked off another item on his list.

Next, he contacted the private jet pilot that had transported Deepak to the US and arranged for him to be at the younger Bhatti's beck and call.

That should square things between father and son.

When the government officials and experts returned to the meeting at FBI headquarters, Vice President Ferdinand "Ferry" Wentworth joined them. "The president wishes he could be here himself, but he's discussing the viability of an evacuation with the Joint Chiefs of Staff."

The Deputy Secretary of Homeland Security, Marc Anthony Hodge, entered behind him.

"Gentlemen," AD Vasko said, "thank you for joining

us. I trust you've been brought up to speed on what's going on."

"It's all anyone is talking about at Homeland," Hodge replied. "I hope you have some answers for us."

"I was hoping Deputy Assistant Secretary Aguta would be back by now," Vasko said. "He seemed to have a handle on what needs to be done. I'm hoping he could open that door."

"Can you be more specific?" the vice president asked.

"Earlier today, he spoke about slowing down neutrons, so they'd die before ever reaching the warheads. He said that might negate the threat."

As if on cue, Aguta rushed in, apologizing for being late. "We have a theory. It's untried, but it's the best we could come up with, considering the time restraint."

"Proceed," Vasko said.

"My colleagues agree that the most likely target is the nuclear arsenal under the Potomac," Aguta continued. "Fortunately, the presence of water may be beneficial because water—in and of itself—will help slow down the neutrons. But it's not enough. We also need to scatter them and throw them off the scent, so to speak. And one scientist I spoke with said prismatic crystals might do the trick. Of course, we don't have a crystal large enough to cover the Potomac, but if we grind lead crystal into small particles and suspend it in a vapor cloud, it should theoretically work."

The VP tapped his pen against the conference table. "Where is the vapor cloud coming from?"

"Liquid nitrogen."

"And you think that will work?"

"We can't be sure. It's untested. So, just to be safe, we think we should add some boron dust to the mix."

"Boron dust?"

"Boron 10 should absorb some of the neutrons, which is why power generating facilities use it in control rods for nuclear reactors."

Undersecretary Pettigrew nodded. "It's like making a cocktail of all the ingredients known to be effective. Together, they just might make a definitive impact. The only question is, can we get our hands on enough of the ingredients to cover the Potomac?"

"Not the entire Potomac," Aguta interjected. "Just 4 square miles. And we're talking about nanoparticles. They'll go a long way in a suspension."

The vice president cleared his throat. "Are we just going to drop this stuff out of a plane, like a bomb?"

"No. We need to release it from a low altitude, so it doesn't carry in the wind."

"Crop dusters," Hodge said. "They fly low and are equipped to disseminate a liquid spray."

The vice president still wasn't convinced. "We need to think this through, first. Will this concoction harm people on the shore if they inhale it?"

"Not as much as a nuclear bomb blast," Tray whispered to Sophia.

"We can put out an announcement," Hodge said. "Tell people we're spraying for wasps or cow killers and recommend they wear masks. Or better yet, advise they stay indoors with the windows closed."

Vasko laughed. "You think they're going to buy that we're spraying for cow killers over the river?"

"Okay then, mosquitoes."

"Can I get this in writing? Something tangible I can show the president?"

"Yes, Mr. Vice President," Aguta replied. "I will have it for you within the hour."

North of the city, a helicopter pilot and his trusted friend put the finishing touches on a Mosquito ML chopper. The pilot had landed with the kit earlier that day, and assembling the lightweight helicopter felt like child's play.

He called Palanivel Bhatti's assistant, Jagan, and said it was ready to go.

"Good," Jagan answered. "Did you bring the *frontiersman* with you?"

"I did. We arrived without incident."

"I need you to place it in the river near the Lincoln Memorial as soon as possible. Mr. Bhatti wants to give the Americans a demonstration."

The pilot tensed. "From what altitude?"

"You're not bombing them. We want it to slide into the water where it can settle on the bottom. Mr. Bhatti's son will take care of the rest. From what I can tell, you have several more hours of sunlight, but the sooner, the better. Contact Deepak Bhatti directly as soon as you have it in place. He'll know what to do."

"Yes, sir." The pilot sighed. He was exhausted, but saying *no* to the people who paid his salary would not be in his best interests. He looked at his friend. "I need a vehicle, preferably an SUV."

"Drop me off at a metro station, and you can borrow mine."

"Perfect. Now, all I have to do is find a small boat or kayak."

"In that case, drive me home, and you can borrow my son's kayak, as well."

"Let's go."

*

THE PILOT WONDERED if his friend's kayak would be functional. It was smaller and lighter than he expected, and it folded flat, which seemed strange, but it had the open hull he needed. His friend showed him how to put it together, and it looked easy enough to do with clamps. The pilot just hoped it would support both him and Davy Crockett.

He found a place along the Potomac to launch the craft, and he got the kayak and Davy Crockett into the water without too much trouble. Just enough space remained for him. Once onboard, he leisurely paddled to the area just west of the Lincoln Memorial.

He looked around. It was a beautiful day, and several people were in the area. *I need to make this look believable.* He swatted at a make-believe bug several times, cursing aloud.

Someone on shore pointed at him, laughing.

Suddenly, he lurched, tipping over the kayak. The warhead brushed his leg as it drifted downward. He managed to flip the kayak back into position but had no luck getting back into it. He put on a good show for the people observing him, although not by choice. Finally, he used the kayak as a flotation device and swam behind it, pushing it back to shore.

THE PRESIDENT ALMOST refused to take the phone call. However, after consideration, he decided to speak to the person threatening America. A synthesized voice told him Americans were in for a treat. Just in case they hadn't seen footage of what had happened in London, they were going to get their own preview. "It will only be a small taste of what you can expect. Tonight, look to the west." The line went dead.

The president turned to his chief of staff. "Tell me we were able to trace that call."

The man shook his head. "He made the call from a military-grade satellite phone. We didn't have enough time to pinpoint where it came from."

"He said, 'look to the west.' Is he talking geographically? Does he mean Rosslyn on the other side of the river, or does he mean the West Wing?"

"It would be impossible for anyone to plant a bomb in the West Wing unless he or she is an insider."

The president went cold inside. "Have a bomb-sniffing dog go through the White House. We need to be proactive."

Aislinn unlocked her apartment door and stepped inside. The late afternoon sun's rays illuminated the picture she had painted of Tray at Main Beach. It still sat on her easel. She placed her handbag on the kitchen counter and walked over to the painting, lifting it high with both hands. *You're no longer welcome in my home.* She looked around quickly to determine the best surface to smash it against. She expected its destruction to feel cathartic. But as she raised it over her head, she realized not only a truth but something else quite unexpected. *If I destroy this, I'll be short a painting for the exhibit.* She lowered her arms. She'd never realized how much Molyneaux resembled Tray. Both were tall and lean yet muscular. Both were handsome and had thick dark hair. Molyneaux's face was more sculpted with his cleft chin and vertical frown lines that formed an eleven between his brows, and his eyes were dark with impossibly

271

long lashes. Tray's face was more relaxed, his complexion fairer, and his eyes a piercing blue.

Tray's eye color is not evident in this picture. If I lengthen the hair and contour the face, I can remove any resemblance to him. And no one needs to know who my new inspiration is.

She returned the painting to the easel, eager to get to work.

Deepak stretched out on his bed at the MGM National Harbor Hotel. His phone rang, and he was surprised to see it was from his father. The more he thought about their previous conversation, the more he thought his father would be happy to sacrifice him to reach a goal. The mechanized box and two-person helicopter both seemed like afterthoughts once Deepak had pointed out that he would be killed doing his father's bidding.

"Is everything in place, my son?"

"Yes."

"Good."

"I have a question."

"I don't have unlimited time. State your concern concisely."

"If I am to leave twenty minutes before the box with Hero's Knot opens, it means the artifact will be left behind and ultimately destroyed. If you're setting off the explosion because America refuses to pay, and the British previously refused to pay—but you've already paid more than five billion Kuwaiti dinar for the artifact—doesn't that boil down to an enormous waste of money?"

Once again, there was silence on the other end of the line.

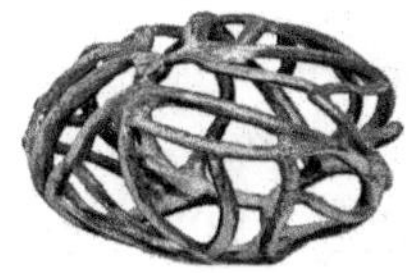

CHAPTER TWENTY-THREE

Aislinn measured carefully, making sure she could exhibit all four of her paintings in the space allotted to her at Guild Hall. She was a newer artist and a late addition to the roster of local talent exhibiting at the show, so even though she didn't like being in the back corner, she knew she was lucky to be included. Everyone else had already placed their sculptures or hung their canvases. She was the last artist to display her work. She hadn't wanted her paintings to look like every other canvas on the wall, so she had hurriedly framed them in driftwood, thinking it looked quite artistic. Now that it was up, she thought it looked hokey and removed the frames from the four pieces she'd decided to exhibit—all seascapes.

They look lost. Unprofessional. Unfinished. Aislinn studied the exposed sides of the canvases. *Sloppy.*

She dug through her bag for black Washi tape and ran it around the canvases' edges. *Not great, but better.* It was a cheap trick, but at least it defined the canvases and looked cleaner.

She walked out to her car, feeling both excited and exhausted. *This is it.*

THE FIRST LADY appeared flustered as she rushed around the White House executive residence, gathering items she needed to take on an impromptu trip. "Why did my mother call you instead of me about my father's heart attack?" she asked. "That is so unlike her."

The president did his best to sound sincere. "She said she would break down in tears talking to you and asked me to intervene. I think she has too much going on and feels overwhelmed. She said the two of you could discuss it when you get there."

He walked up behind her and wrapped his arms around her, kissing the side of her neck. "He's getting the best care available. I want you to take the kids and go. Edwina has already packed bags for them. A car is waiting downstairs to take you to the plane."

She turned and looked up at him, tears rolling down her face. "I feel so helpless."

"I know," he replied, "but the best place for you and the children right now is California with your parents."

ON THE OTHER side of the country in Sausalito, the First Lady's mother was just as confused as her daughter. "Matt only said that she's coming to visit us with the children, and under no circumstances should she be allowed to return to DC, unless we get the go-ahead from him first."

Her husband looked up from his newspaper. "Why?"

"Well, it sounds too far-fetched to mean he's having an affair, so I can only think something is wrong."

"I agree, but what?"

They figured it out several hours later when a news anchor—updating the bombing in London—announced that terrorists had made a more dangerous threat against the US capital.

THE NATIONAL NUCLEAR Security Administration took the lead in securing the Elkhorn National Laboratory in Washington, DC, to create the anti-nuke cocktail. Time was limited, yet there continued to be active discussions on how many parts per million of boron dust they would need to add to a canister of liquid nitrogen. Or whether boron or prismatic crystal particles would be the more effective deflector. All the while, they continued refining the original list of ingredients, calculating the size of the particles and the quantities necessary.

"I'm labeling the canisters BPCLN to designate what's inside them," one worker told Deputy Assistant Secretary Aguta.

"It's not very catchy," Aguta replied, "but it will do. Usually, operations like this have a name."

"Well then," the worker said, "I think we should call it *Operation Smokescreen.*"

"Let me check in case the administration has already given it a different designation. In the meantime, load these canisters for delivery to the airfield."

The National Nuclear Security Administration hired four crop dusters to spray the area, two flying north to south in unison, followed by two more flying west to east, while the first two planes repositioned. Because of the operation's proximity to the Ronald Reagan Airport, officials would need to delay or divert all national and international flights in the region, which would make many people unhappy.

The entire procedure needed intricate precision, yet speed was of the essence.

AT THE WHITE House, the president prayed spraying the Potomac would work. In fact, he was betting his life on it. Although he had arranged for the First Family to leave the area, he had chosen to stay. *A captain goes down with his ship.* He had decided against mass evacuation. There wasn't enough time to do a decent job of it, and it would cause a panic.

Once his family was safely onboard Air Force One, the president announced a large gas leak near the National Mall and points west and said all public places in the area would be closed. People scurried to get indoors or drive home. He hoped it would provide enough of a safeguard against whatever the terrorists had planned.

DEEPAK MOVED AS soon as he got word Davy Crockett was in place. He put the box containing Hero's Knot into a backpack and took the stairs up to the roof of the MGM National Harbor Hotel. Taking a deep breath, Deepak poked his head out the door to make sure no one else was there. It was late in the day, and he didn't expect to see anyone, but better safe than sorry. He stuck a travel magazine between the door and the jamb to keep it from fully closing and settled in an area where he could see Washington from the hotel's height advantage. No one had given him a specific time for the "demonstration." He looked at the position of the sun. *It's now or never.*

The nuke was small, and he was far enough away that he didn't need to worry about his safety. He took out Hero's Knot and waited.

It only took ten minutes for the artifact to complete its job.

THE GROUND RUMBLED. A plume of Potomac River water and smoke shot hundreds of feet into the air, followed by a mushroom cloud. Dozens of people, oblivious to what was going on, remained scattered about the area. They turned toward the noise and were almost instantly doused with radiation and pelted with flying debris. They crumpled to the ground, some crying out in shock or pain. It may have been a *small* demonstration, but it hit its mark.

PRESIDENT MYERS FELT the blast while monitoring updates inside the PEOC—Presidential Emergency Operations Center—located beneath the East Wing of the White House. Some CCTV cameras aimed at areas west of the National Mall flashed white, while others showed the plume of water and smoke. The president watched, knowing the prevailing winds would blow the fallout and smoke toward the northeast. He rubbed his face, feeling sorry for the people he'd seen on camera moments before. *Why the hell are they still outside despite announcements of a gas leak?* His heart ached for an unsuspecting portion of the population, miles from the district, who could still be affected by radiation carried by the wind. His torment was obvious in every line of his face.

"You would never have been able to evacuate everyone in time, Mr. President," a Cabinet member said. "You made the only call you could."

"This was only a small demonstration. The main blast is supposed to destroy Washington in its entirety.' We're talking about unfathomable death and carnage."

"Yes, but a team of scientists is working on a plan to stop it."

The president hurled his fountain pen across the room, the impact leaving a splatter of ink spots across the wall. "There are no guarantees that it will work. It could be nothing more than a pipe dream. We need to increase our terrorist alert code to red."

"Will do."

"Sir," his chief of staff interrupted, "your wife is on the line."

The president faked whatever bonhomie he could muster. "How's Sausalito?"

"Why did you send me away?" his wife demanded, her voice broken. "I should be there with you. At your side. We're a team."

"I won't deny that I wish I had you at my side right now, but this is not a safe place to be. I believe it's more important for you to be with our children and your family, away from this mayhem."

He heard his daughter's voice on the phone. "Daddy, are you okay? Are you still alive?"

"Yes, honey. I've been working down in a bunker below the White House. I'm safe, as long as I stay put. Keep your mother and your brother calm, will you? Tell them I love you all 'as big as the sky,'" he said, using his daughter's favorite expression from when she was little.

"Mom is really upset," she added.

"I knew she would be," her father said, "but I had to make sure she would be with you and your brother, keeping you safe in case anything catastrophic happened."

"But it's over, right?"

"Not yet, honey." *It may get worse before it gets better.*

"But I'm doing everything I can to stop the terrorists who are threatening our country."

"Mr. President," his chief of staff said.

"Honey, I need to go. I'll talk to you tomorrow. Remember, I love you all."

"You've seen a small demonstration of what we can do. Have the money ready to be wired into our account in the morning. If not, by sunset tomorrow, all that will be left of your city will be highly contaminated rubble."

The digital voice disconnected before the president had an opportunity to say anything.

Once again, communications technicians couldn't complete a trace.

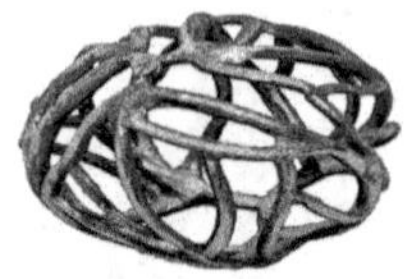

CHAPTER TWENTY-FOUR

Forgoing an introduction, Senator Phineas Paige greeted the media with a simple, "I'd like to thank everyone for joining me." His press conference was initially scheduled to take place on the National Mall, with the senator discussing the dangers of nuclear fuel rods. However, he'd hurriedly switched gears, changing his focus to the overall dangers of nuclear power following the previous evening's explosion in DC. That event also forced him to change his press conference to a virtual one.

Members of the media logged onto the link listed on the press release, hoping the senator would give them information and insight that the president had yet to address.

Paige disliked the idea of a virtual press conference. He enjoyed mingling with the media and felt he made more of a human connection in person. But some lunatic had detonated a bomb, removing that option.

The senator took a deep breath. "I would say *good morning*, but it's not a very good morning for many of us here in Washington. My heart goes out to all the victims, their families, and friends who have suffered as a result of last night's terrorist attack. I offer you my condolences for your pain and loss. I'm Senator Phineas Paige or, as many of you call me, the *anti-nuke senator*. Now you know why. It only takes one disillusioned dissident to turn our world upside down.

"The original intent of today's announcement was to declare my candidacy for the office of President of the United States of America. However, considering last night's tragic event, I'm putting my candidacy on the back burner and instead would like to address the cloud of nuclear threat we all live under every day.

"In our determination to protect ourselves during a World War some three-quarters of a century ago, we developed a weapon so devastating, it could vaporize its immediate surroundings in an instant, with temperatures as hot as fifty to one hundred million degrees. Did it help us win the war? Yes. But that was an extreme circumstance. The reason why any countries or military factions around the globe need to maintain this type of devastating firepower is vexing. And obviously, many of our predecessors felt the same, which is why we have the Nuclear Non-Proliferation Treaty in place. But it's not enough.

"I am vowing today to work toward decommissioning all nuclear warheads on American soil. I am promising you all that I will work tirelessly toward decommissioning all nuclear power plants within our borders. The remnants of nuclear waste can remain a hazard for thousands of years. Are we so egotistical to think that those of us alive during this period in history have the right to endanger future generations for more than a millennium?

"I know my stand on nuclear policies will cause our citizens to take some hits when it comes to the use of radiation in medical testing and treatment, which for many of you has proved invaluable. And I'm not saying people aren't free to leave our borders to seek such treatment elsewhere. But here at home, we must give a little to get a little—give up the perks of nuclear power to prevent the devastation it can cause. And we have to do it now before a possible nuclear winter wipes us all out for good.

"I'm asking you to join me in the fight against nuclear power. I'm Senator Phineas Paige, and I'm demanding safety over politics."

THE COFFEE FLOWED all night while the President of the United States and his Cabinet members debated paying the ransom. The Secretary of Homeland Security argued that it had never been policy to give in to terrorists, and he emphatically stated that he believed the odd cocktail of ingredients—put together by an ad hoc committee to stop the attack—would work. "They're the best scientific minds working in the capital right now, and we must trust them. If we pay the ransom, who's to say it doesn't become an annual fundraising event for the terrorists?"

THE FOLLOWING MORNING, the expected phone call to the president was put on speaker for everyone in the PEOC to hear.

"Are you ready to transfer the money into our account?" the digitally disguised voice asked.

"Absolutely not. We do not negotiate with terrorists,"

the president said in a strong voice, even though he had wanted to pay the ransom.

"It's your funeral. Say goodbye to your loved ones. In a few hours, your beautiful city will become part of your nation's history."

The president disconnected the call, missing the days when he could have had the satisfaction of slamming the phone down. "It's done," he said, rubbing his eyes. "I pray the solution our best minds have devised provides the miracle we so desperately need."

"The planes are loaded and ready for takeoff," his chief of staff said. "As soon as you give the word, I'll tell Ronald Reagan to stop all flights so spraying can begin."

"Do it. Initiate *Operation Smokescreen.*"

PEOPLE GROANED AS every flight information display board in Ronald Reagan National Airport changed simultaneously to show all flights being canceled or delayed. Those standing in line, ready to board, were allowed to proceed but cautioned that their aircraft could remain on the tarmac for a while before authorities cleared the plane to leave the ground.

Everyone else scrambled for seats. Those who couldn't find one, sat on the floor. The buzz of conversation did not sound cheerful.

A short time later, a public announcement sought to soothe aggravated tempers. "Due to turbulent conditions in the atmosphere, we have had to suspend all arriving and departing flights temporarily. We hope to resume service shortly. Thank you for your patience."

It helped that the skies were slightly overcast that day, making the ruse believable.

*

NOT TOO FAR away, four crop dusters took off, reducing their altitude over the Potomac as they sprayed their magic elixir. As soon as the liquid nitrogen met the water, it blossomed into a green-tinged fog that hugged the surface. It looked noxious but had no odor, and no ill effects were expected from it, not even to the neutrons, which would only be dispersed but not destroyed.

As the next few hours passed, each additional layer of BPCLN built upon itself, producing a shroud for the river.

TRAY CALLED JANE as he watched the crop dusters embark on their mission to avert disaster.

Hello?

"Hi, Aunt Jane. It's Tray."

Tray, I've been so worried about you. Where are you?

He turned to face away from people nearby and lowered his voice. "In Washington, DC—"

Thank God! I had no idea what had become of you. Her voice suddenly tightened. *You weren't near the explosion that some lunatic set off, were you?*

He squeezed his eyes shut, feeling the sting of tears start to build. He couldn't believe he might have to put her through the pain of his death all over again. "Aunt Jane, listen carefully. There is a situation in Washington. Something serious. That explosion was related to it, and I'm part of a team working to resolve the problem. But it's a big one. And I want you to know . . . that I love you and appreciate everything you have ever done for Carey and me."

Tray! Jane's voice sounded an octave higher than usual. *You're scaring me.*

"I don't mean to, and hopefully, everything will soon be under control. But I had to let you know what's in my heart in case things take a bad turn.

RRRROOOOWWWWRRRR! One of the crop dusters had circled and descended directly over Tray's head. Over the river, a miasma of green and gray wisps swirled above the choppy water.

Jane's voice quavered. *What was that noise?*

"With any luck, it's the sound of a miracle taking form."

It sounded like a dive-bomber.

"It's a crop duster." Tray shivered as the wind picked up. The sudden breezes threatened to tear the chemical cloud apart and dissipate it—lessening its effectiveness. His limbs tensed as he wondered if all their work had been for naught. "I've got to go, Jane. Remember, I love you." He ended the call before she could say anything else.

Jane grabbed her laptop and sank into the corner of her living room couch. Her neck ached with tension as she scanned all the major media sites, looking for breaking news out of Washington. There were plenty of recaps of the explosion that had already taken place by the Lincoln Memorial but nothing new since then.

She threw her head back and closed her eyes, sniffing as tears rolled down her cheeks. *Tray, what have you gotten yourself into?*

At the appointed hour, Deepak grabbed his possessions and returned to the MGM National Harbor Hotel roof to await the Mosquito ML. He scanned the skies but saw nothing. *Who knows how long I'll have to wait up here to do my father's bidding?*

When he finally saw the helicopter approaching, he stood up and signaled it before setting up the mechanized box. *Mission accomplished.* He grabbed his duffel and boarded the chopper. "Go," he demanded. "The faster, the better."

The crop dusters continued making passes across the Potomac River until they depleted their tanks. They returned to the field they had flown out of and were met with applause from the people who had gathered that morning to speed them on their way.

Very few people on the ground in that airfield were fully aware of the importance of what had just transpired. Many of them believed the government's announcement concerning mosquito spraying, though this operation seemed more controlled than previous spraying events. The spectacle of having four planes crisscrossing the river was enough to clue them in that something extraordinary had just taken place. But they had no idea just how serious this maneuver had been.

Everyone had done what they could. The rest was up to fate.

The Federal Aviation Administration in Washington received a complaint about an unauthorized helicopter landing on the roof of the MGM National Harbor Hotel in Maryland.

"Are you sure you didn't see a small plane disappearing behind the hotel as it got farther away? Helicopters are restricted in that area today because of turbulence in the atmosphere."

"I'm retired Air Force, young man. I think I know the difference between a helicopter and a small plane. I saw a two-seater helicopter land and take off from that hotel roof not five minutes ago."

The FAA clerk took the caller's information, saying, "We'll get right on it."

The transgression was considered so serious that it quickly made its way to the attention of AD Vasko.

She immediately headed to Abernathy's office to tell him about it. "Call it a hunch, but I want your man Lennox, SRR's Brodeur, and an agent from counterterrorism to go check out this helicopter. If it's nothing, it will only take up an hour of their time. But this complaint is unusual enough to warrant our interest. It also makes the hairs on the back of my neck stand at attention, and that's a sign I've learned to trust."

Officials gave the trio their orders, and as soon as the agents were tricked out with Kevlar and weapons, they headed out to the hotel.

Deepak had been in the air—en route to Dulles Airport—for close to fifteen minutes when his satellite phone rang.

It was his father. "We cannot afford to lose the artifact," Palanivel told his son. "Not until we've determined if we can duplicate it. It is too important to sacrifice. You must abort the mission."

"It's too late to abort the mission. It's done. The box will open in a few minutes, and the sun will do the deed. It's too late to go back."

"Your plane doesn't have to leave until you say so," his father said. "You have plenty of time to retrieve the artifact."

"No. I. Don't. If you want the artifact retrieved, you'll have to find someone else to do it." Deepak disconnected the call.

A minute later, the pilot received a private message. The Mosquito ML made a 180-degree turn.

"What are you doing?" Deepak asked.

"I've been instructed to return to the hotel to retrieve the package."

"You can't. We'll be killed."

"If I don't, your father just informed me that his people will murder my mother and father back in India. I cannot allow that to happen. I must retrieve the package or die trying."

"Then touch down and let me off."

"I was instructed to keep you with me at all times."

Deepak unhooked his seat belt, giving himself freedom of movement to grab for the controls. The tiny vehicle lurched as he and the pilot fought for command of the cyclic stick. The battle between the two men in the tiny helicopter made the vehicle bob and weave.

Deepak wrenched the stick toward him, causing the helicopter to bank sharply. Without a seatbelt and with no door to prevent him from falling out, gravity claimed his lower body. He hung on to the cyclic stick with every ounce of his energy, but his weight made it impossible for the pilot to straighten the tiny chopper. The helicopter spun out of control, spiraling downward until it crashed into an empty soccer field at Arrowbrook Centre Park, where it burst into flames.

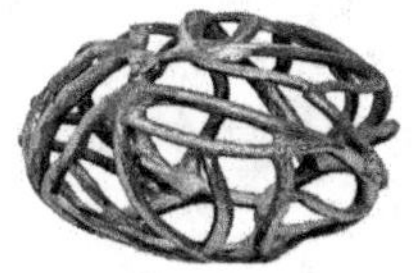

CHAPTER TWENTY-FIVE

TRAY RODE SHOTGUN, and Sophia sat quietly behind him while a special agent they'd just met broke every traffic law to get them to their destination as quickly as possible.

The only sound in the interior of the black Chevy Suburban was the faint hum of road noise. Tray tried to focus on the task at hand, but all he could think about was making a deal with God—something he had done since childhood to protect himself and his brother. *Just help us survive this, and I'll volunteer for public service.* Or, *Keep us safe, and I'll go to church every week.* At this point, he was willing to do whatever it took to stop nuclear warheads from being detonated en masse. He felt sweat beading on the back of his neck. His work for the FBI didn't often put him on the front line. He had never before admitted to himself a fear of dying, but he now realized the possibility had arrived, and it scared the hell out of him.

The MGM National Harbor Hotel towers rose above the landscape as they approached it, and moments later, they arrived.

ON THE HOTEL'S ROOF, the mechanized box popped open, allowing Hero's Knot to triangulate with the sun and redirect free neutrons toward the warheads beneath the Potomac.

Far below, Tray and his companions sweated it out, thinking they would never reach the hotel roof in time. Their elevator stopped on nearly every floor, returning the brunch crowd to their rooms. When the trio of agents finally arrived at the top floor, the assistant manager escorted them to the stairwell that would take them to the roof.

The view was spectacular. Over the past hour, the clouds had dissipated, and the sun cast the surrounding area in its best light. Tray was momentarily dazzled before remembering the task at hand.

"Let's split up. Look around for anything unusual."

The special agent who had accompanied them found indications that a lightweight chopper might have landed. He pulled out his phone, snapped a few photos, and called in his findings.

Sophia moved in a circular pattern around the landing site, looking for additional evidence that may have been displaced by the rotors.

Tray searched the opposite end of the building. He had a large area to inspect that needed more than a cursory once-over. *You can never tell where you might find something important.*

He rounded an air vent and gasped when he saw a familiar-looking object about twenty feet away, lying on an open series of metal squares. He kept his eyes focused on the ground around him for trip wires or additional evidence as he approached the artifact. As he got closer, he knew it was Hero's Knot.

He tried to fold up the metal plates and secure them. It was difficult at first because he couldn't see what held them together. A pin on the ground glimmered in the midday light, and after studying it a moment, he shoved it into a hinge-like edge on two of the sides of the metal contraption, holding them together. He folded over the hinged lid, leaving only two sides unattached, then he removed his Kevlar vest and covered the box, hoping it would help shield the artifact's signal. He wanted to search the ground for the other pins but needed to get the deadly object inside.

Although every one of his muscles tightened with tension, he appeared calm enough. Still, it took him a moment to find his voice. "Over here."

Sophia sprinted in his direction. "What is that?"

"It's what we've been looking for."

"Hero's Knot?"

"Yes."

"How do we stop it from working?"

"I hope closing the lid and cutting off a direct view of the sun is enough, or else I can't be responsible for what happens to us in the next few minutes."

The other special agent contacted AD Vasko, confirming Tray had found the artifact as they headed across the roof. "What do you want us to do with it?"

"Keep the damn thing out of the sun," Vasko said. "I'm sending a bomb disposal unit to pick it up. It may not be a bomb, but I want to ensure it's locked in a place with no access to sunlight."

"We've got to get it off this roof," Tray said. He looked at the assistant manager. "Do you have any gaffer or duct tape I can use to secure this thing? I don't want it to open while I'm carrying it downstairs."

The other special agent called out to him. "The bomb squad is meeting us by the front door, off the lobby."

"Th … that thing's a bomb?" The assistant manager turned pale and started to shake as if he had given some thought to why the FBI was at the hotel, but a bomb scare hadn't crossed his mind.

"It's all right," Sophia said in her most soothing voice.

"We need tape to hold this thing together, so it doesn't pop open," Tray said. "Sophia, perhaps you can escort the assistant manager downstairs to get those items?"

She took the man's arm and led him to the elevator, removing him from the direct vicinity of the artifact.

A few minutes later, she met Tray and the other special agent inside the rooftop structure housing the elevator. She had several rolls of tape, causing Tray to smile at the excess. He immediately started taping the lid to the sides of the box. When he felt confident it wouldn't easily pop open, he wrapped tape around the rest of the container, first from front to back, then side to side. It was a mess when he finished, but a very secure mess. "Where's our friend?"

"He had important hotel business to take care of," Sophia answered, "but he graciously gave me a key for the private elevator so we could go directly down to the ground level without stopping."

The trio quickly descended to the lobby below, hoping the bomb squad was already waiting.

*

"Cradle Hero's Knot like a baby," Sophia told Tray. "But don't get too close to any of the guests here at the hotel."

"A baby swaddled in Kevlar?"

"They won't know that," she surmised. "Just walk quickly and pat it on its back."

"It's a bomb," the other agent said. "Is that wise?"

"It's not a bomb," Sophia and Tray said in unison.

"It's an ancient artifact with special properties," Tray added. "But it won't explode."

"And neither should anything else," Sophia chimed in, "as long as we keep little Tray Junior here out of the sun." She tickled the artifact where she imagined its chin might be.

Outside, the bomb disposal truck had parked a short distance away, within view of the main entrance. It sat with the door to the iron containment chamber already open. Tray huddled over the artifact to shield it from the sun, finally slipping it inside the truck. "It's all yours."

The truck left immediately, and Tray let out a sigh of relief.

"We should head back," the third agent said.

Sophia gave him one of her dazzling smiles. "Lead the way."

The Director of the Federal Bureau of Investigation called the White House to inform the president that the FBI had taken possession of the artifact. While he waited for the call to go through, his outer office filled with people who came to confirm the scuttlebutt. When it came to communications within the bureau, word traveled quickly. It was as if they had never heard the saying *loose lips sink ships.*

The president's voice became hopeful. "You're telling me there's no chance of a nuclear explosion? That we're in the clear?"

The FBI Director repeated the president's words to Tray.

Tray nudged Sophia with his elbow, "Has it been more than fifteen minutes since I called you over on the rooftop?"

She looked at her watch. "More than a half hour."

Tray smiled, nodding at the FBI Director. "We're in the clear."

Everyone in the outer office went wild when they heard Tray's confirmation. Each of them suspected that they might have died on the job that day. It came with the territory, although they had never come so close to death's door.

THE FIRST FAMILY returned to DC later that night. Tray and Sophia received personal calls from the president, thanking them for their service and inviting them to the White House for dinner the following evening.

"I've never been to the White House before," Sophia mused. "It will give me and the PM something in common to talk about."

"I've never been to the White House either," Tray replied. "That should give *you* and *me* something in common to talk about."

"Oh, I'm sure we can find a lot more things in common to entertain ourselves with now that we're back together again."

"Are we back together?" he asked, pulling her into his arms.

"There's no one else I'd rather risk my life with," she replied, before seeking out his lips with her own.

*

THE WHITE HOUSE Social Secretary issued several more invitations to the dinner planned for the following evening. It was very last minute, but no one on the invitation list declined. On the contrary, they were all delighted to attend the affair.

Notice also went out for a virtual memorial service to pay respect to those who had lost their lives or been injured in the explosion near the Lincoln Memorial. The Environmental Protection Agency declared that even though the radiation levels at the National Mall had decreased, it would be several weeks before it would be safe to congregate there. Instead, the service would be televised from the Capitol so that anyone wishing to attend the memorial could do so virtually.

MEANWHILE, IN BETHESDA, the director of the Walter Reed National Medical Center walked into the private room assigned to 'Patient X.' The director's closest friend, a thoracic surgeon, was studying his patient's electronic health record on a digitized screen.

Just a few feet away, the patient's chest rose and fell with the help of a respirator. Aside from the usual monitors and standard hospital furniture, the room lacked decoration. No get-well cards. No flowers from well-wishers. No worried family members waiting for signs of recovery.

"How is our patient doing?" the director asked.

"As well as can be expected."

"Would that include the ability to be in two different places at once?"

"I like to think I'm an excellent surgeon, but that would take a miracle."

"So divine intervention?"

"To be in two places at once? Yes."

"If Walter Reed weren't already 'on the map,'" the director made finger quotes, "this would surely do it. I was contacted today by an insurance company that wanted to know how a patient could be recovering from a concussion in an upstate New York hospital while he's simultaneously incapacitated in a coma in Maryland."

"What are you talking about?"

"They received a bill from both this hospital and a medical center in New York for the emergency treatment of *our* patient."

The surgeon pushed the digital screen out of the way. "First of all, why did *we* submit an insurance claim? That wasn't authorized."

"Blame it on an overzealous clerk. It was a mistake, and we've taken her to task. Regardless, it went out, and now it is raising an intriguing question."

"What was the date of the service in New York?"

"Last weekend."

"I'm surprised the system worked that fast."

"They now want proof that we are indeed seeing to the needs of this patient and that he is indeed incapacitated."

"Not for long. I believe he's ready to rejoin the world of the living."

"Tell me more.

The surgeon checked the patient's wound and nodded to himself. "We induced his coma; however, he's stabilized now. His lung is properly inflated. There are no signs of swelling. The bullet wound has healed nicely. So, I've just ordered that he be taken off Propofol. He should be alert in less than twenty-four hours. I'd even go so far as to say by morning."

*

The president's chief of staff handed him his itinerary. "You have a full schedule for the next few days, Mr. President."

"And to think I just wanted to take a step back and contemplate life."

"Excuse me, sir." His chief of staff stepped away to answer the phone. "Mm-hmm … Yes … Could you repeat that? … I see. I'll let him know right away … Oh? … Hold on, please."

"Now what?" the president asked.

"It's one of your advisors. He wants to speak with you personally." He offered the president the phone.

"This is President Myers." After listening for a minute, the president exclaimed, "Are you kidding me?"

"No, sir, I would never do that," the person on the other end of the line replied.

"I want to meet him."

"Of course, Mr. President. I'm sure that can be arranged."

"Make sure you do."

Sophia invested her morning in looking for the perfect outfit to wear to dinner with the president and his family. Satisfied with her selections, she allowed herself to indulge in an afternoon of pampering at her hotel spa.

She took her time getting dressed in an asymmetrical column of navy blue silk. The length and high neckline made it demure enough for the White House, while the figure-revealing drape made it sexy enough to entice Tray. She slipped on a pair of stilettos and grabbed a beaded clutch. Her reflection in a full-length mirror showed proof of a successful shopping spree, right down to her choice of limiting her jewelry to a stunning pair of faux sapphire earrings.

It's going to be a good night.

TRAY RETURNED TO his brother's apartment and tried on Carey's tux. It hurt to think his brother was dead, but Carey would have loved the irony of his tux having dinner at the White House, even if *he* couldn't.

Tray showered and shaved, his beard soon disappearing into history. However, he still used his beard filler to neaten the uneven growth in what now appeared to be a military buzz cut.

He looked for his watch, not remembering the last time he'd seen it. *The day of the murder?* He checked the pocket of the pants he'd worn that day. *It's confirmed. I'm a creature of habit.* When he pulled out the watch, a piece of metal fell to the ground. Tray stooped to pick it up. *Carey's key—at least, I think it's Carey's. It has to be.* He thought back to the crime scene. *The cord around Carey's neck was broken.* He looked through Carey's dresser and found a black braided titanium neck chain his brother used to wear. It was just the right gauge for the key. Tray threaded the key onto it and slipped it around his neck, under his dress shirt. *I need to find out what this key opens. I wonder if Caterina would know.* Then he realized he would have to break Carey's death to his girlfriend. His shoulders slumped. *How am I ever going to do that?*

But first, he had a White House dinner to attend, followed by his inevitable parting with Sophia.

*

TRAY AND SOPHIA arrived at the White House together. Many members of the president's Cabinet were already there, as well as the FBI and National Security officials who had played important roles in saving Washington, DC. They mingled over cocktails and hors d'oeuvres, happy they had averted a disaster.

The First Lady thanked Tray and Sophia personally for saving her husband and her city.

"All in the line of duty, ma'am," Tray answered. "It's what we were hired to do."

"Surely Wing Commander Brodeur was not hired to protect us."

Sophia smiled. "Anything for an ally."

As the cocktail party warmed up, the decibel level increased until one last guest entered the room. The sudden silence was deafening. If the newest guest had just slipped in the door, he may not have disrupted the flow of conversation. But his wheelchair and his uncanny resemblance to one of the guests of honor made people hold their breaths.

The sea of DC insiders parted as the new guest was wheeled toward the president and first lady.

Tray turned to see who had entered and sucked in a breath as the crystal cocktail glass he'd been holding shattered on the marble floor.

"You're in trouble, now," Sophia whispered before turning around to see what had caused his reaction. "Oh, my!"

Tray dropped to his haunches in front of the wheelchair. "How can you be here?" Overcome by emotion, he could barely speak. "You died in my arms."

"You know, *The Princess Bride* was always one of my favorite movies." Carey gave Tray a crooked smile. "I was only 'mostly dead.' Either that, or I came back to haunt you. However, I know you don't believe in ghosts, so here I am—forced to live. How are you, bro?"

Tray stared, open-mouthed, a second longer before ingrained protocol took over. He stood and turned, saying, "Mr. President, have you met my twin brother, Carey Lennox?"

"I have not had the honor." The president offered his hand to Carey. "Mr. Lennox, it's a pleasure to meet you. I hope you don't mind if I call you Carey. Since there are now two Lennoxes in the room, I wouldn't want the conversation to become confusing."

"The pleasure is all mine, Mr. President. You can call me anything you want."

"Just don't call him late for dinner," Tray joked.

Carey groaned.

"That won't happen tonight, gentlemen," the president said. "I've just been signaled that dinner is served."

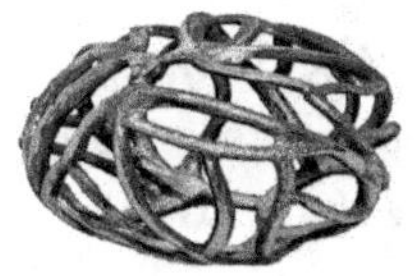

CHAPTER TWENTY-SIX

As the evening wound down, many of the guests departed the White House reception. However, the president, the FBI director, and the National Security Council chairman asked Carey to remain. Carey, in turn, asked if Tray could be privy to the meeting, and Tray requested that Sophia be allowed to stay. Considering the roles Tray and Sophia had played in saving the District earlier in the week, the president agreed.

They all adjourned to the Oval Office, which had a calming effect with its soft shades of cream and blue and its sound-absorbing furnishings. Instead of sitting at the Resolute desk, the president chose an armchair at the opposite end of the room. Everyone else sat on one of two nearby couches except for Carey, who sat opposite the president. Once they all settled, the president nodded at National Security Council Chair Vernon Cruikshank, who turned to Carey. "What have you found out about the saboteur?"

Carey rubbed his head. "Not as much as I would have

liked. Unfortunately, someone stopped me before I could retrieve one last piece of information."

"And what was that?"

Carey paused as if remembering wasn't as easy as he expected. "A journal. It belongs to a politician's campaign manager. It's supposedly here in Washington. I had an appointment to meet with someone about it the day after my premature demise. Considering what happened to me, I don't know if that person will still be willing to risk his neck to get hold of the book."

"Damn," the FBI director stood suddenly and began pacing.

"Do you know where the book is?" Cruikshank asked.

"It could be in the guy's office. It could be in his home. Or he could keep it in an inside jacket pocket, carrying it with him wherever he goes. In other words, I don't know."

Sophia's eyes sparkled. "I do so love undercover work."

"You can't steal the journal," Tray teased. "You're not even American."

She shrugged. "I didn't know US citizens had a lock on thievery."

"If anyone should retrieve the journal, it should be me," Tray said.

"You both could go," Carey said. "Sophia has a much better chance of getting close to the guy. But Tray could hang in the background, seemingly unattached to her, and cover her back."

"I don't think, after what the two of them accomplished this week, and after getting their pictures plastered all over the media, that anyone would consider Tray 'seemingly unattached' to Ms. Brodeur," the president observed.

Carey sat quietly, except for his hands, which seemed

to be having a conversation with his brain, until they, too, settled. "I might have slept through a lot of that."

Cruikshank refused to be deterred. "Can't we mount a case with what you've already collected?"

Carey closed his eyes and shook his head, dejected. When the hospital returned his personal belongings, he looked for a special key, but it wasn't there. "All the evidence is probably gone by now. I locked everything in a safe deposit box at the Bank of America in Arlington. Unfortunately, my attacker must have stolen the key. I used to wear it around my neck to keep it safe. But now it's gone."

"The key!" Tray hurriedly removed his tie and opened the top button of his shirt. He pulled out his chain and dangled the key in front of his brother. "This key?"

"Where'd you get that?" Carey asked.

"It was sitting in a pool of blood next to your body on the day you were shot. All your other keys were gone."

Carey narrowed his eyes. "Is that my chain?"

"Could be. Maybe this is a good time to tell you this is your tux. And shoes."

Carey leaned forward and stared at his brother's choice of footwear. "Tray!"

"But the socks and boxers I'm wearing are my own," Tray rushed to add.

The president burst out laughing.

Sophia shook her head in disbelief.

The director just wanted to know, "So we still have access to the information in the box?"

"Apparently, Tray has," Carey answered. "We can retrieve it first thing in the morning."

"Oh." Sophia sighed. "But that means you don't need me. I guess I'll have no excuse to miss my flight to London."

Tray reached over and grabbed her hand. "What time does your plane leave?"

"Six a.m."

"I'll take you to the airport."

"I need to be there by three o'clock."

"We'll drop off Carey at home, then I'll take you to the hotel to pack. I'll take you to the airport before I go back to Carey's for a few hours of sleep."

Carey groaned. "You haven't been sleeping in my bed as well, have you?"

"Cut me some slack. A man must be allowed to keep some shred of dignity. I've been living in your guest room, where I always stay. Besides, someone trashed your condo and ripped the mattress in the primary bedroom to shreds."

"Living?"

"We'll talk later."

Everyone agreed that Carey and Tray would meet the FBI director and the National Security Council chair in the bank lobby when it opened the following morning.

At the airport, Sophia sadly said goodbye. "I hate going back to England. But it's time to report in and be debriefed."

"I wish you could stay," Tray said. "I'm going to miss you."

"You can always come to visit. I hear there's talk of a never-before-seen Caravaggio discovered in a peer's attic in Wiltshire."

"Really? Or are you just pulling my leg?"

"Scout's honor. Although I would pull your leg if I thought it would get you to stay with me."

Tray smiled. "You have my permission."

Sophia's shoulders sagged. "Unfortunately, not right now. I'm on the SRR's payroll, and my superiors are waiting. However, I'm well overdue for a long, leisurely vacation. Preferably somewhere exotic, where they don't fuss with a lot of clothing." She gave him a slow wink and a smile. Then she turned and walked to the front of the airport security checkpoint without looking back.

Tray watched her hips sway, already missing her. "I'll see what Abernathy has on the Caravaggio and get back to you," he called out, just before Sophia used her diplomatic passport to become next in line.

She was glad she was allowed through security quickly. She didn't want Tray to see her cry.

The Bank of America Financial Center's manager opened the bank on his day off just to escort the gentlemen and lady down to the safe deposit bank vault. AD Vasko had accompanied the FBI Director in case she needed to mobilize agents immediately.

The bank manager and Carey inserted their keys. The lock released, and they removed the box to a private room.

The manager left them to sort through the contents of the box. As Carey explained the significance of each piece of evidence, Chairman Cruikshank's eyes grew wider. "You have more than enough information here to nail the bastards."

"Perhaps," Carey agreed, "but isn't a lot of it circumstantial? If I only had that journal, it could seal the deal."

"And who did you say the journal belonged to?"

"A man named Achille Pasquarelli."

Cruikshank grimaced. "Senator Paige's campaign manager?"

"I'm not sure who he works for. I'm still a little hazy on a lot of the details from just before being hospitalized."

"Pasquarelli works for Paige," Cruikshank answered. "I wouldn't trust the guy to lend me a penny. His record is clean, but let's just say some of my personnel have implicated Pasquarelli several times in connection with actions that border on shady."

"Is there anything we should be doing immediately?" Vasko asked.

"I'll get a search warrant," the director said. "You assemble a team. Maybe we can close the book on these nuclear plant incidents before something else goes haywire."

"Do you want me to break the news to Aunt Jane?" Tray asked Carey as they ate takeout in Carey's condo.

"Don't you think it would be better if I did it in person?"

"You're in no condition for a long car trip. But I have a Zoom account. Let me set up a call, get you connected, and then I'll text Aunt Jane and ask her to Zoom me because I have something serious to discuss."

A few minutes later, they were all connected, although Carey had moved off camera so she wouldn't see him right away.

Jane sounded out of breath. She ran her fingers through her hair, forcing a few strands out of place. "Tray, what is it? Has something else happened?"

"Nothing bad, Aunt Jane."

"Please, we've been through this before. Just call me Jane." She picked up a cup of coffee and took a sip.

Carey shifted the laptop, so it faced him. "Hey, Just Jane! I'm not dead."

She spit the coffee out all over the screen. "Uh ... uh ... uh ..."

"You idiot," Tray said. "Are you trying to make her have a heart attack?"

"We buried you," Jane cried.

They watched Jane disappear behind a handful of tissues as she wiped the screen. "No, you didn't," Tray cut in. "You buried me."

"How can this be?"

Carey gulped a swig of beer before answering. "It's true. Tray thought I was dead when I passed out in his arms after somebody shot me. I guess I'd lost a lot of blood and barely had a heartbeat. Even the police thought I was dead, but the medical examiner figured it out. He also discovered that I'd recently been exposed to radiation. When he wanted to learn where *Tray Lennox* might have come in contact with radioactivity, he tried calling his nearest relative. *Me.* He couldn't reach me, so he called the EPA, which called the NRC, which had a report on file that said Carey Lennox had been exposed to radiation the night before the shooting. The NRC knew I was working undercover, so they told the ME to refer to me only as Patient X. They asked the coroner to attend to me and then transfer me to Walter Reed Hospital in Bethesda, where I've been ever since, mostly in a coma.

"The head of the FBI also knew I was alive," Carey continued, "but said nothing because he wanted to flush out the killer. So did Tray, who made everyone believe he was the victim."

"So, no one died!"

"Nope," Carey answered.

Someone died, Tray thought. But he would only discuss that particular death with FBI officials. He leaned in to put his arm around Carey's shoulder. "So here we are, together again, one not-so-big happy family."

"No wonder they wouldn't let me have an open coffin," Jane said. "They told me they had to keep it sealed because of time constraints. Now that I think of it, that's ridiculous."

"Was anyone in the coffin?" Tray asked.

"I don't know," Jane replied. "But if he thinks he's getting a free ride in my burial plot, he's got another thing coming. I want that coffin exhumed."

"Keep that on the back burner," Carey said. "We can't go into details right now, but Tray and I will be inundated with work over the next week. After that, we'll assist you in exhuming and evicting any freeloaders."

By early afternoon, federal officials had the warrants to move forward on their investigation into a nuclear saboteur. Carey was still too weak to take part. However, Tray received permission to join the operation. At this point, he knew as much as his brother did about the acts of sabotage that had taken place.

Achille Pasquarelli lived in the end unit of a nicely maintained brick row house on Capitol Hill. Tray whistled when he saw the house. "Where does a campaign manager get the money to afford digs like this?"

Bob Sarinana, who oversaw executing the warrant, studied Tray. "You're not from around here, are you?"

"New York. Manhattan, actually," Tray answered.

"DC is different."

"Apparently."

"You're the one from the Art Crime Team, aren't you?"

"*Mea culpa.*"

"Let's get one thing straight. You being here is a

courtesy. You're only here in an observational capacity, so stay out of my team's way."

It wasn't just Sarinana's team waiting to execute the warrant. The SWAT team and DC police were also there as backup. Sarinana gave the signal, and his people fanned out around the house in case Pasquarelli tried to make a break for it. When everyone was in place, he banged on the door.

Fifteen seconds later, he banged even louder.

"Overkill," Tray muttered to himself.

Ironically, Achille was sitting in his second-floor office, updating his journal, when he heard the pummeling on his door. The ferocity of it made him angry. *Who the hell is that?* He locked the journal in a shallow opening, hidden behind a section of baseboard that was held in place magnetically. Then he thundered down the stairs, yelling, "Hold your horses."

Sarinana handed him the search warrant and waved his team into the house.

Hercule rushed for the door and began barking. The one-hundred-pound dog was bigger than most labs and was a force to be reckoned with.

"Please restrain your dog," Sarinana stated.

Outside, a crowd gathered to see what all the commotion was about. It was a weekend, so a lot of people were at home, and the glut of federal and police vehicles with bubble gum machines on the roofs acted like a beacon saying, *something's happening here.* Social media alerted the reporters, and soon, police were forced to set up barricades to keep onlookers back.

"Put your dog out in the backyard before someone accidentally puts a bullet in him," one agent snarled.

"Stand down," Sarinana told him. He turned to Achille. "Your dog will be safer outside."

Achille sent Hercule into the garden with his favorite chew toy. Then he sat in his living room, reading the search warrant. His blood boiled. *How the hell do they know I have a 'written record, diary, or journal detailing transactions I made with people?*

As much as he wanted to scream his head off, he sat quietly, not offering any information that could be used against him. He watched as FBI agents seized his computer, tablet, cell phones, answering machine, the Echo Show in his kitchen that his sister had given him last Christmas, and the contents of the desk in his office.

Sarinana handed Achille a receipt detailing everything they had taken. "We'll be in touch."

THAT EVENING, ACHILLE received a call from Senator Paige. "What the hell is going on?"

Achille took another sip of his single malt scotch. He carefully placed the glass down on his desk. "The feds served me with a search warrant today."

"What are they looking for?"

"Evidence of tampering at nuclear power plants."

"How can you say that so calmly?" the senator practically screamed.

"Because they didn't find what they were looking for. So, relax."

The sound of Paige's hand slamming the desktop was loud and clear. "How can I relax when everyone on the Hill is calling me to find out why the FBI was all over my campaign manager's home?"

"*We* have not done anything. I've got it all under control. I'll admit today's visit was a bit of a surprise, but that's all it was. Sleep well, Senator. No matter what anyone says, your star is still rising."

CHAPTER TWENTY-SEVEN

Early Monday morning, federal agents swarmed the Dirksen Senate Office Building before entering the offices of Senator Phineas Paige with a search warrant.

They confiscated Achille Pasquarelli's work computer and all the paperwork from his desk but did not disturb the senator's inner office or his paperwork.

Pasquarelli tried to enter the office, but was stopped in the hallway and prevented from going in. As he stood in the corridor, seething, his phone rang. He looked at caller ID and walked a short distance away, but judging by the guys with guns now stationed all around him, he dared not go further.

Paige was on the other end of the line, calling to tell him the FBI was ripping Pasquarelli's desk apart. He sounded more upset than the campaign manager had ever heard him. "I'm waiting for them to barge into *my* office and confiscate everything of mine as well, which would make it impossible for me to do the job I was elected to do!"

"I'm on it, Senator. I'm cooperating with officials to get to the bottom of this boondoggle." He lowered his voice. "You have nothing to worry about. Just try to remain calm."

"I'm running for president, Achille, in case you've forgotten, and appearances are everything!"

Achille could tell that the senator spoke through gritted teeth. *I'm going to have to sacrifice something.*

SARINANA PUSHED AWAY the last box of paperwork taken from Achille Pasquarelli's home. "We've been through all these files twice, and there's no mention of a journal in here or suspicious references to any of the nuclear power plants across the country," he told his boss. "I feel like we're spinning our wheels."

AD Vasko sighed. "I'll inform the NRC. Maybe they'll want one of their people to look at what we have."

The Nuclear Regulatory Commission called back, saying it definitely wanted to do so and that someone would come by to pick up the boxes that afternoon.

Sarinana nearly blew a gasket when he heard about the call. He immediately called the NRC back, saying, "I'm sorry you were misinformed. We are not sending these boxes to your office. We're responsible for everything, and it's staying right here. If your people want to take a gander, they're welcome to come here to see it."

An hour later, Tray pushed Carey's wheelchair into the National Security Branch offices. Sarinana set them up in an unused conference room with the boxes of files officials had confiscated. They worked for several hours, discussing little bits and pieces they saw, with Carey filling in background information.

"I've seen this same odd name a few times," Tray mused, "and can't help picturing the guy as rangy, with a crew cut, and one eye that opens bigger than the other."

"Sounds like Steiger, a guy on the maintenance crew who's always bumming cigarettes off people."

"That's the name! Steiger. Is that his real name?"

"It is on his employment records. But why is his name in Pasquarelli's files? One is a political campaign manager, and the other cleans nuclear power plants."

Tray pushed the box within Carey's reach. "You tell me. He's in the top file and the bottom one. And one in the middle, but I couldn't say which one right off the bat."

Carey studied the top file. His eyes widened, and he removed a piece of paper, waving it at his brother to attract his attention. "It's a canceled check made out to Steiger Bob. This opens up a much bigger can of worms. Why would Pasquarelli be paying a power plant maintenance worker?"

"Good question," Tray answered. "Maybe we need to bring him in for questioning."

He informed AD Vasko of what they'd found, and she asked Sarinana to pick up Steiger Bob. "I hope this is the break we need," she told the twins. "If we could resolve two major cases in the same week, that would be a big win for us."

STEIGER HAD EVAPORATED into thin air. The last power plant he had worked at said he just stopped showing up for work. He had cleaned out his apartment, and none of his known associates knew what had happened to him. He was just gone.

Achille Pasquarelli heard about the inquiries and sighed with relief that he'd had the foresight to send the man on an extended vacation under an assumed name. But it also limited him. He had thought about offering Steiger up on a platter. Now, he would have to give up Mark Allen instead.

Allen already had a black mark against him. He had committed fraud by impersonating Pete Majewski and getting a job with the dead man's credentials. It didn't matter that Mark had his own Reactor Engineering degree. He had been fired from a previous position for negligence and had ended up blacklisted.

Pasquarelli gathered whatever evidence he would need. The FBI had not yet tried to access the safe deposit box he kept outside of DC. As soon as the fiasco at the Dirksen building ended, he would placate the senator in person, then drive out to retrieve the necessary paperwork for a meeting with federal agents.

ALL THE PUZZLE pieces fit. Achille had created a timeline of Mark Allen/Pete Majewski's employment. He listed—in detail—every act of sabotage Mark Allen had committed. Achille had previously requested copies of Mark Allen's and Peter Majewski's college records and affidavits showing that they were friends and roomed together. He had pictures of the two of them together and yearbook pictures of each of them individually. And he had a copy of Peter Majewski's obituary, as well as both Mark Allen's and bogus Peter Majewski's job applications.

He wrote in his notes:

Mr. Allen was enraged when he lost his job at the hands of Carey Lennox. He asked us for help, but I told the senator we shouldn't get involved, even if he was a constituent. I had a bad feeling about Mark Allen from the get-go. I didn't think a person fired from a highly perilous job should be allowed to work again in such a dangerous sector. Who knew what type of revenge he might try to exact?

I did not want to stay in contact with Mr. Allen, but he kept badgering me, and in the interest of courtesy, I forced myself to return his calls. You can probably see proof of those returned calls in my phone records. Mr. Allen also texted me, but not as often, and I sometimes replied. But I would have preferred not to be contacted by him at all.

Then he did the unthinkable. He threatened to disclose that my younger sister had turned to prostitution in her youth to support a drug habit. While true, she has since cleaned up her act, married, and has a husband, two children, and a respectable job. Rather than have him ruin her life, I began paying him regularly to keep him quiet.

This man, who is already perpetrating fraud against his employer and blackmail against my sister, should be considered a person of interest, brought in for questioning, and possibly arrested. I realize telling anyone about him puts me in a precarious position because I believe he will try to implicate me

in his crimes to save himself.
My only role is to offer him the courtesy
of this senatorial office and protect my sister.
Nothing more.

Achille looked over his collection of evidence before re-reading the latest addition to the journal and thought he may have missed his calling as a fiction writer. He kept one copy of his evidence regarding Mark Allen at home, hidden in his secret baseboard compartment, and he took another to work, where he locked it in his desk drawer. He meandered down to the Dirksen Senate Dining Room, cell phone in hand, and placed a bogus call where he knew he'd be overheard.

"It's protected," Achille said in a voice that sounded like he was trying to whisper. "The FBI already searched my desk and seized everything in it, so it's the safest place to hide something because lightning won't strike twice in the same place. Please," he added dramatically, "your secret is safe with me."

He returned to the office and told Senator Paige there might be a secondary search warrant. He suggested the senator head over to Capitol Hill and work in the Environment and Public Works Committee room to avoid being disturbed.

Paige didn't need to be told twice. The last place he wanted to be was an office under siege.

Over the next few hours, Achille put together supplies and copies of files he would need for his desk. He accomplished a few of the work-related items he needed to take care of before Sarinana and his men converged on the senatorial office.

"Not again," he complained.

"Step away from the desk." One agent grabbed Achille's arm as soon as he stood up and dragged him across the room, where he held him in place.

Achille watched an agent use a lock pick to jimmy his locked desk drawer. He observed the slight widening of the eyes as the agent went through the evidence, followed by the hushed discussion between her and Sarinana.

The lead agent approached Achille. "Mr. Pasquarelli, we would like you to accompany us to the J. Edgar Hoover Building for questioning."

"Am I being arrested?"

"Not at this time."

Achille huffed, not showing how delighted he felt that they had responded to his plan the way he'd hoped.

Almost everything Achille had put together on Mark Allen/Pete Majewski was true. Except for blackmailing his sister—which Achille had used to disguise ongoing regular payments for *services rendered*—he had built a solid case against the reactor engineer. He just hoped when the shit hit the fan, it wouldn't splatter all over the senator. Or him.

MARK ALLEN OWNED an industrial loft in the Manchester area of Richmond, Virginia. It was a three-story property with sweeping views from a rooftop deck. He would have never been able to afford it, if it hadn't been for the monthly automatic payments deposited into Pete Majewski's bank account. The money didn't come from paychecks—those he received from the North Anna Nuclear Generating Station, where he had previously been on staff. The automatic payments came from an agreement he had *with a government official* to compensate him for the private work he did.

He'd been staying out of town ever since the Diablo Canyon incident but needed to fly back to DC for the day to close up his condo and pack some personal belongings.

Unfortunately, his healthy bank account and ownership of a trendy loft did nothing to stop an army of federal agents from invading his home with an arrest warrant.

His first mistake was trying to save himself. As he fabricated reasons why he had taken a specific step or been in a particular place at a given time, federal agents refuted Allen's answers with copies of the evidence they had seized from Pasquarelli's desk. He kept tripping over his own lies, and agents stopped him cold when they produced proof that he had illegally assumed Pete Majewski's identity.

His second mistake was offering up Achille Pasquarelli on a platter. He claimed the campaign manager and Senator Paige had hired him to tamper with the equipment in power plants and even paid him regularly. "You can check with my bank."

Federal agents refuted that argument, saying they had a copy of a diary listing the blackmail payments he received.

"I don't know anything about blackmail." Unfortunately, by then, agents believed they had enough evidence to bury him.

He had one last piece of information that might save him, but he wanted a lawyer first. He'd done enough damage thinking he could defend himself. "I won't say another word without an attorney."

GRACE ESMOND WALKED into the interrogation room, where she would interview her new client. She was in her fifties, a Harvard graduate, and had a lengthy resume as a successful defense attorney. She took a seat across from Mark Allen, who was already waiting, and sized him up. She thought he looked smarmy and acted like he was smarter than everyone else around him. However, he was ready to make a deal, so she heard him out.

After hearing the evidence, Grace took the case. "I'll do my best to push for a deal. But I have to be honest with you. It appears they have enough evidence for a conviction."

"But some of it is made up," Mark complained. That stuff about blackmail payments is a lie. Those payments were to reimburse me for systematically damaging nuclear power plants."

Grace stood and stretched. She went over the finer points with him again as she paced the tiny room. She looked down at him, "Why would anyone want you to damage a nuclear power plant?"

"We're talking about Senator Phineas Paige—or at least his campaign manager. Paige hates nuclear power plants and wants to abolish them. If problems start popping up all over the place, it makes them easier to close down. I received regular paychecks because this was a concerted effort to get the job done so Paige could run for president. 'Safety over politics' is a lot of hogwash. He should change his slogan to 'winning at any cost.'"

"That's a very serious accusation. Do you have proof?"

"No. But I know the name of a guy who helped me do some of the mischief around a couple of power plants."

"Mischief?" Her voice was hard. "Isn't that downplaying it a bit? If any of those reactors had melted down, we'd be talking about lives lost. Mass murder."

"Except I have no vested interest in wanting to see a meltdown or people dying. I'm an engineer. I know about the dangers of nuclear power and how to avert them. This alleged sabotage is not something I came up with on my own. I'm just trying to make a living. Senator Paige and his presidential campaign would benefit greatly from such an event. It would give him ammunition to put the lid on nuclear power. That's why he paid me. But I couldn't handle everything they wanted me to do by myself, so they sent someone else to help me. His name is Steiger Bob, and I don't think he only helped with minor acts of sabotage. I'm pretty sure he killed Carey Lennox, an inspector for the NRC. He even boasted to me about his impromptu visit to the Hamptons on the weekend Lennox was killed."

"Where can I find this guy?"

"I don't know. It's almost like Steiger disappeared off the face of the earth after the murder."

Grace Esmond immediately set to work finding Steiger, but it proved to be an impossible task. Her detective found an employment record for someone with that name at the same power plant Mark Allen had worked at, but the social security number turned out to be fake. No one named Steiger Bob lived at his listed address, and the detective couldn't find birth records under Steiger Bob's name in the system. There was no such person as *Steiger Bob.* No matter how hard anyone looked, there was no substantial proof that he existed. Legally. Just little snippets here and there that were circumstantial. Like pictures of the man known as Steiger playing darts with Achille Pasquarelli. And another of him clocking into work at the power plant. She had also retrieved a copy of Steiger's application for employment, but a background check based on the information in that application proved he had fabricated most of it.

Grace repeated the findings to her client. "What we have is a person calling himself Steiger Bob, but we can't find the man, nor do we know his true identity."

"Isn't that enough to provide reasonable doubt?" Mark Allen asked.

"Reasonable doubt of what? It makes it sound like you're making him up."

"But there are pictures of him."

"The man in those photos could be anyone."

"I swear, he's real."

"I'll enter the photos and the limited information we found into evidence. Let's hope the FBI picks up on it and goes looking for him. They certainly have more resources than we do."

THE FBI REVIEWED the new evidence entered by Mark Allen's attorney and started its own search for Steiger. Agents tripped on the same stumbling blocks as Esmond's detective, but they found something additional. Almost obscure. A case file in the social services system detailed a family's complaint about a twelve-year-old foster child whom the family said had sociopathic tendencies. He had broken their natural-born son's arm—without remorse. The caseworker noted *the youngster insists on calling himself Steiger Bob instead of his real name, Steiger Roberts.* This revelation helped the FBI put together a much more comprehensive file on the man but provided no help in locating him.

"We're not getting anywhere with this," AD Vasko said at a special meeting with her team at FBI headquarters. "I think it's just a stalling tactic while Mark Allen tries to concoct a new way to cast suspicion elsewhere. We already have proof of fraud. Book Allen on that."

"Too bad we can't prove he tried to kill Lennox," Sarinana said.

Vasko leaned back in her chair, causing the metal to squeak. "You know who I think tried to kill Lennox?"

"Who?"

"The phantom, Steiger Bob."

"What makes you say that?"

"Sherlock Holmes. 'When you have eliminated the impossible, whatever remains, however improbable, must be the truth.'"

"You're basing your deduction on the words of a fictional detective?"

"That and the fact that facial recognition programs crosschecked with traffic cameras show the image of a man identified as Steiger Roberts in East Hampton for only the half-hour window during which the murder occurred."

"So, the phantom did it."

"Let's face facts. It's not really a murder, and we can't find the person most likely to have committed the crime. So, I say we bow out and hand it back to local jurisdiction. Let them go crazy with it."

"You have a macabre streak."

"I like to think of it as a sense of humor. Let's discuss charges against Achille Pasquarelli."

"We have nothing concrete," Sarinana said.

"I agree. There's nothing that will stick to Pasquarelli. Nothing that will stick to Senator Paige, either. We should table the investigation into those two—put it on the back burner—but continue to collect information on them and Steiger. None of them are clean." She closed the file in front of her and tucked it under her arm.

"So, we're telling the NRC what, exactly?" Sarinana asked, standing.

"That we only have enough information to prosecute one person but believe him to be the main perpetrator, considering he is a reactor engineer who had the means and opportunity to commit the crime."

"What about his motive?"

"His motive could be similar to what's known as firefighter arson. Maybe he's bored or wants attention. Maybe he wants to be a hero by stopping a meltdown."

"Okay. I'll write up the report, and you can present the NRC with the findings."

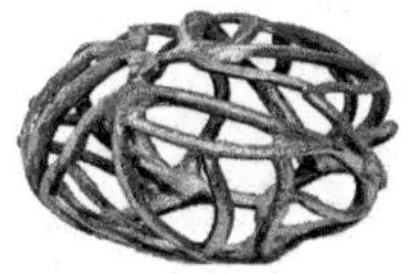

CHAPTER TWENTY-EIGHT

PIER WILLIAMS DUMPED the trash from another resort hotel room located along one of the pristine beaches in Ambergris Caye, Belize. He was used to being on a cleaning crew, and this job was a lot easier than working in a power plant. It was mindless work. Besides, he only worked four hours a day. The rest of the time, he lazed on the beach, drinking beer and turning as brown as a cashew nut. Sometimes, he went fishing. Sometimes, he hustled the tourists. Not enough to get him arrested, but he enjoyed besting them because they all thought they knew better than him. *If they only knew.*

Pier Williams wasn't the name he had used to travel into this country. It was the name on the passport of a man whose pocket he had picked right after he arrived. Lucky for the new Pier Williams, his mark had been a tourist on his way home. Besides, he had felt compelled to target this particular man. *I had to do it. The guy looked just like me.*

The airport was always a good place for easy pickings. Not that Pier needed it. He had nearly a quarter-million dollars in the bank, and between that, his job, and his hustling, he was set.

Now he had settled in—a regular Belizean—and he didn't care if he ever returned to the States again.

Tray returned to New York, knowing he would have a lot of explaining to do to Aislinn. He had left her in a lurch and had seen how badly she took his "death" when he'd witnessed her reaction to his funeral. Trying to make sense of what had happened wouldn't be easy. Breaking up with her would be even harder.

It wasn't fair to Aislinn to lead her on. After spending time with Sophia, he knew he and Aislinn were not meant to be. He liked her. He especially liked her family. But he was pretty sure he still loved Sophia.

Even though he knew what he had to do, it didn't mean he was eager to get started.

Molyneaux did not know why the FBI had asked him to visit their field office in Melville, but he had never been there and was curious to see what it looked like.

Google Maps directed him to the location, and he was surprised to find the office was just another ubiquitous building, identical to so many others in that area.

Flores didn't keep him waiting long. "Detective Molyneaux." They shook hands. "Thank you for coming. I want to dot the i's and cross the t's on the Lennox case and thought you might want to know the final resolution." He showed Molyneaux into his office and asked him to take a seat. "Coffee?"

"No thanks. I get the feeling in a building like this one, it's probably no better than the swill we drink in Yaphank."

Flores laughed. "About the case. We've established that the victim's identity was switched almost immediately after the shooting. The injured was, in fact, Carey Lennox, an investigator for the NRC searching for a nuclear saboteur. His twin brother, Tray Lennox, works for the FBI's Art Crime Team and was investigating the trail of a stolen and dangerous artifact.

"Let me remind you that everything we discuss here today is classified and is not for general dissemination.

"Anyone who reads a newspaper regularly is aware of the explosion in DC. What most people will never learn is that the blast was part of a terrorist threat caused by the artifact Tray Lennox was chasing down. That artifact has now been recovered and is in government custody, where it will be buried deep, never to see the light of day again. We also learned after the DC explosion that Carey Lennox survived the gunshot wound he received in East Hampton, even though many people, his twin brother included, had written him off for dead. The Suffolk County ME saved his life and got him to the Walter Reed Medical Center, where doctors nursed him back to health.

"So, East Hampton murder number one was not a murder. It was a shooting. We believe someone named Steiger Bob committed the crime, but there is still some discussion about whether such a person exists. If he does, he remains at large. And it's no longer my case, nor yours. The FBI's top honchos in DC have taken it over.

"But then there's East Hampton murder number two, the death of Calam Fergus at The Old Salt House. That murder did happen. Fergus was apparently on the trail of

Tray Lennox and was tossing his room when Lennox walked in. There was a struggle, and a gun went off. However, it was Fergus's gun—Lennox wasn't armed—and the FBI has determined the cause of death as self-defense in the line of duty by a special agent.

"So, that's two case files you can retire. I thought you'd want to know."

"To most people," Molyneaux said, "this would look like Tray Lennox killed a guy and walked away because he's FBI."

"What most people won't ever know," Flores answered, "is that Tray Lennox prevented a much bigger nuclear explosion from knocking Washington, DC, into orbit and got to sit at the right hand of the president at a White House dinner held specifically to thank him for his service. It was at that dinner that Carey Lennox's survival was revealed, much to his twin brother's surprise.

"Tray and Carey Lennox, together, helped unravel another threat against the country the following morning. That will probably ensure more White House dinners in their futures."

"So, he's not just another pretty face?"

"No. Tray Lennox is a bona fide hero, and so is his identical twin."

TRAY AND CAREY laughed when Jane said she wanted to attend the exhumation. "What satisfaction could you possibly derive from looking inside the casket?"

"I want to see who I was subsidizing and evict him. Why are you two here?"

"Because we said we would be."

"Well, we should all know what's happening in a little while."

Even with the permits in place, the cemetery crew took hours to dig up the casket. Tray eventually left to pick up lunch, and he, Jane, and Carey had an impromptu picnic while they waited. By early afternoon, they were ready to open the casket and see who was inside. Workers unlocked the lid, lifting it to view the remains.

Inside, they found a young man, probably in his twenties. A gargling sound erupted from Tray's throat.

"You okay there, bro?" Carey asked.

Tray didn't answer. He just stared at the man he had inadvertently killed inside his hotel room on the day of Carey's murder.

"Tray?" Jane said.

He blinked. "How big a plot did you buy?"

"It's just for one person. I was so rushed, I didn't think ahead."

"I'll reimburse you."

Her mouth opened, then closed, her eyes narrowing. "Why would you do that?" She pointed to the coffin. "He's a stranger, isn't he?"

"Just believe me. It's for the best."

"Tray—"

"No more questions." He looked at the cemetery workers standing beside a large pile of loose dirt. "You can rebury him now. I'll take care of the paperwork. Thank you."

IT TOOK A FEW days, but Tray finally sucked up his pride and headed to the Hamptons. It was dinnertime, and he thought he and Aislinn could have one last meal together.

When he showed up at her door, he didn't expect the reception he received. She looked spectacular in a short, baby blue dress, with her hair pinned up off her neck. *She's so pretty, she could be a model.* But then he thought about Sophia in the emerald-green dress she'd worn in Paris and the navy blue one she'd worn to the White House, and he felt his heart race and his senses come alive—suddenly followed by a sense of emptiness. It gave him courage.

He had expected Aislinn to run into his arms. *Nope.* He expected to face buckets of tears and recriminations about not telling her he was alive. *Not happening.*

Instead, she just stared at him.

He stood motionless, feeling awkward and not knowing what to say.

"Who are you?" she asked, although her inflection made it sound more like a rhetorical question.

He realized he looked nothing like the guy she was initially attracted to. "I know I look different. A lot has happened. Can we talk?"

She shook her head. "I thought we had something special. I even told you I loved you. To me, you were perfect. And then I thought I'd lost you. Mourning you was the most difficult thing I ever did. It was heart-wrenching. Until I learned you weren't dead at all. Was it all a game to you? Was I just another notch on your bedpost?"

She narrowed her eyes at him and opened her mouth to continue but turned away, distracted. Her face lit up as a sleek Porsche 718 Cayman pulled up to the curb.

Tray turned and recognized the well-dressed guy who walked up to the door. *Molyneaux.*

The detective stared at Tray for a moment before pushing past him to gently kiss Aislinn and hand her a bouquet of wildflowers. "Are you ready for dinner?"

She smiled and nodded.

He turned to Tray. "Lennox."

Tray nodded.

Aislinn took the flowers over to the sink and ran water into a vase for them.

Molyneaux lowered his voice. "It's not nice allowing your girlfriend to believe you're dead."

Aislinn stepped around Tray and closed her front door, taking Detective Molyneaux's arm. "Just tell me," she turned back to Tray, "is your name really Tray? Or are you Carey?"

He opened his mouth to answer, but she cut him off.

"No. Don't tell me. I don't care anymore. You'll have to find yourself a new girlfriend. I still have feelings for you, but none of them are very positive. I hope you're more considerate of other people's feelings than you were of mine." She turned abruptly, pulling Molyneaux with her.

"Goodbye, Lennox," he said as he and Aislinn walked away. "I thought I'd get to arrest you for the murder of Calam Fergus but was informed it happened in the line of duty. I hear you've been doing a lot of things in the line of duty over the past week and that we may not be seeing much of you around here anymore. At least, I hope not."

He helped Aislinn into the passenger seat before walking around to the driver's side of the Porsche. He took one last look at the special agent. "Before you go, let me just say thank you for your service."

Then, Molyneaux slid into his car and drove away.

TRAY FELT LET down after watching Aislinn leave with Molyneaux. Yes, he had intended to break up with her, and she had made it easy for him to do so. But losing someone as nice as Aislinn to another guy still hurt.

He cranked up the radio in his car, and by the time he reached the Queens border, he started thinking about Sophia. He had a lot of vacation time coming to him. A trip to London might be a pleasant diversion.

His phone rang, but he ignored it. He just wanted to get home and unwind.

Once inside his apartment, he called Sophia. "I sure hope that Caravaggio is the real deal and has a shady past. I could use the distraction."

"Oh, Tray, it was stunning," she replied. "We didn't know what Caravaggio had titled it, so we called it *The Conception*. It was an outstanding example of tenebrism and chiaroscuro. The modeling and the contrast between light and dark brought the painting to life right before our eyes. I swear, I could almost see the Madonna breathing."

"You know, you're talking about it in the past tense—"

"That's because someone stole it from right beneath our noses. It had to be an inside job, and I'm waiting—as we speak—for the sign-in logs for the National Gallery in Trafalgar Square. We need to interview everyone who was in the building."

"I thought it was in a peer's attic?"

"That's where they found it, but we couldn't very well leave it in a neglected manor house that's vacant six months out of the year. When the family is in London, there's only an older man on-site at the manor, and he lives in a caretaker's cottage. We brought the painting to the National Gallery to study it."

"Interviewing everyone in the building sounds like a huge job."

"Not as bad as it could have been. The museum is mounting a new exhibition and was closed to the public yesterday when the theft happened."

A line of text appeared on Tray's cell phone. *We need you in Lon …*

"Sophia, wait," he said, clicking on the text.

We need you in London to investigate the theft of a previously unknown Caravaggio.

"Sophia, count yourself lucky. The FBI reassigned me—something about London—the theft of a previously unknown Caravaggio."

"I thought you were more of an expert on artifacts."

"And old masters. I hate to cut this short, but I need to go into the office and get my travel papers. The sooner I do that, the sooner I can see you."

"Well, in that case, Mr. Lennox, get going."

"Consider me gone."

EPILOGUE

PHINEAS W. PAIGE
MAINE

WASHINGTON, DC 20510-2004

September 12, 2022

Dear Mr. Bhatti,

Let me introduce myself. I'm Senator Phineas Paige of the United States of America. I am currently one of three members of the US Senate who sits on the Board of Regents for the Smithsonian Institution and was recently named chairman of that board. In that capacity, I have become aware of an artifact that I've heard has an affinity for materials that are prone to explode. We have been asked to hold said artifact indefinitely here in the Smithsonian Archives.

I've been alerted that this item can be dangerous when exposed to light, so we are doing our best to store it in a deep, dark location, where, unfortunately, it could be forgotten if not properly documented.

Someone mentioned that you know a lot about this antiquity, being both a fan of Hero of Alexandria and a former owner of the item, although the records of its exact provenance seem to have been misplaced.

Our archives are vast, serving almost twenty museums, galleries, and gardens, not to mention a zoo. So, it's understandable that many of the items we hold for future display are sometimes mishandled or lost.

As the chairman of the board of regents, I would hate to see a piece with so much potential stored without proper documentation or forgotten through the ages. I think it would be beneficial to us both if we could meet to discuss the item further. We would like to correctly catalog the artifact's strengths and weaknesses before archiving it. Is it possible for you to assist with a small demonstration? In return, we could allow for a reciprocal exhibit of the artifact at one of your national venues, should the need suit you.

I look forward to hearing from you.

Sincerely,

Phineas W. Paige
Phineas W. Paige
United States Senator

Reply To:
Dirksen Senate Office Building
Washington, DC 20510-2004
www.paige.senate.gov

Would you like to know more about the origin of herotite?

You can read a free short story by signing up here:
https://mailchi.mp/50be34c94064/origin-of-herotite

If you enjoyed reading *Artifact*, please help others discover it.

Review it: Most readers rely on reviews to decide what to read next. Help them out by describing what you liked or did not like about this book.

Recommend it: Tell your friends or book club about it. Ask your local library to carry it.

Talk it up: Social media is a great way to start a conversation about the characters and issues brought up in this book.

Lend it: Share it with your friends.

ACKNOWLEDGMENTS

I often feel like I write my books in a vacuum, all alone, holed up in my office for long periods of time. However, if that were true, this page wouldn't exist. No matter how isolated an author feels—outside comments, suggestions, and assistance affect the completed work. And this is my opportunity to say *thanks for your help*.

First, of course, I need to thank my husband, Andrew, who keeps my life running while I'm lost in my imagination, or tearing out my hair uploading manuscripts, or handling all the supplementary publishing work that's not nearly as much fun as writing. And a big hug to my cousin Joann Colucci, my TSAB, sounding board, and staunchest supporter. Another hug to my nephew Dan Mealie who pointed out how a ransom demand in an early version of my book was laughable and helped me come up with a number that works better. My sincere thanks to my wonderful friends, Barbara, Carol, Chris and Ken—who agreed to give me feedback during the different phases of my manuscript. And there were lots of phases. *So many phases.* A huge thank you to my developmental editor, Maryssa Gordon, who took the time to answer my questions, even on the weekend she was getting married, and to Ceara Nobles, my line editor. A shout out to Rich Glanzer, who answered my questions about police procedure when responding to homicides in the Hamptons. And my deepest gratitude to Pamela Stratton, who answered my questions about the FBI, although, in the end, my protagonist stretched reality more than would probably be allowed. But hey, it's fiction. I also want to thank Terrie Wolf and Joe Brosnan, an agent and an editor (although not my agent and editor), whom I met through Thrillerfest, and who both gave me invaluable feedback.

Right in the middle of it all, I gained my certification as a copy editor and proofreader. I have to say, what I learned opened my eyes—immensely—to the whole process of writing. However, commas are still the bane of my existence.

ABOUT THE AUTHOR

C. A. Pack is an award-winning former journalist, who gave up fact for fiction. Being the daughter of a twin, the niece of twins, and the aunt of twins, she felt inspired to write *Artifact* after wondering what might happen if someone were killed and his twin switched their identities after death. Please note, this was just a *musing,* and she in no way wishes harm to any member of her family.

She is the author of the Library of Illumination series. The first book in that series, *Chronicles: The Library of Illumination,* was named one of the "Best Indie Books of 2014" by Kirkus Reviews, who gave it a starred review.

C. A. is also the creator of the *Evangeline's Ghost* books — historical fantasy thrillers about an assassinated WWII spy who helps prevent catastrophes while seeking to avenge her murder.

As Carol Pack, she co-authored several non-fiction, self-help books on aging including, *Over-Sixty: Shades of Gray,* a lighthearted yet informative journey through life's later years (on the road to fossilization); its companion puzzle/coloring book, *Mind Games & Soporifics*; a humorous look at the COVID-19 pandemic in, *Our Coronavirus Diary;* and the *Book of Lists,* which boils down to bullet points a lot of what older adults may find interesting about life.

And finally, in her reinvention as a copy editor and proofreader, Carol wrote the *Indie Authors User's Guide* for independent authors who need help with self-publishing.

The author lives on Long Island with her husband.

You can learn more about her on her websites:

www.carolpack.com

www.capproofreading.com

www.ingramcontent.com/pod-product-compliance
Lightning Source LLC
Chambersburg PA
CBHW060428310726
48977CB00001B/101